when she vanished

KAITLYNN FLINT

when
she
vanished

To all the women in my life—my mother, grandmothers, sisters, and friends. As Alice Hoffman wrote, "There's a little witch in all of us."

"Like a heartbeat drives you mad
In the stillness of remembering what you had
And what you lost."

—Dreams, Fleetwood Mac

PROLOGUE

AN EERIE LAYER OF FOG HOVERED carefully over the dark bayou. Thick clouds blocked out any sliver of moonlight, casting a sinister shadow on the cypress trees.

The frogs moaned, and the crickets softly laughed as the yellow-eyed alligators crept around the black waters like slithering snakes.

Out in the middle of the river, tiny air bubbles began to rise to the surface, a sign of life below the blanket of turbid water. Ripples formed circles around the popping bubbles before a figure slowly ascended, pale and drenched. Her black hair hung over her face, hiding all but her trembling lips. She was dressed in a white nightgown, discolored from the muddy bayou, matching the gray bark of the surrounding trees that stood like decaying skeletons dressed in Spanish moss.

The woman stopped rising when the water was just below her chest.

Her blue lips opened slightly, murmuring, *"Dreams and visions will show you the way."* The thin, shaky lips repeated this message again and again in a delicate whisper. *"Dreams and visions will show you the way. Dreams and visions will show you the way. Dreams and visions will show you the way."*

Her whispers echoed throughout the murky swamp until they began to morph into desperate cries.

"Dreams and visions will show you the way. Dreams and visions will show you the way. Dreams and visions will show you the way."

CHAPTER ONE

JANE'S EYES SHOT OPEN, and she gasped for air as she awoke. She blinked a few times and looked around the small sedan before coming back to her senses. The dream, if that's what it was, vanished the second she left it, leaving her scared and disoriented—just as it always did. She's been having the same thing happen for weeks now, and she still can't understand the cause. No matter how hard she tried, she could not remember anything about her strange nightmare.

"Sorry, I didn't mean to wake you. We hit a pothole," her mother said from the driver's seat. "These backroads are in worse shape than I remembered."

Jane wiped the sleep from her eyes. "I didn't mean to doze off. Where are we now?" She looked out at the road ahead. Tall water oaks and longleaf pines tunneled the long concrete path. Through the thick trees, Jane couldn't see anything besides a tangled mess of green vegetation.

"We're ten minutes away from Belles Parish."

"When did we get off of the interstate?"

"Half an hour ago," she answered, her green eyes remaining on the road.

The silence returned again, the same silence that had lingered in the car most of the drive from New York. It was nothing new, of course. Jane wasn't very close to her mother. She was hoping that would change on this spontaneous trip. Wasn't that the point of all this? The more time went by, the more confused she felt, though. The thick silence between them only grew stronger.

Recently, she's had a lot of suspicions about her mother. Mostly about if she was hiding something and what that something could be.

She turned her attention to the window. There was a small white church the size of a shack in need of a good pressure wash on the side of the road. It had a marquee sign out front that read;

RENOUNCE ALL EVIL.

An image of the strange card Jane had seen on her mother's desk just before they left popped in her head again. She couldn't stop thinking about it. She just wanted to know what it meant.

She and her parents were not religious people, not in the slightest. She had never even stepped foot in a church before. Her mother always said organized religion was nothing but nonsense—and her father was an atheist.

So why did her mother have that card? What did it mean?

Her mother didn't know she saw the card, and Jane was too nervous to bring it up. She didn't know how she would bring up such a question. But most of all, she didn't know how her mother would react.

She took a deep breath, doing her best to push the image out of her head. It was probably nothing, she assured herself.

"Here we are," her mother muttered, her voice coated in defeat. "Belles Parish."

Jane looked ahead and saw the tunnels of trees opening, revealing a town in the distance. She sighed in relief at the thought of finally getting out of the car. Driving for three days straight made her body feel beat, and the silence of the long ride made her feel crazy.

As they drove through the small southern town, she observed every store and restaurant and tried to imagine what it must have been like for her mother to call this place home. Her mother had left for New York when she was eighteen-years-old to study engineering at a university in the city. And although she tried to hide it, she was born and raised in Belles Parish, Louisiana.

She never spoke about her childhood. Doing so made her feel vulnerable. As if the past could, at any moment, catch up to her and bring her back. She didn't want to dig up the old memories, even if that meant forgetting the good ones.

All that Jane knew about her mother's life in the small town was that she had a tight-knit group of friends that she considered sisters and that her grandmother had passed away while giving birth to her mother.

With her mother being one of the most respected architects in the city, she wasn't around much. And when she was, she didn't want to discuss her complicated past with her seventeen-year-old daughter.

Her mother's fingers tightened around the steering wheel as they drove through the quaint town, her mind crowded with so many thoughts and worries. When she got the call from one of her sisters about how she had to come back to Belles Parish *right away*, she initially wanted Jane to stay in the city with her husband, David—but before she had time to ask, she and David got into a heated discussion unrelated to their daughter, the trip, and the whole emergency down in Louisiana.

"How could you lie to me this whole time?" she had asked him the night before leaving. Jane was out having dinner with a few classmates, the house was empty. But they kept their voices low, nonetheless, as if they didn't want the walls to hear them. They were standing in their kitchen when the fight broke out. She had a hand pressed against their glossy marble countertops, fingers curling and tinted red.

"She cares about me more than you do," he had yelled at her. The comment made her feel a pinch of pain deep in her chest, and it stirred the embers of her past, reminding her of the heartaches she had endured long ago.

When Jane got home that night, her mother told her they were going to take a small trip together—something they had never done before—and that her father could not go with them because of a conference trip. Jane believed her, not suspecting anything more. Her mother was good at making everything seem like it was okay. She knew she had to tell Jane about David's affair and how he wanted to file for a divorce sooner than later—but in the meantime, she tried her best not to think about it too much. She had more important worries on her plate.

They passed a diner with a sign in the window that read: *Come in and try our famous fried chicken.*

"Is that where you worked?" Jane questioned, bringing her mother back to the present moment.

She heaved a sigh in response. "Yeah. Looks like it hasn't changed a bit."

The car turned down a street that was in worse condition than the old two-lane highway. Thick bushes covered each side of the beaten road, and Spanish moss hung from the power lines like tangled, wet hair. The concrete was cracked and worn, the paint separating the lanes long since faded.

Just a little way ahead, the ingress to a driveway caught Jane's eye. Beside the driveway was a large white mailbox with an address that read; *1111.*

A large gate made of brick and black iron stood open, inviting them through its entrance. It was intricately designed, with vine-like spirals climbing the bars to the pointy arrows at the top. It looked like something that could be found in a cemetery.

Giant oaks lined the dirt driveway like guards at a castle. The yard was immaculate. There were no weeds or fallen leaves, only the big, beautiful oaks and the greenest grass Jane had ever seen. Even though the grass was shaded by the big branches of the trees, it was glowing vibrantly.

At the end of the driveway was a large two-story house— no, *mansion*, more like— painted a fresh white with a roofed porch on each floor. Jane counted four windows, a tall purple door on the first floor, and five glass French doors on the second. It was a Southern Belle's dream.

At the sight of it all, Jane felt a rush of emotion wash over her that she could not describe. Almost like a sort of familiarity. She had never seen the place until just now, and still, it was like she had been here before. Like she was returning home.

A woman her mother's age stepped out of the big house and waited patiently as they drove down the driveway. She was shorter than her mother and had brown hair that fell to her hips. She wore a flowy green kimono that blew elegantly in the breeze like the Spanish moss that hung from the surrounding trees.

Jane could see a soft smile on her face.

"There's Mary Grace," said her mother. "Remember to be polite. I didn't tell her that I was bringing you, so mind your manners."

She looked over. "Why didn't you tell her I was coming with you?"

"I didn't have time. Like I said before, this visit wasn't planned. We're only staying for a week or two, okay?"

Jane wanted to ask more questions, but she nodded instead. "Okay."

When they made it to the house, Mary Grace walked towards them with an air of wisdom about her.

Jane got out and was immediately greeted with warm and sticky air that smelt like mud and muck. She couldn't help but scrunch her nose at the odd smell.

As if her mother could read her mind, she mumbled to her, "It's the swamp. The smell? It's the smell of the bayou. It'll grow on you." The scent set off a million memories, and she focused on her friend walking over to keep them all at bay.

Mary Grace gasped in awe at the sight of her childhood friend. "My lord, what did you do to your hair?"

"I..." she sighed, rolling her eyes. "It's nice to see you too, Mary Grace." She didn't realize until then that she had been so anxious to finally see Mary Grace again. After years and years of not speaking to her, shutting her out, and trying to forget she even knew her. As confident as she already was, she found that she was subconsciously building up the courage to face her childhood friends the entire drive down. Not every worry, but most of her worries were released with Mary Grace's sarcastic remark. It was reassuring to know her friend hadn't changed.

"Oh, Margaret, you can't even *imagine* how much I've missed you," she cried, wrapping her in a tight embrace.

Jane listened to their conversation, surprised at the heavy southern drawl coated in the woman's voice. Compared to her mother's voice, it sounded almost like a different language. Every syllable and suffix were coated in honey.

Her mother kept her wall up. "It has been a long time," she said flatly, pulling away from her friend.

"You must be Jane." Mary Grace walked over to Jane, grabbing hold of her shoulders softly.

"Yes, ma'am."

"You can call me Mary Grace. I will not stand for *ma'am* or *miss*. My name is Mary Grace, and that's it."

"Yes, ma'am—" Jane stopped herself. "Yes, Mary Grace."

The woman smiled up at her. "You look just like your mother. Tall and skinny with those jade green eyes and dark hair. *Mmhmm*, you're your mother's daughter alright. Even got that short haircut like her too." She lowered her voice to a whisper. "Did she make you cut your hair, darlin'?"

The question made Jane run her fingers through the ends of her bob, and she laughed.

"Mary Grace, not everyone wants their hair down to their hips," her mother said from behind them.

"Oh? Well, you didn't think that when *you* had long hair."

"Well, I'm not a little girl anymore, either," she snapped.

"Maybe not on the outside," she muttered back.

Before Margaret could add to her friend's quick statement, the front door swung open and out came the golden-headed Lucille Callaway in a scarlet mini dress and high heels.

"Good God almighty, if it ain't the old crone herself!" exclaimed the woman, putting her hands on her sharp hips. Her high-pitched voice had the same heavy drawl as Mary Grace had.

After a moment's hesitation, Margaret pulled her lips back. "Hello, Lucille." She walked up to her and gave her a quick hug.

"Y'all took *forever*. My flight landed *three* hours ago, and I've been *bored outta my* mind just *waitin'* for you. Y'know how *borin'* Mary Grace is," she laughed and, after a quick embrace, she grinned. "Look at you... all sophisticated." She looked her friend up and down, shaking her head in disbelief.

"If you're about to insult me on my hair, Mary Grace already beat you to it."

"I'd never do such a thing." Then her smile softened when she remembered why Margaret was really here. "I'm sorry we have to reunite for such a terrible reason."

Margaret didn't know what she to say.

Jane's stomach tightened at her words. What terrible reason? Her mother never told her about any *terrible* reasons.

Lucille looked over Margaret's shoulder at the shy girl who stood beside Mary Grace, her smile returning.

"Jane," Margaret called, bringing Jane's attention back. "Come meet Lucille."

She gave a small smile to Mary Grace, who was staring back at her wistfully, and then walked up the steps to greet the blonde woman. "Hello."

"My lord," gasped Lucille. "Aren't you a *doll*." Unexpectedly, tears filled the corners of her eyes. "I'm so happy to finally meet you." She looked like a movie star from the 1950s. Her golden hair was put up in a neat side bun, short wavy strands framing her flawless face. Her lips were a cherry red that matched her dress, and her eyes, now pooling with fresh tears, were the color of a clear sky on a summer day.

At first, Jane didn't know how to react. No one had ever cried in front of her before. Especially not when meeting her. Awkwardly, she replied, "It's good to meet you, too."

The woman pulled her in for a tight hug before saying, "I have a strong feeling we're gonna be friends."

Mary Grace walked up the steps and opened the front door. "Alright, Lucille, let them be so I can show them to their rooms."

Margaret and Jane followed Mary Grace through the door and into the old house.

It was like stepping into a dream. The house was in the same order and condition as it was when Margaret last visited seventeen years ago. Nothing was different. There was even the same antique mahogany console table on the wall beneath the stairs with the same crystal bowl on it full of butterscotch candy.

The house smelt the same, too. Dust and sugar. The combination made Margaret's head spin. She felt she was walking into her childhood again. For a split second, she expected Mary Grace's mother to walk down the stairs and greet her. But Mrs. Abel was deceased. She pushed the disappointing expectation in the back of her mind and focused on the present moment, knowing she would never be able to return to the past.

"Follow me. Your rooms are upstairs." Mary Grace said, starting for the narrow stairs. Margaret let Jane go first.

Lucille stayed back on the porch and lit a cigarette, an addiction she started as a teenager right after her first heartbreak.

"It is very kind of you to let us stay here, but I don't mind checking into a hotel if you think we'll be intruding," Margaret told her friend, half-hoping Mary Grace would let her leave. The old house was terrifying. She could feel the memories of her past slowly grabbing hold of her, and the faded wallpaper of blue-colored roses caved in on her a little more each second.

"Nonsense!" laughed Mary Grace as they reached the top of the stairs. "I won't have my best friend and her daughter stayin' at some bug-infested hotel. Plus, the closest hotel is in New Orleans."

The wood floors creaked and cracked as they walked down the hall. There were rooms on each side of the wall, each door closed. Margaret noticed the smell of dust was even more pungent on the second floor.

Margaret's hands began to shake. She hid her sudden nervousness by crossing her arms and lifting her chin.

"My room is downstairs, so it's just you three up here. I set you all up on the front side of the house because of the porch, but if you don't care for the room, please feel free to move. There are eight rooms in total. The room at the very end, on the back side, is locked—but other than that one, you can move to any room you like."

Margaret assumed she was saying all of this for Jane, so she let her thoughts wander from the conversation. She smiled to herself, remembering the times when she and the other girls would play up here. She let the tips of her fingers run across the wallpaper as they walked. Happy memories that had been muddled under the pain of what had happened rushed back to her. She didn't think she'd ever feel them again.

Faint, high-pitched giggles suddenly stormed the hallways. Margaret stopped abruptly. The hairs on the back of her neck stood.

Mary Grace and Jane turned around.

"You okay, Mom?" Jane questioned with a furrowed brow when she saw the paleness on her mother's face.

Margaret swallowed, her mouth dry. "I'm fine." She looked at Mary Grace and pressed her lips together.

Mary Grace could sense that she was lying, but she simply continued down the hall instead of saying anything. She understood how hard it was for Margaret to walk through the old house again after trying so hard to detach herself from the trauma.

Mary Grace opened a bedroom door and stepped inside. "Jane, this is your room. I hope you'll feel comfortable here."

Jane looked around and smiled. The room was small, much smaller than her large bedroom back in the city, but it felt homey. There was a twin bed against the wall to the left and an antique secretary desk on the back wall to the right. Two glass French doors took up almost the entire back wall between the bed and the desk. A wooden chest sat at the foot of the bed and a nightstand by the pillow. On the nightstand was a bronze reading lamp accompanied by a stack of books. She glanced at the titles and let out a gasp, walking over to the nightstand.

She ran her fingers across the spines. Almost all her favorite classics were there: Frankenstein, The Bell Jar, Jane Eyre, and The Catcher in the Rye.

Mary Grace smiled and nodded her head, happy with the girl's reaction. "Do you like to read?"

She never considered herself a big reader, only picking up a book whenever she was bored or lonely. But she realized she spent quite a lot of her time reading. "Yes, I love to."

"Good. I picked out a few paperbacks from my library downstairs that I knew you'd like."

Jane turned away from the books. "How did you know I liked these?" she asked, a little shocked. Hadn't her mother told her that she hadn't even announced that she was bringing Jane?

Instead of answering, she just shrugged her shoulders and laughed under her breath.

Margaret sighed as if the question was rude. "Jane."

"Thank you, Mary Grace," she said, picking up on her mother's tone. "The room's perfect."

"You are most certainly welcome. Oh, and the bathroom is directly across from you. It's already stocked with all the toiletries you may need." She looked over at Margaret. "Mar, let me show you your room."

"Oh, you don't have to. I still know my way around, just tell me which one you set up and I'll—"

"Margaret, let me show you your room," Mary Grace repeated with a stiff smile before turning to the door. "Right this way."

They walked out of the room, leaving Jane to get settled. Lucille ran up the stairs, holding a suitcase in each hand.

"Hey, y'all, I'm just dropping these off for Jane," she said, taking a deep breath. The heavy suitcases seemed to be dragging her down a little.

"Good. She's in her room now." Mary Grace nodded her head, then started for Margaret's room. Margaret wanted to warn Lucille not to say anything outrageous and crazy around her daughter, but she was already walking away before Margaret had the chance to.

Lucille walked into Jane's bedroom, gasping for air, and dropped the suitcases. "My lord! What *did* you pack? It's so heavy!"

"Oh, you didn't have to get those!" Jane giggled softly. "I was just about to get them."

"No, it's fine," she breathed, her cheeks flushed from exhaustion. "Man, I'm out of shape. I mean, I'm *really* out of shape. Too many beignets, that's what that is."

Not knowing what a *benyaay* was, Jane just responded with a laugh.

"And the heat don't help, either. Georgia is *freezin'* compared to this swampy town. I'm never gonna complain 'bout the hot summers in Savannah *ever* again," she rambled, throwing her hands in the air.

Jane heaved a sigh in agreement as she used the back of her hand to wipe a forming line of sweat from her hairline. "You live in Savannah?"

"Yes, ma'am. Ten years now."

"I heard that place is pretty haunted," she said with a small smile.

"It is home for many lost souls, yes."

She raised an eyebrow. "So, you believe the ghost stories are real?"

Lucille grinned, flashing her pearly white teeth. "And you don't?"

She hesitated. "No, I don't."

"Stick around here long enough, and you'll start believin' in ghosts. I can promise you that."

She brushed her discomfort off and forced a laugh. "Well, thank you for bringing me my suitcases."

"So polite," she giggled. "Your mama never had manners. She was a wild child without a care in the world."

Jane grabbed the suitcases and placed them on the bed. "Really?"

"Hard to believe, ain't it? Now that she's all *professional* and *rich*."

It was hard to imagine her mother being carefree and wild. If that was true, what happened to her that made her so... cold?

Jane looked at her suitcases and back at Lucille. "Lucille, how did you know these were my suitcases?" She was still a little taken back by how Mary Grace knew about her favorite books.

Lucille put her hands on her hips and made a face as if she had asked why the sun was hot. "It says your name on the zipper, silly." And after a quick smile, the modern-day Marilyn Monroe left her alone to unpack.

CHAPTER TWO

"JANE DOESN'T KNOW," Margaret told Mary Grace once they stepped in the room and closed the door.

Mary Grace simply nodded. "I know."

"Of course, you know," she grumbled. "Well, I just wanted to tell you in case you *didn't* know. I don't want Jane finding out about us. About... what we are."

"You make it sound like we're monsters!" She laughed, keeping her voice down. "I can't stop her from finding out, but I'll try to keep my lips sealed. Lucille, on the other hand... that'll be a challenge."

Margaret paced the room. "It was a mistake to bring her here." But she had no other option. Even though Jane was almost eighteen years old, she couldn't leave her in the city by herself.

"Margaret, can't you sense her power? I felt it the very moment you guys pulled down the driveway. In fact, that's how I sensed you were here. I felt... *her*," she whispered. "You need to tell her."

"Are you crazy?" she crossed her arms over her chest. "I will not tell her—and you better not, either."

"But think about how hurt she will be when she finds out and realizes that her mother has kept her heritage hidden," Mary Grace said, shaking her head in disgust. "Like it's some dirty secret."

"I am here for one reason," she snapped, her eyes narrowing with irritation. "Not to unbury my past or practice magic again. I came back for Vivian, understand? So, if you're going to coach me on how I should raise my kid, I *will* leave."

Mary Grace nodded after a solid minute of silence. "Okay, I understand."

"Lucille knows as well, right?"

The door swung open, and Lucille came in with Margaret's suitcases. "Yup! Mary Grace told me as soon as I came."

"Good," she said. "So be sure to keep your loud mouth shut."

She dropped the suitcases at Margaret's feet and then huffed. "I'll try."

Pleased, Margaret said, "Thank you guys for agreeing not to speak of or practice any witchcraft around—"

"She's coming," Mary Grace interrupted, cutting her eyes to the doorway.

After a few seconds, Jane appeared just as Mary Grace predicted. She looked at the staring women and took a step back.

Jane hesitated. "Sorry, I didn't mean to interrupt. I was just going to let you guys know that I'm getting in the shower now."

"Not at all, dear. Enjoy your shower," said Mary Grace with a knowing smile.

"Thank you," she said before heading back to her room.

When they heard her door close, Margaret turned her attention back to her two friends. "I should unpack."

Mary Grace took her cue. "We'll leave you."

Before walking out, Lucille said in the most reassuring tone she could manage, "And don't worry about Jane. She won't find out."

Mary Grace softly laughed when Lucille closed the door behind them, and Margaret could hear her say, "Oh, yes, she will."

Margaret collapsed on the twin-sized bed, letting the hours of driving and the stress of it all melt into the mattress.

Now that she was really here, back in Belles Parish, she thought of Vivian. It didn't feel right to be here without her.

She shut her eyes and fought the urge to scream.

The idea of wearing anything sounded miserable to Jane, but she picked out a pair of jean shorts and a white tank before getting into the shower. It was hot outside, far too hot, and she ended up taking a cold shower just to cool off.

Her mind wandered as she rinsed herself, leading back to the question she had the moment she arrived here. *Why was she really here?* She was excited about staying in the old house and seeing everything the town had to offer, but now that she realized there might be more to her stay than she was told, she couldn't think about anything else.

'I'm probably overthinking this,' she thought to herself when she got out of the shower. She decided to worry about it later when she could talk privately with her mother. For now, she tried to appreciate where she was, knowing she wouldn't be able to go on a trip like this often.

She walked the hall toward the stairs and looked at the framed pictures hanging on the walls. Most of them appeared to be family portraits of generations taken in front of the white house. Some looked as dated as the early 1900s. The most recent family portrait was of Mary Grace as a small girl and her parents. Jane realized this meant Mary Grace never had a family of her own.

The thought of the kind woman living all alone made Jane's heart heavy.

The following picture that caught Jane's eye was of four little girls no older than ten, playing by an oak tree. Two tire swings were tied up to one of the long branches, holding two of the girls. The other two were pushing them, their faces glowing with laughter and joy.

Jane smiled to herself as she realized that her mother was the little girl on the swing to the right. The girl swinging next to her had blonde pigtails tied with pink bows, undoubtedly little Lucille.

Pushing them were two other girls—Mary Grace and someone she did not recognize.

The picture after that was of the same group, but years later. They were now teenagers, almost the same age as Jane. They were sitting on the steps to the front porch of the big house, smiling out at the camera. Mary Grace looked almost the same now, only slightly younger in many ways. Lucille was wearing jean overalls, and her golden hair was longer with hundreds of curls. She had her arm around Mary Grace's shoulders. On the other side of Lucille was Margaret, her features softer and her long much longer. Her smile stuck out to Jane. It was almost outlandish to see such a wide and genuine grin on her mother's face. She couldn't remember ever seeing such a smile in the family pictures placed around their penthouse.

The energy in the room shifted when Jane moved her gaze to the girl next to her mother. She had dark eyes, the same shade as her hair, and a soft smile.

A wave of remembrance passed through Jane just then, making her blood run cold. She knew this girl. She had never seen her before, yet she knew her. Somehow.

A lurking presence surrounded her, watching her. Goosebumps rose on the back of her neck and down her arms.

Time paused in the hall as she stood frozen before the framed picture.

The sound of dishes clanking together downstairs brought her back to the present moment, and she broke her gaze with the girl in the picture.

Shaking off the shrouded darkness that seemed to hang over her now, she continued to make her way downstairs.

A faint peppery smell filled the house. The closer she walked to the kitchen, the stronger it smelt. It made her stomach growl and her mouth water.

She hadn't realized just how hungry she was until she could smell the cooking food. *'Eat first, then worry later,'* she decided as she pushed aside the strange feeling of déjà vu. She wasn't sure who the girl in the picture was, and more importantly, why she felt like she knew her. But she was sure she would figure that out soon enough, along with any other questions she had for her mother. Like, why were they really here?

"Jane, is that you?" squealed Lucille from the room left of the front door. "C'mon in the kitchen. We're makin' gumbo!"

She followed the smell and Lucille's cheerful giggles into the kitchen. Steam and smoke lingered around the three women gathered around the big pot on the vintage stove.

"It smells great," Jane said as she looked around the kitchen. She had never seen a kitchen like this. Dried herbs and flowers hung from brown twine on the back wall above a white dining table. Clay pots full of lively plants that she could not possibly name were placed on the counters and windowsills.

The walls and glass cabinets were painted a soft shade of white, allowing natural light to spill in from the long windows and brighten the room.

Mary Grace pointed a copper ladle at Jane.

"You ever had gumbo, Miss Jane?"

Jane thought about it for a second before shaking her head. "No."

Lucille's red lips parted as she let out a gasp.

Before Jane could reply, Mary Grace was walking over to her with a bowl.

"Here you go. It's hot, so be careful," she said as she handed her the bowl. "Go take a seat at the table." She returned to the pot, filling a bowl for Margaret next.

"Thank you," Jane smiled. "Your kitchen is beautiful, by the way. Your whole house is, really."

Mary Grace raised her eyebrows in surprise. "Why, thank you, dear. That's very kind."

When Jane sat down at the small table, she got a good look at the brown soup, trying to ignore the fact it resembled chunky vomit and, instead, focus on how good the steam rising from it smelt.

Not long after, her mother took a seat next to her. Margaret blew at her own bowl, waving the steam away with her left hand as she stirred it with her right. The last time she recalled having gumbo seemed like forever ago. The spicy smell made her think of Lorraine and all those Wednesday nights at Belles Parish Baptist Church. Every week, without failure, Lorraine would make gumbo for the townspeople and bring the girls with her for the Wednesday service and bible study. Though most everyone looked down at the Abel family, not a single person in that church refused a bowl of the delicious gumbo.

Jane softly nudged her mother's arm with her elbow.

She looked up from her bowl as if snapping out of a daze.

"You okay?" she whispered.

Her mother raised the corner of her mother into a small smile. "Try it," she said, nodding to Jane's bowl. "I know you're a picky eater, but I promise it's not going to kill you."

Jane never thought of herself as a picky eater, but instead correcting her mother, she just smiled and raised a spoonful to her lips. The flavor exploded in her mouth, making her mouth water and her stomach grow hungrier. She took a few more spoonfuls before she felt the heat from the spices dance on her tongue. Just as she was about to look around for water, Mary Grace placed a tall glass of iced tea in front of her.

"You might want this," she said and returned to the stove to finish making bowls for Lucille and herself.

Jane could feel her face turning red as the fiery flavor took over. She lifted the glass to her mouth without hesitation, and the liquid abolished the heat like a fire extinguisher. She swished the tea in her mouth, letting her tastebuds recover. The tea was thick and sweet—and not a little sweet. No, this tea was *sweet*. It tasted like liquefied sugar.

She had heard about this. About how the people down south added a lot of sugar to their tea. For some reason, she had always thought this was just a rumor.

Lucille sat across from Jane and laughed at her. "What's the matter, sugar?"

'*Sugar.* That *was the matter.*' She laughed under her breath. "Nothing. Everything tastes great. Just wasn't expecting the tea to be this sweet."

"How's that gumbo?" Mary Grace asked the table when she sat down with her bowl.

Lucille took a bite of andouille and shrimp. "Truly amazin', Mary Grace. You outdid yourself!"

Margaret set down her spoon. "Tastes just like how your mom used to make it."

The kitchen filled with a sweet silence as the three women thought of Lorraine. They knew she would have loved to see this. Her not-so little girls gathered around the kitchen table, savoring the same recipe that had been passed down multiple generations. But what would she think of the empty chair? It didn't feel right without Vivian here—but Jane's presence sort of eased their worries, keeping them at bay for tonight.

The rest of the evening went well. Jane helped Mary Grace clean the kitchen while Margaret went upstairs for a shower. Lucille painted her nails a fresh coat of red at the table as she asked Jane more about herself.

"Do you like living in a big city?"

The question repeated in Jane's head a few times. She hadn't lived anywhere else so she wasn't sure if she could have a real preference or not. "Um—I don't know. It's not bad."

"I bet you have a lot of friends," Lucille added before blowing on her nails.

"Not really."

"You got a boy back home? I'm sure you do, don't you?"

"No." She shrugged, grabbing the wet dishes Mary Grace washed and drying them off with a rag. The kids in her high school never seemed worth her time. She was a natural introvert. She wasn't a shy person, but she found peace in being her own company.

Mary Grace looked over her shoulder and narrowed her gaze at Lucille. "Stop pesterin' the poor girl."

Lucille rolled her eyes. "I'm not persterin' anyone. We're just talkin'—ain't that right, Jane?" She rolled her eyes at Mary Grace.

"Sounds more like interrogating to me," she muttered.

"Okay, I'll be quiet," Lucille sighed in response.

Mary Grace washed out the last cup, and looked over her shoulder at Lucille. "Oh, don't be so dramatic."

They treated each other like sisters when they were annoyed with each other. It made Jane laugh a little.

"I drove over that single-lane bridge on the way here," Lucille said after a few moments of silence. "Remember? The one we jumped off of in fifth grade?"

Mary Grace smiled and she turned off the faucet. Of course, she remembered. That was one of the best summers of her childhood. Every day felt like its own adventure.

It was Lucille's idea to cannonball from that worn bridge. The bridge wasn't very high, but for a kid, everything looked bigger.

"There's no way I'm doing that!" whined little Margaret as she stood on the bridge, looking down at the water below. "Lucille, you're crazy!"

Young Lucille slowly climbed on the wooden railing with caution. "Don't be a scaredy-cat, Mar."

That summer, Lucille fell from a tall tree and busted her left front tooth right out, so she had only one tooth that whole summer. Fortunately, it was just a baby tooth, and the adult tooth grew in right before school started, but during the summer months, she tried her best to keep her tiny lips shut in hopes of hiding the missing tooth.

"I'll do it!" young Mary Grace had said, standing up on the rail next to Lucille. She grabbed her hand.

Quiet Vivian climbed up next to Mary Grace and grabbed ahold of her hand. She looked down over her shoulder at Margaret. "C'mon, Mar. It's not that high. I promise." She reached her hand for Margaret's.

With a decided sigh, Margaret took her friend's hand and joined the three girls on top of the railing.

Hand in hand, they all peered down at the moving water below them.

"Ah, yes," Mary Grace sighed in awe. "How could I forget?"

"We did some *wild* stuff back then, didn't we?"

"We did."

Mary Grace and Jane left the sink and sat at the table with Lucille as she proceeded to tell the story of when they all jumped off a bridge.

Margaret came downstairs just as Lucille was explaining how Margaret was scared out of her mind at the idea of jumping off the bridge. She cleared her throat, cutting the story short.

"Margaret!" Lucille cheered, clapping her hands together. "You remember that time we jumped off the bridge?"

Margaret locked her jaw. "I don't," she lied. She didn't *want* to remember. Not tonight, at least. It was already enough being back in Belles Parish without remembering each and every bittersweet memory. She had to remind herself she was here for one reason.

And it certainly wasn't to reminisce on the past and who she used to be.

Later that night, when everyone had said goodnight, Margaret found herself sitting up in bed, staring down at the list of missed calls and unread text messages on her phone. They were all from David. Talking to him was the last thing she wanted to do today, but she knew she would have to talk to him one day. She pressed his contact, swallowing a knot in the back of her throat as she waited for him to answer. Even though she never wanted to speak to him again, she had to be mature. He *was* a good father to Jane and a good husband to Margaret—at least, he used to be.

She tried to imagine what he was going to say when he answered. He'd ask how things were going, and she'd say perfect—even though they were far from perfect—and then he'd ask how Jane was, and she'd say she was doing fine, and the conversation would go stale. They'd run out of things to say to each other, and the awkward silence of the call would echo their recent fight.

"Margaret," he said when he finally picked up. In their seventeen years together, he was always an optimistic man. Always smiling, joking around—but his voice now proved he was still thinking about the argument they had had before she left. "How are you doing?"

Margaret couldn't help but frown, holding the phone to her ear. "Fine. I just wanted to let you know we're at my friend's house now."

There was a pause. "I know. Jane texted me."

"Oh."

"Look, Margaret, I'm sorry about how I acted. If you had just told me about your friend first, I wouldn't have brought up…"

"Go on," Margaret spat.

"I don't know—" he took a deep breath. "I guess I would have waited until you didn't have to leave. I feel awful."

She clenched her teeth.

"Does Jane know yet?"

"Know what?" she rolled her eyes.

"Know about me and—"

"No, why would she need to know?"

"Because she's going to be a part of our lives—"

"I need to go now."

"Margaret, wait—"

"Goodbye."

She ended the call and dropped her phone on the nightstand, turning the lamp off to let the darkness of night swallow her whole.

CHAPTER THREE

JANE WAS RESTLESS THAT NIGHT. She tossed and turned on the unfamiliar mattress, her mind refusing to silence.

It was too hot to find comfort. She kicked off the sheets but still could not escape the thick blanket of heat that lay heavily over her body.

After what felt like forever, she finally fell into a light sleep—only to be awakened around three in the morning by her burning discomfort again.

She took a deep breath, unable to take it anymore. Sitting up, she eyed the French doors beside her. If she opened one of the doors, she might get some sort of breeze to circulate the sticky air in the room. Slowly, she crawled out of bed and reached for the glass doors. Upon opening them, she felt a small draft blow through her hair, filling her with relief. The smell of the swamp was still there, but she was more focused on the cool air to care about the stench.

She walked out on the porch, gazing out at the beautiful driveway. It looked different in the nighttime. Eerie yet romantic.

Above the tall oaks, she found a full silver moon shining down on her and the plantation. Her lips pulled upward into a soft smile.

"Pretty, ain't it?" a voice whispered beside her.

Jane jumped and then sighed when she saw it was only Lucille. She rocked slowly in a rocking chair, a cigarette in between her index and middle finger. It looked to be just lit, which meant she must have just woken, too.

"Can't sleep?" Jane asked, leaning against the rail.

"Oh, I always wake up at three." She took a drag and tried to blow the smoke away from Jane's direction.

She thought about it for a moment. "Why?"

"I don't know," she shrugged. "Guess that's when my mind wants to think and worry."

"Worry about what?" She shut her mouth as she realized she let her nosiness get the best of her. "I'm sorry—that's none of my business."

She took a drag of her cigarette and looked at Jane. "No need to waste an apology, honey. So many people go around apologizin' for things that don't matter anyhow. It's mostly the women who are always sorry. And for what?"

Jane shrugged her shoulders.

"Exactly. Nothin'." She looked ahead again. "To answer your question, the normal stuff. Fears. Sometimes regrets," she said with a sigh. "How 'bout you? What's got you up?"

"It's too hot." She knew how silly her excuse sounded after what Lucille had said and was not surprised when she started to laugh.

"You'll get used to it."

The nightmare that haunted Jane's sleep made her jolt awake when the morning sun shone through the glass doors. She sat up in bed and found her own hands clutching at her throat. She gasped for air as if her lungs did not work.

She released her fingers and dropped her hands to her side. This was new. She had never tried to strangle herself in her sleep before.

Was that what she was really doing? Strangling herself?

She stood up from the small bed and made her way into the bathroom to catch a glance at her reflection. There were no bruises on her neck, no tiny scratches from her nails.

She splashed her face with cold water and thought, *'I need to get a grip on these dreams before I really do choke myself.'*

Just as she glanced up at the mirror, she caught a shadowy figure moving just behind her.

She whipped around to find there was no one in the bathroom. It was just her and the sound of the *shushing* water pouring into the sink bowl.

'I need to get a grip—'

"Mornin', Jane," a voice called from the open doorway. It was Lucille. She was already dressed, wearing an orange sundress adorned with ruffles.

Jane felt herself take an involuntary step back, clasping her chest as if her heart was going to escape from the scare. Water was now filling the sink. With a deep breath, she turned off the faucet, avoiding the mirror and anymore shadows lurking behind her.

"Didn't sleep well, I take it?" the woman said with a laugh. "I just came to let you know breakfast will be ready soon."

"Th—thank you," she said when she could feel her heart begin to slow to its regular beat.

Lucille smiled and then disappeared down the hall.

Jane thought about what Lucille had said yesterday. About believing in ghosts. She contemplated asking her if she saw any ghosts of the plantation—but she shut this idea down almost immediately.

First the nightmares, and now this? What would her mother think?

After getting dressed in a light T-shirt and a pair of jean shorts, she made her way downstairs. She glanced at the family portraits on the wall, finding the unknown dark-haired girl. It made her brain itch, trying to remember where she had seen her before. She decided she'd ask her mother and the women at breakfast.

The smell of breakfast filled the space downstairs, along with a cheerful hum.

Mary Grace stood in front of the stove, cooking eggs and bacon as she sang to herself, tapping her foot to the rhythm. When she heard Jane enter, she turned around and gave her a welcoming smile.

"Good mornin', darlin'. How'd you sleep?"

Jane returned the smile, hoping she didn't look as tired as she felt. "Fine, thank you."

"You weren't too hot, were you?" she asked, turning back to the stove.

'How did she know that?'

"It can get a little hot here sometimes," she went on. "There's a small fan under your bed for your nightstand."

"Thank you."

It was odd talking with Mary Grace. It was like she knew what Jane was going to say before she even did.

She took a seat at the kitchen table. Lucille and Margaret weren't here yet, and for some reason, this made her uncomfortable. Silence made her nervous. Mary Grace made her nervous.

"Would you like some orange juice?" she asked, already pouring a glass.

"Yes, please."

She placed the glass in front of her and then took a step back and looked at her as if studying her image. "You really do look like your mama."

The right corner of Jane's mouth lifted. "I think I took all my mom's genes. Everyone always thinks we're sisters," she joked. "I barely look like my dad at all."

"Perks of having a daughter at nineteen, I suppose," Mary Grace laughed with her.

Just as she said this, Margaret walked into the kitchen, and they stopped laughing.

"I need coffee," she grumbled, wanting to know what they were talking about before she came in. The kitchen was set up the same way it had been when she lived in Belles. She walked over to the coffee pot by the refrigerator, pulling out a pottery mug from the cabinet above. She could probably walk this house blindfolded. It sort of warmed her heart that Mary Grace hadn't changed anything, even after Lorraine had passed.

Mary Grace moved to the stove again, flipping the cheesy scrambled eggs around the pan. She cut her eyes to Margaret and gave her a sarcastic look. "Whatever happened to *good mornin', Jane*?"

Margaret rolled her eyes. "Please stop doing that," she hissed.

"Stop what?"

She filled the mug to the brim with black coffee. She knew, of course, that no matter how much coffee she drank, there wouldn't ever be enough caffeine to help her cope with being there. She lowered her voice as if Jane wasn't right there. "Oh, you, of all people, shouldn't try to act clueless." She picked up the mug with both hands and brought it to her lips. She missed this taste. Rich, smooth, with hints of chicory. The way Lorraine used to make it. Half coffee grounds, half chicory.

"I don't know what you mean." She moved around the kitchen to grab plates and silverware.

"Stop always *judging*."

"You and I both know that's never gonna happen. I will always judge. When are you gonna learn that that is just part of my unique personality?"

"Ha! Unique is one way to describe it."

"Well, at least I'm not plain," she shot back.

Lucille then entered the kitchen, her eyes glaring with irritation. "Y'all sound like little girls. What did your mama always say, Mary Grace? *If you ain't got nothin' nice to say, don't say anythin' at all.*"

Jane tried not to laugh.

"She started it. It's not my fault she's got a bad temper."

Margaret laughed without amusement, taking a gulp of black coffee. "I have a bad temper?" She left the counter and helped set the plates of the table.

"So, what's the plan today?" Lucille asked as she took a seat across from Jane. Her orange dress swayed as she moved, and the sunlight pouring in from the big window made the fabric glow.

Mary Grace answered her when everyone was seated. "I think we should go into town. I told the Sheriff we'd stop by."

"Sheriff," Lucille repeated with a smile.

Jane looked over at her mother for an explanation. Why would they need to speak with the Sheriff?

"Today?" her mother sighed, looking up from her plate. She avoided Jane's concerned gaze. It's not that she didn't think Jane could handle the truth. She was worried about the danger it could put Jane in if she knew.

"We can't waste any time, Margaret," Mary Grace said. "She's been missin' since Wednesday."

"Wait," Jane spoke up. "Who's missing?" She set down her fork, her appetite leaving that instant.

She was right. Her mother *was* hiding something.

She thought of the illustrated card and shuddered.

Mary Grace didn't understand. She looked over at Margaret, her blue eyes filled with disbelief. "You told her about Vivian, right?"

Margaret clenched her teeth together.

"No, she didn't," Jane answered for her mother, anger boiling in her stomach.

The kitchen fell silent.

"Vivian is our friend," Margaret finally said. "She went missing a few days ago. That's why we're here. To find her."

The dark-haired girl in the pictures. That's Vivian.

Jane processed her words. That was a *very* big secret to keep from her. The anger in her stomach only grew stronger. "Why didn't you tell me?"

It was like her mother wasn't sure how to answer. She sat there, mouth agape. There was a look of betrayal in her daughter's eyes, but she pretended not to notice, averting her gaze.

"Mom?" Jane pressed, a sharpening edge to her voice.

"I was going to tell you," Margaret replied with a huff of a sigh. "Eventually."

"*Eventually*?" A *V* formed between Jane's thick eyebrows.

"I didn't need to because that is not the reason why *you* came. I came because I made a stupid promise when I was ten to return home if something happened—" she spat, her pale face turning pink. Mary Grace and Lucille looked at each other and let out a hurt sigh. "—and you came because your father couldn't watch over you while I was away because of *work*." The words slipped out before she could stop them.

Jane rose from the table quickly, almost knocking down her chair. "And for a second I thought maybe you just wanted to spend time with me."

"Jane, wait. That's not fair." She grabbed her wrist, but Jane pulled away instantly and rushed out of the kitchen.

Margaret glared at her friends. "Thanks a lot," she growled, pushing her chair away from the table.

"No, no," Mary Grace snapped. "You're not allowed to blame *us*. This is your doing. What were you thinking? Not telling Jane about Vivian?"

She didn't bother answering her, leaving the antebellum kitchen to chase after Jane.

As she rushed to the top of the stairs, she heard Jane's bedroom door slam shut. Before knocking, she took a deep breath, trying her best to settle her nerves. When she felt calm enough, she knocked on the door three times, but there was no response. She wasn't surprised by this. Still, she knocked instead of barging in. After waiting five seconds, she creaked open the door.

"I don't want to talk right now," Jane muttered from her bed. She was sitting against the headboard, holding her knees to her chest, fresh tears pooling the corners of her eyes.

Margaret stood in the doorway.

Jane shook her head. "Dad told me that you were *so* excited to spend time with me. He said that this trip would make us closer." She sighed. "I guess he and I were both wrong."

'If only you knew the truth about your father,' she wanted to say but held her tongue.

Jane's throat felt swollen, and her heart ached. She rubbed her eyes, preventing any tears from escaping. At least, not anymore. She had never spoken to her mother that way. They weren't ever together long enough, until now, to have a chance to start an argument.

There was a separation in their relationship—if it even could be called a relationship. Jane realized it was more of an obligation. Margaret *had* to be a mother, and Jane *had* to be her quiet, well-behaved daughter. There was no *real* relationship going on. It was all an act, a performance. And deep down, Jane had always suspected this, but like her mother, she'd try to ignore it. But now, the tension was visible and it was as though everything at that moment came to fruition. She felt hurt. And the fact her mother still hadn't said anything made it ten times worse.

Margaret stood frozen, her own heart tearing at the seams. She had to apologize. But how? Her eyes narrowed on the bed sheets, avoiding her daughter's stare.

The room was painfully silent.

"Jane, I'm sorry that I haven't been entirely honest with you."

"No, you aren't sorry."

Margaret sighed, "I truly am. I should have told you about Vivian." She sat down on the end of the bed. "And," she went on, "you were right."

Her daughter pushed her eyebrows together, not understanding what her mother meant.

"I didn't want you to come. But not because I don't love you," she said, easing the tension a little. "I didn't want you to come because I was scared."

Jane inhaled deeply. "Why?"

"Well," she thought of her next words carefully. "I was worried this all would be too much for you. I mean, with my friend missing. I don't know what happened to her or where she could be. It's all a little... scary." That wasn't the entire truth, but enough of it.

Jane's face softened. "Mom, you should have told me."

"I'm sorry."

"I can handle the truth." She thought about the Devil card. "And I prefer the truth— no matter how dark or scary it is. I'm not a little girl anymore."

Margaret placed her hand on Jane's hand, the corners of her lips turning upward. "I know that."

"Can you grab my watch for me?" her father had asked her the morning before they left for Louisiana. Her mother was taking a shower while her father was down the hall cooking breakfast. Jane was at the kitchen island watching him, enjoying the aromas of charring bacon and freshly baked biscuits, which filled the space with warmth.

"Your lucky one?" she had asked teasingly.

"The one and only," he gave her a quick wink with his chocolate-brown eyes before returning to the eggs. Conversation was easy with her dad. Sometimes, she felt he was more of her best friend than her father. He was the kind of man anyone would trust. Always happy, always seeing the best in things. Jane loved that she was close with him.

She had moved off the stool and bounded down the hall of the modern apartment, slipping into her parents' bedroom. As always, the room smelt of fresh sheets and cologne. She could hear the water running in the master bathroom.

She was walking to the dresser when she saw it.

The card.

It was placed in the center of the desk, the red-horned creature glaring back at Jane with two black, shadowy, unnatural eyes. Even though she was quite frightened, she stood there and stared at it for a beat longer. She had never seen anything like it. Especially not in her parents' room.

"Jane, I love you," her mother's words brought her back to the small, muggy bedroom at the plantation. "You know that, right?" Her green eyes searched Jane's.

Jane couldn't bring herself to ask her mother about the card right now. She decided it was better to leave it a mystery.

"I love you too."

CHAPTER FOUR

MARGARET AND JANE MADE THEIR WAY downstairs to the kitchen after their argument diffused. Margaret's friends had already cleaned up the kitchen and moved across the hall to the grand living room. Sunlight shot rays through the long windows around the room, filling the space with golden warmth.

Old jazz music played from a vintage record player beside a massive mahogany bookcase filled with dusty spines that seemed like more of a decoration than part of a library.

Mary Grace was sitting on an antique red velvet couch, which was positioned in the middle of the room in front of a long wooden coffee table and two matching wide tufted chairs. She was peacefully rereading a worn copy of *Gone with the Wind*, her eyes wide and focused as she consumed the story's words.

Lucille was sitting in the wide tufted chair to the right, looking slightly bored as she read through a fashion magazine. She shut the magazine the minute Margaret and Jane walked in and tossed it on the coffee table.

It was obvious they were waiting for Margaret and Jane to make amends, which only made Margaret feel even more awful. She felt she should apologize to them for causing a ruckus earlier. But Mary Grace spoke first, sensing her friend's discomfort.

"*Sheriff Jones* called while y'all were upstairs," she told them, lifting her eyes from the pages. "Said he has something to show us."

Margaret nodded, pressing her lips together. "Okay. "

Lucille jumped to her feet, almost twisting her ankle in her high heels. "Let's go then!" The longer they stayed here the more time felt wasted, every second slipping away from them like sand in a bottle.

"I'll drive," said Mary Grace— even though they already knew this. Margaret needed a few driving-free days after the long trip down, and Lucille was dropped off by a taxi.

Mary Grace rushed out of the living room and down the hallway to her bedroom, disappearing for a moment before meeting them all on the front porch, wearing a floppy, wide-brimmed hat and the same green kimono she had worn yesterday.

Margaret turned to Jane. "Do you want to stay here?" she asked, half-hoping her answer would be yes.

Mary Grace and Lucille were already walking down the steps to the side of the house where the cars were parked.

"No, that's okay," she replied, shaking her head. She'd rather not be left alone in the big house, especially after what she thought she saw in the bathroom that morning.

"Okay." She didn't have the heart to tell her to stay, not after their argument.

Mary Grace's car was a twenty-year-old hatchback, its once forest-green paint faded and chipping, starting on the hood.

As they piled into the car, Lucille laughed to herself and asked, "Where did you get this lemon?" She sat in the back with Jane, leaning forward to watch Mary Grace's reaction.

Mary Grace slipped the key in, bringing the engine to life. She looked offended. "Lemon? No, no. Might not be a *fancy* electric car like Margaret's—but I like my car."

Lucille laughed.

"At least I have a car," Mary Grace mumbled, holding back a smile. The hatchback made its way down the long driveway, leaving the old white house behind.

Jane looked out the back window as they entered the downtown strip of Belles Parish, eager to see more of the quaint town.

Shady magnolias and pines lined the sidewalks, draping in gray Spanish moss like most of the vegetation in the area. All of the magnolias were in bloom, displaying the beautiful white flowers like pearls placed between wide, green leaves.

Small shops and colonial-style houses were on each side of the clean street, with an American flag waving in the breeze at almost every entrance.

It was a classic southern town with charm and history.

Margaret sank into her seat as they drove through the downtown toward the sheriff's office at the end of the street. Being back in town made her skin crawl. So many memories surfaced in her mind.

She swallowed the knot in her throat and pushed the memories away.

She had to focus on the present moment, not what happened in the past.

Mary Grace pulled into a parking space, a little too close to Randy's tan 1981 Chevy Blazer.

Margaret remembered this truck from when they were teenagers. It was his father's. The cranky alcoholic died when Randy was sixteen. At first, he wanted to sell the truck. He said he didn't want to keep anything that belonged to his old man, mostly because it didn't feel right. Mr. Jones was barely there for Randy, and when he was, he was almost always drunk and in a sour mood.

When Randy Jones became Sheriff, he had decals put on each door that read *"BELLS PARISH SHERIFF"*. The white stickers were now faded and torn after ten years, but still readable.

"Jane," Margaret started, turning around to look at her. "Why don't you check out some of the shops while we're in the office? You could grab something to eat at the diner if you want. I'll give you some cash."

Jane took off her seatbelt, thinking over her mother's offer. Why didn't she want Jane to go to the office? After everything she said this morning, did she still not trust her to handle the truth?

She nodded, coming to the realization that she didn't have a choice here. It was better than being stuck at the plantation, at least. "Okay," she finally said, suppressing a sigh of disappointment.

They all got out of the car and were immediately greeted by a hot, sticky breeze. Margaret pulled out a twenty-dollar bill from her purse and handed it to Jane, saying, "We won't be long. *Do not* go anywhere far. Stay on this street, understand?"

'Where else would I go?' she wanted to ask back. "I will," she said instead of the snarky question, taking the money. The cash felt heavy in her palm, weighed by her mother's bribe. She stuffed it in the back pocket of her shorts.

For a split second, Margaret almost took back the offer. Even though Jane was almost eighteen years old, the idea of her wandering alone in the town made her stomach tighten. She had to remind herself that Jane walked the streets of New York City alone almost every day to school. She could handle a small town. But it wasn't just the town that worried her. It was who might be in the town that made her worry for Jane's safety.

"Why don't you want her to meet Randy?" Mary Grace asked Margaret as they watched Jane walk away on the shaded sidewalk.

Lucille went into the building first, not wanting to wait around in the heat any longer than they had to. It must have been one-hundred degrees in the direct sun.

"It's not that," Margaret answered as she followed Lucille inside, meeting a wave of cold A/C. "I just don't want her to be... too involved, okay? I don't need her worrying about this." The icy air danced on her bare arms, and the sweat on her upper lip magically evaporated.

"She might need to."

"What the hell does that mean?"

Mary Grace didn't answer, instead joining Lucille at the front desk. An old lady wearing thick-brimmed glasses and flamingo-pink lipstick sat behind it. She looked tired and, quite frankly, annoyed by their presence.

"How can I help you ladies?" she asked, pulling back her lips in the shape of a smile. Her teeth were stained yellow and were partially covered in pink lipstick.

As always, Mary Grace was the first to respond. "We're here to talk with the Sheriff."

The building was small and quiet with few police officers and secretaries about. Anyone could tell that not a lot of crime happened in Belles Parish by the lack of officers.

This caught the receptionist's attention. She lifted an eyebrow. "Is it about that missin' woman from New Orleans?" She asked this in a hushed tone, as if the disappearance of Vivian Banks was a secret. But it was likely that everyone in town knew about it by now.

Just as Mary Grace was going to answer, a deep voice called out from their left.

Randy Jones.

The man was an average height with a beer belly and rosy cheeks. He had a brown walrus mustache that shrouded his wide smile. He wore a tan uniform, his gold badge displayed proudly above his chest pocket.

"Randy?" gasped Lucille. She ran over to him to get a closer look. Margaret and Mary Grace followed. "Well, look at you! You're fat!"

The man scratched the right end of his mustache with his thumb as he processed the insult. Or was it—the hard truth.

"Well, it's good to see you too, Lucille," he grumbled. "You're old now."

Lucille gasped. "Am not!"

"Sure," he laughed softly. He looked over at Margaret. Her hair was chopped just beneath her sharp jawline, and her pale face was almost unrecognizable. She didn't look like the same wild-hearted girl he had grown up with. She was the reason he was friends with the four girls. Because they were direct neighbors, it was only natural that they became friends.

Margaret remembered the many times Randy used to sneak into her trailer during the night, desperate to escape Mr. Jones, with a fresh black eye or a split lip. She had always felt like she had to look out for him and protect him like he was her brother.

"Margaret," he breathed, the past echoing in his words. "Good to see you, too."

Margaret looked in Randy's eyes, realizing just how many years had gone by. The last time she saw him he was just a gangly boy with not a speck of hair on his chest. But now, not only was he a grown man, but he was also the Sheriff of Belles Parish.

"Same to you." She couldn't help from tearing up a little.

Mary Grace clapped her hands and heaved a sigh. "I hate to rush our reunion, but I was hoping to see what you had to show us."

Randy nodded once. "Of course." He almost forgot the real reason Margaret and Lucille were back in town.

Besides talking briefly over the phone that morning, Randy hadn't spoken to Mary Grace since the night Mary Grace realized her friend had disappeared.

Mary Grace had called him Wednesday night, just after Jones had finished eating dinner while he was scraping leftover potatoes and sirloin into his labrador's bowl. His wife heard the phone ring first. She turned off the sink, drying her hands on her jeans before picking it up from the dining room table.

"It's Mary Grace," she had said, holding out his phone.

He set his plate on the counter beside the dog bowl and then took the phone. Mary Grace's voice was shaking. She sounded scared, which made him worry because she was never scared.

"Mary Grace, calm down," he had said. *"I just saw her last weekend."* He had decided it was time for a road trip with the family,

so they drove down to New Orleans for a mini getaway. There, he ran into Vivian at a local café.

"Yes, and now she is gone!"

"How do you know?"

Mary Grace huffed into the phone. *"Because I know. She's my best friend, and I just know. You need to send out a search team at the crack of dawn."*

Jones almost laughed. *"What? She lives in New Orleans, not in Belles Parish."*

"I'm serious. You need to find our friend," her voice remained solid.

He still didn't know how Mary Grace knew Vivian had gone missing.

Randy led the women over to his office.

"I'm not sure why I'm even showin' y'all this video," Randy said as he sat before his old friends. "But I promised Mary Grace I would let y'all know if I found anything, and I'm a man of my word."

"Video?" Lucille leaned forward.

The office room was small and cluttered with random papers and books. The once white walls were stained a light tan from the many years of smoking inside. The cramped space smelt of cigarettes and ink. There were two ashtrays on the desk beside the outdated computer, filled to the brim with cigarette butts.

On the solid wall behind Randy was a pinboard disarrayed with small handwritten notes and photographs of things involving Vivian's case.

"Well," he began, clearing his voice with a single cough. "A surveillance camera caught footage of her in a convenience store a few minutes from New Orleans—" he looked at Mary Grace. "—the night you called me."

Mary Grace could feel her heart sink in her chest. "And?"

"Well," he sighed. "It recorded her exiting, but we couldn't see anythin' after that. The place had electrical problems that night, and all the cameras shut off."

Mary Grace pressed her lips together. "How convenient."

"Her car was found there too. No damage or anythin'. It just looked like it was abandoned."

"Vivian wouldn't leave her vehicle like that," Mary Grace huffed, shaking her head. She tapped the desk. "I would like to see that video."

He hesitated. "Just don't tell anyone I'm showin' y'all this, okay? You know I can't share any evidence with the public right now. The case is still fresh and it's not even in our jurisdiction to investigate. The boys down in New Orleans are already on my ass." He leaned back in his chair and inhaled a deep breath, his belly inflating like a balloon.

Lucille nodded. "We understand. Our lips are sealed." Those were rich words coming from her—the only one out of the friend group who could spread gossip around the entire parish in less than twenty-four hours.

After two seconds of hesitation, he finally turned to his computer and searched his files for the video. As he did so, Margaret noticed a framed picture on his desk of Randy and, who she assumed to be, his family. The woman had her arm interlocked with his, her head resting on his shoulder like two high school lovers. She had brown curly hair and big round eyes and was tall and slender with a warm smile that just proved she was a kind person. The teenage girl standing next to her shared an uncanny resemblance except for her button nose and round cheeks she undoubtedly inherited from Randy.

Randy noticed Margaret looking at the picture. "That's my wife Melissa and my daughter Bobbie Jo."

Lucille giggled. "You named your daughter *Bobbie Jo* Jones? Kind of a tongue twister, ain't it?"

"Her birth certificate says Barbara Josephine Jones," he replied, shaking his head and laughing. "Barbara was my great-aunt's name, and Josephine was Mellisa's grandmother's name. But we haven't called her by her full name since she was a baby. I don't think she would even reply if someone called her that."

"She looks just like you when you were a kid," Lucille awed.

Mary Grace coughed and nodded to the computer. Her whole body was tense as she awaited the video.

He gave her a look like *'right, my bad'* and scrolled through the files some more before finding the one he was looking for.

He clicked the file.

The screen changed, and the three women all leaned in closer as he hit play, making sure to absorb every detail on the screen.

CHAPTER FIVE

THE WARM SUNSHINE BEAT DOWN ON JANE without sympathy. The air was thick and difficult to breathe. A bead of sweat rolled down the side of her face, emitting a quiet *hiss* as it hit the hot pavement. There was no relief even in the shade of the magnolia trees.

She walked down the sidewalk, studying each shop she passed. She only went into a few of them, just to receive a break from the heat, and majority were boutiques. She browsed through the homemade crafts and tacky overpriced clothes with cow prints and southern sayings on them, such as *"HEY Y'ALL"* and *"BLESS YOUR HEART"* and *"G.R.I.T.S: GIRLS RAISED IN THE SOUTH"* and—Jane's favorite— *"I'M FROM THE SOUTH: I LIKE MY TEA SWEET, MY FOOD FRIED, AND MY MUSIC COUNTRY"*.

Every sales associate she encountered gave her a hopeful look—like she was the first tourist they had seen in a long time. And maybe she was. The town wasn't crowded with vacationers on summer break or tourists in golf carts. Maybe it was because Belles Parish was just too small to be a vacation destination, too desolate and removed from the busyness of New Orleans.

On the corner of the street was the diner she and her mother had passed when they first drove into town. The smell of canola oil and grease emanated from the diner and, it being almost noon, she made the decision that she would grab lunch. There wasn't much else to do, and she wasn't sure how long her mother and her friends would be.

A small bell tied above the door rang as she entered. The diner looked like a place right out of the 1950s. The floor was made of black and white checkered tiles, popping against the scarlet-red leather booths that sat by the large windows. Bright, yellow sunlight leaked in from the windows, allowing heat to travel inside—but it was balanced by the A/C and whirring overhead fans. Across the booths was a bar that stretched the entire length of the kitchen, complimented with red swivel stools.

Besides a few people eating at the bar, the place was practically empty.

Jane slid into the last booth, near the window. She rested her hands on the sticky plastic tabletop, intertwining her white fingers. She looked around the diner, trying to imagine her mother working there, trying to picture what type of person she was back then. She must have been different because Jane knew her mother would never even eat at a place like this.

She noticed a curly-haired girl around her age sitting at the bar by herself. Her head was down, completely buried in a large book, hiding her face.

An older woman with bleached blonde hair and blue eyeliner walked over to Jane's table, carrying a small notepad in one hand and a menu in the other. "Hello, doll. How are you today?" She chomped on a piece of gum, placing the menu in front of Jane, her free hand settling on her hip.

Jane smiled at the waitress. "I'm doing good. How are you?"

The woman didn't reply to her question, didn't even hesitate to think of an answer. "You need some time to look at the menu or are you ready to order?"

She noticed the girl at the bar squinting at her. When they locked eyes, she turned around to her book again. Jane looked back at the waitress. "Um—I need a minute to look at the menu." She felt like all of the customers were watching her, sniffing her out as a tourist instantly.

The waitress kept chomping the gum in her mouth. "Alright," she sighed. "Take yer time." She trailed back into the kitchen, sort of waddling from side to side like a tired penguin.

Jane glanced at the people of the bar, catching a few of their curious stares. The girl with the book was watching her again. She smiled and shut her book before sliding off the stool. She walked toward Jane with a pep in her step.

She was tall and thin, her limbs lanky and quite awkwardly proportioned. She had a freckled face and a head full of chestnut-brown curly hair. Her oval eyes matched the color of her hair and were perfectly outlined by her thick lashes. She smiled again, displaying her crooked teeth. She was unapologetically imperfect, and yet smiled with a beauty so kind that none of her flaws mattered.

"I know every face in this town—but I don't know yours. Are you new here or just visitin'?" Like Mary Grace and Lucille, the teenage girl's accent was thickly coated in the same southern twang.

"Um," Jane stuttered. "Just visiting for a few weeks."

The girl slid into the booth across from her, setting her big book on the table.

Jane glanced at the book. *'Stories of True Crime and Mysteries'* was written in chunky silver letters on the spine. She looked back at the slender girl.

"I hope you don't mind if I sit with you. I hate sittin' alone, and seein' that you're alone, I figured you might want some company," she told her, her friendliness slightly off-putting.

Jane shrugged her shoulders. "I don't mind at all."

The girl shot her hand over the table. "My name's Bobbie Jo."

Warily, Jane shook the girl's hand and was surprised by the firm grasp. There was something in the girl's eyes that told Jane she was a lot tougher than she looked. "I'm Jane."

When they dropped hands, Bobbie Jo sat back in the booth. "So, where you from and why are you visitin' Belles Parish?" Her left eyebrow raised, and she squinted her brown eyes again as if trying to interrogate Jane.

"Well," Jane hesitated, wondering if she should tell her. Was the disappearance of her mother's friend a secret? It was hard to tell, considering how her mother made it a secret. "I'm from New York, and my...*aunt* just went missing, so my mom and I are here to help find her." It was easier to think of her mother's friends like aunts—especially since they treated each other like sisters.

Bobbie Jo's eyes grew wide. "You mean to tell me *your* aunt is Vivian Banks?"

Hearing the name made her blood run cold. It shouldn't have surprised her that this girl knew about Vivian. It *was* a small town, after all. "Yes," she said with a single nod. "Not by blood, of course. Do you know her?"

"Know her?" she gasped. "She's one of my father's childhood friends. And she was piano teacher for a few years. I used to see her every week, up until last year when she moved to New Orleans."

"Really?" The condescendence left her speechless.

Bobbie Jo grinned and shifted her weight as she crossed her legs. "This is so cool! We can look for her together!" She made it sound like they were going on a fun scavenger hunt together, not searching for a missing person.

The waitress returned just then, forcing them to halt the conversation. "So, what are you gettin' today, sweetie?" she asked, bringing out her notepad and pen. She looked over at Bobbie Jo as if she hadn't noticed her sitting there. "Oh, hi, Bobbie Jo."

"Hi, Mrs. Opal. How are you doin' today?" she asked, out of politeness and obligation.

She huffed at the question. "Just peachy-keen, honey."

Jane realized then that she hadn't read over the menu once while the waitress was gone. She looked up at Bobbie Jo for help.

"What do you normally get?"

Bobbie Jo smiled, waving her hand at Jane. "I got you. Mrs. Opal, can you get my new friend my favorite plate?" she winked.

"That all?" Not needing to write anything down, she tucked her notepad in her apron's pocket.

"Oh—and can I get a cheeseburger and fries to-go? It's for my dad. Oh—and a strawberry milkshake. For me." She looked at Jane and then back at Mrs. Opal. "Actually, make that *two* strawberry milkshakes."

Mrs. Opal sighed, walking away. "One favorite plate, two strawberry milkshakes, and a cheeseburger and fries to go, coming up," she called over her shoulder.

Bobbie Jo returned her attention to the new girl. "They have the *best* strawberry milkshakes."

Jane laughed and ran a hand through her short hair. She was happy by how smooth this interaction was going. It was like she had already met Bobbie Jo before.

"So, you said you came here with your mom?" she questioned, looking around as if to find her mother in the small diner.

"Yeah. She's at the sheriff's office right now talking with the Sheriff."

Her jaw slowly dropped open. "No way," she gasped, her eyes growing wide. "My *dad* is the Sheriff."

Jane just raised her eyebrows.

"This is crazy," she went on, talking faster. "I mean—I can't believe this. Our parents grew up together! That practically makes as *cousins*."

"I guess it does," Jane replied with a laugh.

"Who's your mom?" she asked.

"Margaret."

"I remember hearin' 'bout her before. So basically, the gang reunited to bring back Vivian?" she grinned, overflowing with excitement. "This is great. Not that Vivian is missing, but that y'all are here again. My dad tells me stories from his childhood 'bout his friends all the time."

For some reason, Jane felt slightly jealous. It seemed the curly-haired girl knew more about who her mother was in the past than she did. She wanted to pry a little, maybe ask if the girl could tell her some of the stories her father shared—but she didn't know how to ask, so she didn't.

"Do you have any theories on where Vivi is?" She figured if anyone had theories about Vivian's disappearance, it would be Vivian's niece. After all, they were family, right?

The question came out so fast that it took a second for Jane to hear it clearly. Does *she* have theories?

"I don't. I—um," she stuttered. "I didn't know Vivian very well. Actually, I didn't know her at all until a few days ago. I'm just here because my mom wanted me to come with her."

Bobbie Jo hesitated. "Oh." Her face dropped. It was like all her hope and enthusiasm evaporated into thin air.

Jane could see her disappointment. "My mom never talks about her past with me. I didn't know any of the women until Thursday morning."

"Huh," she exhaled.

"I want to help, though," she said, nodding. "What about you? Do you have any theories on where she might be?" When she asked this, the bell above the door chimed, and Jane saw three girls around their age walk in.

Bobbie Jo looked over her shoulder at the group of girls and sighed a loud breath. "Oh, great," she whispered to herself.

The girl walking in first looked like a Barbie doll. She had straight blonde hair that was cut in a perfect line across her collarbone, and her skin was a fake orangey tan that made her teeth look unnaturally white.

"What? Do you know them?" Jane questioned.

Bobbie Jo rolled her eyes, letting out an annoyed breath. "They're Belles Parish's *finest* clique," she quickly whispered.

To the blonde's left was a shorter girl with curly dark hair, pale skin, and red ruby lips. She looked irritated. She was talking about some clothing store or dress, Bobbie Jo and Jane couldn't exactly hear from across the diner.

"Oh, shut up, Trista. We'll go shopping *after* I get somethin' to eat—" the Barbie doll's eyes landed on Jane and Bobbie Jo, and she stopped.

"Charlotte is the leader of the pack, and Trista and Laney are the other girls. In school, they call themselves *The Angel Trio*, but most kids call them *The Triple Brats* behind their backs," Bobbie Jo told Jane as the three girls stopped and stared at them from across the diner.

The girl to the right, Laney, had dark skin and coily hair. She wore gold glasses that magnified her brown eyes as she stared dumbfoundedly at Jane.

"What—are they mean girls or something?" Jane asked in a hushed voice, dodging the six gawking eyes.

The blonde, Charlotte, whispered something to Trista and Laney, and they nodded without hesitation as if agreeing to whatever she said. They then began to take quick strides towards Bobbie Jo and Jane.

"Something like that," Bobbie Jo answered before they made their way to the booth.

"Hi," Charlotte greeted Jane, pulling her lips back in a tight smile that looked like it was plastered on her face like plastic. "Are you new here?" she asked, her blue eyes wide. The girls didn't look over at Bobbie Jo.

"Yeah," she answered with a nod, casting a quick smile.

"Where are you from?" the girl Laney questioned.

"New York City."

Charlotte gasped, and she looked at her two friends with astonishment, as if finding out Jane was from New York suddenly made her a thousand times more interesting.

"Do you want us to give you a tour 'round the parish? We're not doin' anythin' today," she offered with another fake smile.

Jane looked forward at Bobbie Jo, who looked beyond bothered by the Barbie doll.

Bobbie Jo coughed, as if to make her presence known. The girls' smiles dropped as they turned to look at the freckled-faced girl. Bobbie Jo ignored their gawking stare and rolled her eyes at them. "Leave us alone. She doesn't want to go with you."

Charlotte scrunched up her face. "Well, look who it is, girls. It's Detective White Trash," she hissed. Her voice was high-pitched and squeaky, like that of a mouse.

Jane raised her eyebrows, shocked by the rude greeting. *Detective White Trash?* The nickname was childish. She didn't see how the three girls could take it seriously, but from the way Bobbie Jo's face lit up pink, Jane could tell *she* did.

"Good to see you, too," mumbled Bobbie Jo, gracefully lifting her middle finger to the girls.

Laney sucked her teeth, taking a step forward. Jane could see the thick layer of foundation caked on her skin. "You better watch it," she told Bobbie Jo through her teeth.

"Why are you calling her *Detective White Trash?*" Jane asked, knowing she had just opened a can of worms that she wouldn't be able to close.

The three girls flicked their eyes in Jane's direction, their once friendly smiles vanishing in an instant.

"Well—" Charlotte stuttered, blinking multiple times as if the question hurt to think about. She flipped back her blonde hair draped over her right shoulder. "Who are you, anyway?"

No more tours around town.

"My name's Jane," she said, knowing the girls wouldn't know who she was by her first name.

The corners of Bobbie Jo's mouth lifted like she knew a secret the girls didn't. "Her aunt is Vivian Banks."

The three girls took one giant step back.

Jane lifted an eyebrow at their response.

"You're related to the *Witches of Belles Parish*?" gasped Laney.

"What?" Jane didn't know how to react. She didn't know if she should laugh or be concerned by her sneery remark. They looked disgusted and a little scared. Like at any moment, Jane could jump up and yell *'boo!'*.

"Oh, Laney, please," Bobbie Jo shook her head. "Not this again."

"You said *witches*?" Jane pressed, moving a strand of hair behind her ear.

The devil card she found in her mother's bedroom popped into her mind, and out of nowhere, a strange burning sensation started to spread in the back of her head. Like she was remembering something. Or maybe she was forgetting. She shut her eyes, trying to ignore the headache, and opened them again and focused on the girls.

Trista rolled her eyes. "We all know your family's history. So, you ain't foolin' no one by actin' dumb."

Laney pulled Charlotte's arm. "Let's get out of here before she puts a *spell* on us or somethin'."

"What do you know about *my* family?" Jane snapped, crossing her arms over her chest—truly interested in what she had to say.

Bobbie Jo shook her head. "It's nothin'. Just mean rumors—"

Trista cut her short. "I know about your *weird* aunts, and they all used to dance *naked* under the *full moon*."

Jane laughed, shaking her head. "You can't be serious."

"Trista, just shut up, will you?" Bobbie Jo snapped.

But the girls didn't stop. "I heard that they sold their souls to the *devil*," barked Laney, her eyes wide with terror.

Her headache was growing stronger as an unnerving feeling filled her. Her words repeated in Jane's head. The sinister drawing lingered in her thoughts—grinning at her in mockery.

"And I heard they all practice *black magic*," Charlotte said, taking another step back.

Her head was starting to pound with the sudden pain. She dropped her eyes to the table as she tried to breathe through the rapid headache.

"Alright, ladies," another voice spoke up from behind the three girls, making Jane's headache disappear. It was a waiter carrying two strawberry milkshakes topped with fluffy cream and cherries. He was probably in his mid-seventies, tall, and walked a little hunched over, with starch white hair and a mouth full of crooked yellow teeth from the many years of drinking coffee. He walked around the three girls. "Well, hello, girls!" he said. "Good to see y'all. You all dinin' in today?"

Charlotte took a deep breath, forcing her lips upwards into that fake smile she came in with. "Yes, sir. I think we'll be sittin' at the bar today." And then, without hesitation, the Triple Brats marched away from them, their chins lifted like they were of high importance.

The white-haired waiter set the pink milkshakes down at the table along with two paper-wrapped straws. His face lit up when he saw Bobbie Jo. "Hi, darlin'! How are you today? Those girls botherin' you again?"

"Not anymore, Jim," she giggled.

The waiter, now known as *Jim*, looked over at Jane. "I hope you don't mind me askin', but who are you? I don't recall seein' your face before."

"This is Jane," Bobbie Jo answered excitedly. "She's here to help find Ms. Banks."

Jane nodded in agreement.

He raised his eyebrows a little and gasped like he just now remembered something. And then, his face lit up with joy. "Now, hold your horses. Are you Margaret's daughter?"

"Yes, I am," Jane smiled, opening her straw and sticking it in the fountain glass.

"Well, I'll be!" he laughed, clapping his hands together. "You're a spittin' image of your mama, alright—minus all the hair she has. She still got that long hair, right?"

"No, she cut it when I was born."

He sighed, "What a shame. Your mama was a sweet girl. I miss seein' her big 'ole smile in here." He shook his head, getting rid of the memory. "Well, my name is Jim—I own this place, so if you got any questions 'bout the food or anythin', come and find me."

When he was gone, Bobbie Jo put her straw in her milkshake and took a big sip.

"So," Jane started, looking around them. The mean girls were seated at the bar with their backs facing them, but she kept her voice down in case they were listening. "Does everyone in this town think my mom and my aunts are..." she felt ridiculous saying it. "witches?"

Bobbie Jo lifted her mouth from the straw, and she rolled her eyes. "It's just a stupid rumor, really. I wouldn't worry about it."

"How long has this rumor been going on?"

She frowned. "Long time. It's kinda like Belles Parish's folklore. I thought you would have known about it."

"Like I said, my mom doesn't talk about her past."

"Right," Bobbie Jo sighed. "Well, don't let them get to you. The rumor isn't real or anythin'. It's just another stupid lie they can spread."

Jane couldn't help but think about the strange card again.

Jim came back with a big plate and a Styrofoam box, carefully setting both down on the table as if they would shatter.

After he set the plate and box down, he wiped his shaky, long, bony hands on the front of his white apron.

"Here y'all go. One cheeseburger to-go, and one *Bobbie Jo's Breakfast*."

"Thank you, sir," Bobbie Jo said, a smile tugging at her lips.

Jane looked down at her plate. The *Bobbie Jo's Breakfast* consisted of two slices of French toast buried in cinnamon sugar and syrup, two thin slices of burnt bacon, and cheesy scrambled eggs sprinkled with pepper.

"Hey, Jim, mind if I borrow a pen real quick?" Bobbie Jo asked, pulling out a napkin from the napkin dispenser by the window.

Jim turned around and smiled, pulling out a pen from his front pocket. "Sure thing, sweetie."

"Thanks," she said, grabbing it from him. She scribbled something on the napkin and then handed the pen back to the old waiter, letting him return to the kitchen.

The curly-haired girl slid the napkin to Jane and then stood up, grabbing the Styrofoam box. "Well, I need to give this to my dad. If you find out anything 'bout Vivian's disappearance or you just want to talk—call me."

Jane looked at the napkin, finding Bobbie Jo's number written in blue ink. She smiled and nodded. "I will, thank you."

"Anytime. See you around." As she walked out of the diner, she said goodbye to the three girls at the bar. "It was great talkin', girls. I'll see y'all in church."

CHAPTER SIX

BACK IN THE OFFICE, RANDY JONES replayed the scene where Vivian was leaving the store. The cramped room smelt of dusty cigarette smoke. As time went on, the smell intensified, burning the back of Margaret's throat. She used to smoke. Most people did back then. But she dropped the bad habit the moment she found out she was pregnant with Jane. Now, after seventeen years without one cigarette, the smell was almost unbearable.

She checked the watch on her left wrist, hoping Jane was doing okay.

"There! Pause it!" commanded Mary Grace, pointing her finger at the computer screen.

The man quickly did as told, looking over at Mary Grace for an explanation. He had already watched the video about twenty times before even showing it to Mary Grace.

"You see her face?"

Margaret and Lucille nodded, staring at the paused video.

"Her face changed the minute she walked outside," Mary Grace stated, nodding at the paused clip. "She saw something."

"Or some*one*," added Lucille.

Randy Jones raised one eyebrow. "Ladies, you don't know that for sure. It's a grainy video, I can barely see her face. And plus, why would the suspect approach her as she was still exiting the building? Don't you think that's a bit risky?"

"That depends on who it was. They got the rest of the video erased, so who knows? Maybe it was someone who worked at the place?" Mary Grace pressed her lips together, waiting for his response.

"Erased? No one erased the video. The place had electrical problems, remember?" Then the Sheriff gasped, his rosy face turning a ghostly white. "*Unless* that was just a lie..." He grabbed a notepad from inside his desk and began frantically writing something.

Mary Grace looked at Lucille with a look that said something along the lines of, *'Can you believe this guy?'*

She snorted.

Randy stood from his office chair and took the note to the pinboard. He stuck a tack in the top of it and then found his seat again.

Margaret stared at the note on the board, trying to swallow the knot in her throat that came after watching the video the first time.

WAS THE VIDEO ERASED???

An eerie silence hung dense in the office but was interrupted by a knock on the door.

Randy rubbed the back of his neck as he called out, "Who is it?"

The door crept open, and Ms. Wilma, the woman who sat at the front desk, popped her head in. She stared at the Sheriff over the brim of her glasses.

"The new detective is here. He's waitin' in the lobby," she said with a deep sigh. She turned around and closed the door before Randy could respond.

Randy sat there for a second before standing up from his chair.

Mary Grace stood up with him, grabbing her keys from the desk. "You hired a detective?"

"Yes, I did. We only got one detective in this town and he's on vacation for the next few weeks."

"That's good then," Mary Grace nodded. "Thank you for callin' us in today. Make sure to tell me everythin' you find, okay?"

He nodded. "I'll keep you posted." He looked over at Lucille and Margaret. "It was good seein' you girls again. We should all meet up for dinner sometime. I'd love for you to meet my family."

"We should," Lucille agreed.

"See you tomorrow, Randy." Mary Grace smiled and then headed for the door. Margaret and Lucille followed her as they all walked out of the sheriff's office and dove into the hot, humid weather of Summertime in Louisiana.

Lucille wiped the back of her hand across her face, gasping. "It's hot," she said, as if her friends didn't know already.

Margaret pulled out her phone and pressed Jane's contact. Jane answered the call immediately. When Margaret returned her phone to the back pocket of her jeans, she looked at Mary Grace and Lucille, who were standing by the car.

"Jane's at the diner. She said she's almost finished."

Lucille perked up. "Let's go meet her! I'm just about starved anyway."

The idea of going back to the diner made Margaret's stomach turn. She held her breath, not liking her friend's sudden enthusiasm. "I don't know. I'm kind of tired. We should just wait—"

Mary Grace shook her head, smiling. "There's no way in hell I am waitin' in the car when it's this hot. Let's just go. For old times' sake."

Being back in town and seeing Randy was enough *walking-down-memory-lane* for Margaret.

"Pretty please, Mar?" Lucille pushed out her lips and held her hands together dramatically. "Pretty, *pretty*, please?"

She sighed in defeat, knowing there was nothing she could do to change their minds.

As they walked down the sidewalk, under the sweet fragrant magnolias and past the boutiques and antique shops, they all felt a spark of the past. It was almost like they were teenage girls again, walking together through the town. But, without Vivian, it felt wrong. Walking down the same sidewalk they've walked a million times growing up wasn't nearly the same. And despite the hot weather, it left a cold feeling in each of their chests.

Up ahead, a teenage girl was headed in their direction. "Hi, Mary Grace!" the girl cheered when she walked past the three women. She had orange freckles sprinkled across her cheeks like pixie dust and curly brown hair that bounced with every step she took.

Mary Grace smiled at the friendly girl. "Hello, Bobbie Jo. I'll see you in church tomorrow?"

The girl was obviously in a hurry, but she slowed to a sort of stop and nodded her head. "Yep!" she simply said and then continued down the sidewalk towards the sheriff's office, holding a to-go box in her hands.

The three women kept walking.

"Was that—" Lucille started to ask.

"Yes, that was Randy's daughter," Mary Grace finished for her. "She's a sweet girl."

"How come no one is staring at us? Or calling us names?" Margaret asked while releasing an uneasy laugh. She looked at the few people walking the sidewalks. They were oblivious to the women, smiling and waving at them as if the three women were... well, *normal.*

"Are we under some *spell*?" Lucille teased but seriously wanted to know as well.

Mary Grace shook her head, still smiling. "No, we're not under a spell. It's not like how it was twenty years ago. People here know me. They respect me. Sure, there are a few people in town who still talk trash about us, but most don't care anymore."

"You think it's because the coven broke apart?" questioned Lucille. "People just forgot about the weird group of girls?"

Mary Grace answered with a simple shrug. She liked to think that it was because the townspeople liked her for who she was—but maybe Lucille was right. Maybe without the whole group, people just let go of the *'Witches of Belles Parish'* story.

Dread and anguish smacked Margaret in the face as she followed her two friends through the door to the diner. The familiar bell chimed overhead, a pleasant sound. But it was almost worse revisiting the nostalgic diner than it was when she set foot in Mary Grace's house for the first time in almost twenty years. It seemed like everything that had happened in her teen years, the good and the bad, boiled and thrived in this restaurant. And when she entered, the past she thought she had buried long ago bubbled in her gut.

She saw Jane eating by herself at the table across the diner. She smiled, trying her hardest to lock the discomfort away. The past couldn't actually hurt her. No matter how hard it got revisiting the areas from her past—the memories couldn't actually do her harm. She had to repeat this as she walked toward Jane.

When they slid into the booth, she took a deep, shaky breath and focused her attention on the sounds of the diner. Coffee pots brewing, customers chatting in graceful voices, and pots clinking in the kitchen.

"How was the Sheriff?" Jane asked her, anxious to tell her that she had just met his daughter.

Margaret looked around the diner nervously. The past couldn't hurt her.

"Mom?"

"Huh?" she snapped her attention back to their table.

"How was the Sheriff?" she asked again.

"Oh—he's fine."

"I met his daughter," she told her, gesturing to the napkin with Bobbie Jo's phone number scribbled on it. "She's really nice."

Margaret could hear her heart beating louder. She was starting to get a headache from being in the diner. "Really? That's great," she muttered, her head someplace else.

She then zoned them out as Mary Grace and Lucille shared their favorite stories of the diner, picking on Margaret for the years she worked there as a waitress. They made it sound like the diner was this amazing restaurant, but to Margaret, it was just a cheap place to eat, filled with truckers and locals who reeked of sweat.

A song started to play from the radio propped up against the fountain machine. The song was an old one and chillingly familiar.

'Sweet Jane' by the *Cowboy Junkies*.

It was a song she could never forget. She had played it so many times that she knew every beat and lyric by heart. But hearing it now, as a grown woman, reminded her of when she was eighteen—and she loathed it.

She wanted to throw up, she wanted to run home. But her daughter was sitting right next to her. She had to keep it together.

"Hi, ladies," a deep voice spoke from in front of the table. "Here are some menus." Four laminated paper menus were placed on the table. "Do we know what we want to drink?"

She knew that male voice. Or she *once* knew it.

She used all her strength to drag her eyes from her menu to the waiter beside her.

Goosebumps covered her arms and neck as panic swept through her.

It couldn't be. It was impossible.

But there he was, nonetheless.

Her first love.

Margaret stopped breathing.

The waiter was a haunting ghost from her past. A teenage boy, not much older than Jane. He had crystal blue eyes that sliced through Margaret's heart, a wide, crooked smile and a hooked nose, and messy brown hair that turned a dirty blonde when the sun hit it. He was charming and handsome with not a single imperfection.

"We're actually ready to order, if that's okay," Mary Grace said, her voice suddenly light and soft.

Margaret looked at her friend ahead of her and almost shrieked.

Mary Grace was young— a teenager. Her crow's feet had disappeared, and her eyes seemed brighter. She looked youthful and happy— like she had never faced stress in her entire life.

Lucille was a teenager again, too. Her hair was lighter and filled with twirly curls. She wore her favorite blue baseball cap and a muscle tank that was about two sizes too big.

"Of course. What can I get you?"

Margaret found herself looking back at the waiter and down at the nametag on his white apron.

Wyatt.

"I'll take a hotdog with ketchup and mustard and a side of fries. Oh, and sweet tea, please," young Mary Grace told him.

Young, lively Lucille perked up. "I'll do the exact same, please."

He nodded, then turned his attention over to Jane. Margaret almost forgot about Jane. She looked to her right, finding that she was gone. Instead, shy and innocent Vivian sat next to her. She was how she remembered her to be. Her black eyes flicked up to find the charming waiter, and she stuttered as she usually did when she spoke.

"Can— can I get the cheeseburger and fries?" she asked— as if asking for permission. That was Vivian. Too kind for her own good.

"Sure can," smiled the ghost boy. "What can I get for you to drink?"

"Water," she said, almost in a whisper.

Then his eyes settled on Margaret, like a fly would stick to honey. His blue eyes made her insides freeze. He licked his lips and smiled, showing off his perfect teeth. As she stared up at him, time seemed to freeze as well. Her goosebumps left and were replaced by a sudden heat in the diner. The song continued to play in the background.

She found her cheeks blushing, the same way they did when she first met him.

But this *was* the first time meeting him. This was the day that he introduced himself and asked her out on a date. This was the day that she fell in love.

But that day was years ago. That day was far in the past.

"Margaret?" Mary Grace called, her voice growing deeper. "What would you like?"

The song ended, and the air became cold. She moved her eyes to the menu and did her best to read the options before her.

"I'll have... er..."

"Oh, come on. She ain't got all day!" Lucille snapped. Margaret's gaze lifted. Lucille's hair lost its curls and lightness. Her blue cap was gone. Her cheekbones looked more defined and sharper, and the innocence in her eyes had faded.

"Just get what I got. It's the best thing on the menu, you know that," Mary Grace said, the softness in her tone gone too.

Margaret looked at the two women and realized that they were now matured. But just a few seconds ago, they were teenagers!

She looked to the right and found Jane staring back at her with concern. She shook her head, trying to understand what was happening, what kind of tricks her mind was playing.

"I can come back, if you need more time to decide...?" a female voice offered.

The ghost of Margaret's past was gone, and instead an older woman stood in his place.

"No, I'll take what she got," Margaret nodded her head to Mary Grace. "Sorry."

The woman shook her head. "Don't worry about it, hon. I'll get y'all's order in right away."

Jane squinted her green eyes at her mother, confused by her strange behavior. Margaret looked sick— her face a pale shade of green, her eyes bloodshot, and her hands were trembling in her lap.

"So," Lucille started, trying to fill the awkward silence at the table. Mary Grace and Jane turned their attention to Lucille. "What—"

"Girls?" Jim exclaimed from behind the bar. He quickly made his way over to the booth. "Oh my—" He panted, too shocked to find his breath. "It's—It's—"

"It's so good to see you again, Mr. Jim!" Lucille finished for him, clapping her hands together in excitement. "Good golly, you haven't changed a bit!"

Margaret looked up at the old man, her first ever boss, and felt like she was just about ready to have a panic attack from her recent interaction with the boy from her past. She told herself everything was fine and faked a smile.

They talked with Jim until drinks and food came, and no matter how hard she tried to focus on the conversation, her mind was gone. She didn't—*couldn't* care about anything that was happening at the table, not when the young man's face unforgivingly burned in her head like scalding water.

Margaret didn't understand why her past was revisiting her the way it was. She felt like she was dreaming. Or hallucinating. The memory felt so real. Why did her past have to confuse her like this? Haunting over her like a dense cloud, always lurking somewhere just beyond her vision. Why couldn't she just shut off her mind and forget about her childhood? It was the past, after all. Why couldn't it *stay* in the past?

The rest of the time in the diner felt like one long fever dream. She remained silent, even on the ride back to the plantation. She was stuck in a trance, all her energy left behind in the small town. All she could think of was the boy's smile. It played in her mind over and over again, and she couldn't find the strength to stop it. She couldn't find the will to push his memory to the back of her mind where all the other painful memories resided.

She could hear Jane and Lucille talking in the backseat, but she couldn't decipher their words.

She could feel Mary Grace's pitiful stare from the driver's seat. She didn't want her pity. She didn't need anyone's sympathy. It only made her feel weak. Was she not capable of facing her own problems? She was tougher than this. Braver. She ran away from home without a plan and built a six-figure business from the ground up—she did not need anyone to pity her.

But, nonetheless, she couldn't deny the awful, gut-wrenching feeling she had. Visiting the diner again was just too soon.

When they turned down the long dirt driveway, a sudden force seemed to pull her in. The house was a black hole, and she was its victim. It sat patiently as it pulled her nearer, ready to swallow her and all of her shadows. The shadows of her past. The shadows she kept hidden. How long would it be until all of the shadows were brought to the light? Dragged to the surface for everyone, even Jane, to see? To judge?

The minute Mary Grace parked the car, Margaret started to head for the door.

"Mom, are you okay?" Jane asked, walking after her.

As she was about to answer, she heard Mary Grace whisper, "I think your mother needs some time alone. To reset, you know? Why don't you and I get some *ice* tea and sit out back and enjoy this lovely evenin', hm?"

Margaret pushed open the heavy doors of the house and fell through the doorway. She dragged her feet up the stairs to the second floor, racing down the hallway. She ignored the quiet laughter coming from the walls, the nostalgic memories etched in the wallpaper and carved into the floorboards. It was like the house was smiling at her pain, feeding her more and more memories just to watch her suffer. Just to watch her crumble beneath the weight of her own shadows. Just to remind her that everything she was feeling was all self-inflicted. That all of this was her doing and that no matter how fast she ran, the shadows would always be right behind her.

CHAPTER SEVEN

"THE GARDEN IS OVER two hundred years old. Almost everything, except the statues, is how it was when it was first designed," said Mary Grace as she led Jane out the back doors of the house. "The herbs, the roses, the cobblestones—the layout has not changed since this house was built."

The backyard was perhaps even more immaculate than the front side of the plantation.

Worn, gray cobblestones were placed along the soft ground, creating a meandering path through the lush garden. A stone water fountain stood in the center, its running water a serene offering to a few red cardinals that swooped by.

Four angels made of stone stood at each corner of the fountain, standing together in a ceremonial circle.

Jane was taken back. "It's so..." she gasped, walking over to the nearest angel to get a closer look. "...*peaceful* here." A rose bush was planted at the bottom of each stone angel, so she couldn't get too close.

"Indeed," Mary Grace agreed as she sat down at a round iron table next to the fountain.

The female angels looked sad. Frowns pulled their faces down, angled to the ground. Their palms were stuck together in prayer, desperation in their stance. Their wings were massive, hunched over their shoulders and around their cloak-like robes.

A shudder ran down Jane's spine. She looked away from the angels and turned to Mary Grace.

"It's a beautiful evenin', isn't it?" she asked Jane as she looked around the yard. She tried not to notice Jane's interest in the statues. She had promised Margaret she wouldn't tell Jane anything, and she was planning on keeping that promise for as long as she could.

July was a very lively month at the plantation; cicadas hummed with energy, birds sang peaceful melodies, and the bees and butterflies graced their presence around the garden's roses. The sky was a light shade of royal blue, and there wasn't a single cloud in sight. A soft breeze blew through the Spanish moss-covered oaks, making the humidity easier to bear.

Margaret didn't come downstairs, and Mary Grace said it would be best to leave her alone for the night, so they did.

Around midnight, Jane found herself struggling to shut off her mind. She worried about her mother. Her reaction in the diner made Jane wonder what was going on in her head. And of course, what the three girls had said didn't make her concern any easier.

Witchcraft? It wouldn't have bothered her as much as it did if she hadn't found that card in her mother's bedroom. She didn't know what to think of all this—but she couldn't deny that there must have been truth, even if it wasn't *all* true, in the rumors.

She lay wide awake in bed, staring up at the ceiling, not fighting the thoughts came and went. She wished morning was here. She wished she was brave enough to speak with her own mother. She wished she didn't feel as scared as she did now in the darkness of the small bedroom.

The stack of books on the nightstand fell with a loud thud. She shot up in bed, holding her breath as she stared down at the books. She didn't understand how they got on the floor. It was like they were pushed off the nightstand—but by what force?

She scanned the empty room, finding only shadows that lingered in the darkness like figures.

A chill prickled her skin, and she shuddered.

The crickets outside silenced.

A noise outside her door drew her attention away from the books. It was squeaky, amplifying, as though it grew closer.

Footsteps. Walking the hall slowly. It had to be.

Was her mother awake? Or was it Lucille or Mary Grace? What were they doing up? Of course, it had to be one of them. Who else could be in this house?

She planted her feet on the cool, wooden floors and picked up the books, putting them back on the nightstand.

She crept across her room to investigate. Her body was stiff as she did this, careful not to make any sounds.

The footsteps walked past her door, a shadow flickering under the bottom. Out of fear, she flinched, and in doing so, the wood moaned under her weight.

The shadow paused, then turned to face the door.

She held her breath, cursing herself for foolishly making a sound before.

The shadow didn't move.

Her heart pounded against her chest, flittering at the base of her throat.

Who was it?

After a stretched silence that seemed to last forever, the doorknob turned left.

The hairs on the back of her neck stood.

The doorknob then twisted right.

Her door wasn't locked, but yet, whoever was outside couldn't come in.

She stared at the antique doorknob, the air in her room cold and stiff.

"Who's there?" she asked out in a whisper.

The doorknob stopped turning, and the shadow soundlessly floated away.

She stood in the middle of the pitch-black room, finding it hard to breathe. Her heart drummed with panic, and the blood in her veins boiled.

She wasn't ever afraid of the dark—but at that moment, she wanted to scream, run back to bed, and hide under the covers until morning came.

Someone was in the hall.

Someone was trying to get into her room.

Her gut feeling told her it wasn't her mother or her aunts. Of course, that would be absolutely crazy. And yet, the feeling clawed against her throat, finding a home in her chest. It wouldn't leave.

She had to find out for herself.

Jane, more curious than frightened now, grabbed the knob and took one last steady breath before pulling the door open. Perhaps it was adrenaline, or maybe she was insane herself, but some sort of desperation overcame her, and she couldn't resist it.

The hall was dense with dark shadows, shrouded by the twilight. It felt like a thousand eyes were burning in the back of her neck as she stepped out of her bedroom.

She stared down the hall in the direction the footsteps had gone, but no one was there. At least, not that she could see.

She stood still in the dark hallway as she listened for any noises. But there was nothing.

The Abel Plantation mansion was a different house in the night. It was as if the high ceilings and glossy floorboards morphed into something dark and menacing. The shadows of the longstanding plantation oozed out of the walls, tasting of history and secrets.

Just as she thought she made the footsteps up in her head, a female voice whispered, "Jane."

Goosebumps blistered along her arms, and the blood in her face drained.

"Jane," it repeated, the voice echoing throughout the house, bounding off the walls.

The voice was coming from the end of the hall. She wanted to believe that it was just her mother calling her—but this voice didn't sound like her mother. Not at all. It didn't sound like any voice she recognized.

She had to see who it was. That same curiosity, it wouldn't budge.

She made her way down the hallway, tracing the walls with her fingertips to guide her through the dark.

The voice called out to her again.

The wooden floors creaked and moaned as she walked.

Before she knew what was going on, she found herself standing in front of the door across from her mother's room.

"Jane," the voice said behind the door, pulling her in closer.

Mary Grace had told her this room was locked. Who was in there?

She watched her hand lift, grabbing ahold of the silver doorknob.

The door creaked open, miraculously unlocked, and Jane found the bedroom empty.

The voice had stopped. Jane let out a gasp when she saw no sign that anyone was ever there.

She didn't understand. Who was calling her name? She had hoped she would find one of the women, but it was just her in that small room.

She stood in the middle of the bedroom and looked around. White light from the setting moon shone through the window, tarnishing her ability to see.

Who unlocked the door?

There was a twin-sized bed pushed to the wall on her right and a vanity in front of the window. Behind her was a small bookshelf stocked with worn novels of poetry and classic fiction and a rocking chair that was placed in front of the shelf.

A thick sheet of dust covered every surface; it was obvious that no one had been in the bedroom for a long time. Paintings of nature and wildlife, now yellowed, hung on the walls around the room. A framed photograph stood on the vanity next to the bed. She walked over to it and picked it up to get a better look, wiping the layer of dust off the glass. It was a picture of Mary Grace, Lucille, Margaret, and Vivian. They were standing in front of the diner downtown, smiling happily at the camera. There was a message written in neat cursive at the bottom of the photograph. It said: *We love you so much, Vivian. Happy birthday. I hope sixteen treats you well,* and then directly below it, *With love, Margaret.*

Jane was standing in Vivian's room.

She quickly put the picture down, taking a step away from the desk.

What was she doing? Creeping around in someone else's room? It was so unlike her to be this nosy, yet here she was, looking around Vivian's bedroom. But then again, where did the voice come from?

'I heard someone,' she thought to herself, turning to the door. *'I know I did.'*

A knock on the vanity sounded from behind her. She whipped back around. Her eyes fell on an open drawer that she hadn't noticed before. She could have sworn that it wasn't open just a few seconds ago. Something in the open drawer caught her eye. She knelt in front of the vanity and looked into the drawer. It was filled with random items, like small leather books, pens, and what looked to be a black velvet jewelry bag, sticky with tarnish. She stuck her hand in the drawer and began pulling out the odd items with curiosity, studying each mindlessly. Dust swarmed the space around her.

She pulled out one of the leather books, opened it to a random page, and scanned the inky words written so carefully on the cream-colored pages.

'To bring the deceased back to life' the heading of the page read. She flipped to the first page of the book. *'Vivian's Spell Journal'* it read in elegant cursive. She scrunched her eyebrows together, shutting the journal.

Spell Journal?

She thought of what the girls at the diner had said to her. It was *just* an old rumor. Witchcraft wasn't real. But why did Vivian own a notebook filled with handwritten *spells*?

The next thing she grabbed was the black velvety bag. It was heavier than she expected and solid. Inside was a deck of cards, beautifully illustrated with stars and moons.

She turned the deck over and instantly dropped it as though it burned the skin on her hands.

They scattered across the floor.

The same card that had frightened her back in New York was staring at her once again with its red eyes and evil grin.

The Devil.

It was a different drawing than the card she saw in her mother's room, but nonetheless, it was the same card.

What did these cards mean? And why did Vivian have them, too?

Her mind was a tangled mess of thoughts and emotions. She had to make sense of what was going on. It couldn't be just a coincidence that her mother *and* Vivian owned the same cards. And what about the book of spells?

She took a deep breath and shook her head. She couldn't go on pretending everything was fine.

There was a gray cloud lingering behind the reality she lived in. Her current world, where she felt safe, comfortable, and protected, was starting to crumble, splitting at the seams.

Something else was going on here. She just needed to figure out what.

'What is my mother hiding?'

She took the Devil card and slipped it into the pocket of her pajama shorts. Quickly, she gathered the rest of the cards from the floor and shoved them back into the bag. She returned everything to the drawer and pushed it closed, jumping up to her feet. She looked around the bedroom again, the two devil cards still burning in her mind. She thought of the sign in front of the old church on the side of the road. *RENOUNCE ALL EVIL*, it had said. She thought of the four creepy angel statues in the garden, recollecting her aunts, the photograph of Vivian, and her mother's heavy secrecy.

'I heard they all practice black magic,' the girls at the diner had said.

Her heart beat rapidly, and she couldn't stop her hands from shaking. Dread clutched her throat and held to her tightly.

After seeing the notebook and cards, she feared the rumors about the women were true.

"Jane," a voice, the same female voice that led her there, snapped her attention to the door.

She flicked her eyes across the room.

That's when she saw her.

Vivian Banks.

Jane was so stunned, the edges of her vision blurred, tunneling.

The woman stood in front of her, watching Jane with her ghostly stare. Jane swallowed back dry tears that curdled behind her eyes.

"You must listen, Jane," she whispered, her voice light and soft but hauntingly clear. As if she was expecting her.

She wore a dripping wet white nightgown that clung to her body. The bottom of the dress was caked with mud and was just long enough to hide her bare feet. Her greasy black hair shrouded her pale face like black curtains.

Jane could hardly manage the words out. "Vivian? How—"

"Now's not the time for that," she avowed rather gloomily. Drops of water dripped from her nightgown to the wood floor. "Jane, listen to me. You must remember. You're the only one who can save us."

Her head started to feel dizzy. "What?" Her legs felt weak, and her eyes lost focus.

"You must remember," she repeated, her bottom lip quivering. *"You must remember."*

And then Jane was falling. Her legs gave up and sent her to the floor. When she hit the ground, it all went black.

CHAPTER EIGHT

WHEN JANE AWOKE, SHE WAS DROWNING. At least, that's what it felt like.

Gasping for air, she sat up in bed and looked around her bedroom. Her body shivered with waves of cold sweat. Once she ripped the canvas covers off, she pulled her knees to her chest and tried to steady her breathing.

She swallowed the thick lump in the back of her throat, gripping her shins to stop her hands from shaking.

The nightmare. Again.

Back home, she had researched multiple articles on the frequent, reoccurring nightmares that vanished the minute she woke, but there was nothing on the web related to what Jane was going through.

When the fear and confusion of the fleeting nightmare settled, she felt strange. A fuzzy feeling clustered from her toes and slithered up to her head, leaving her nauseous.

She grabbed her phone from the nightstand, surprised at the time.

It was exactly nine on the dot. She had never slept this late before—not even as a kid.

Standing up slowly, she saw something fly out the left pocket of her pajama shorts and slide underneath the bed.

She wrinkled her nose and went down on her hands and knees to see what it was.

It looked like a piece of paper.

She reached out her arm cautiously and grabbed it, whatever it was, and stood back up as she looked at it.

The card. The devil card. Just like the one she found in her parents' room.

But how?

How did she get this? And most importantly, why was it in her pocket?

"What the hell," she exhaled, shaking her head a little.

She replayed everything that happened last night in her head as she stared down at the evil drawing. She had dinner, said goodnight, went to bed—nothing happened that would explain why she was now holding the sinister illustration in her hands.

Where did the card come from?

She began to feel even more nauseous. It was like her head was spinning around on her neck. Her heart pounded in her chest, drumming a beat that told her to leave. To run.

Two knocks on the door made her almost drop the card. "Jane?" Mary Grace called from outside. "Are you up?"

She tucked the card under her pillow and whipped around just in time to watch Mary Grace open her door and walk in. She held a pastel-blue sundress with ruffle short sleeves in her arms, a wide smile on her round face.

"Oh, you are up—that's good. We're leaving for church in twenty minutes."

"Church?" She had never been to church.

Mary Grace held the dress out. "You'll be fine, I promise. I figured you didn't bring any church clothes, so I found one of Vivi's old dresses. And I know how much you like this color."

"This was Vivian's?" she asked, lifting her eyebrows. Not that she wouldn't wear it, but knowing it belonged to her missing aunt made her feel a bit wary. It's not like she was dead or anything.

"Do you like it?"

"Yes, thank you," she said and took the dress when she realized she was hesitating for too long.

"Good. Vivian left a lot of things behind when she moved to New Orleans. I know she won't mind if you borrow it. And, I know for a fact you're too tall and skinny for my clothes," she stated, her tone indicating that she could sense Jane's discomfort.

"Thank you," she said again, looking at the dress. It was a beautiful sundress. Simple yet elegant. Something she would never wear back in New York. It was far too country for the busy streets.

"How did you know I liked this color?" she questioned, eyeing her quizzically.

Mary Grace was already walking to the door. She hesitated for a split second. Long enough to make Jane wonder. "Your mother told me," she stammered. She let out a dismissive laugh.

She could hear the lie in her tone, and it annoyed her. "Oh, okay," she said.

"Well," Mary Grace cleared her throat, then smiled. "I'll leave you to get ready." She took a step backward but stopped when she stepped in a puddle of water. "What's this mess from?"

Jane wrinkled her nose, looking down at the water Mary Grace was standing in. "I... I don't know."

"Miss Jane, I will not tolerate a mess." She shook her head, looking around. There were no cups anymore, no footprints, no drops of water to explain the reason for the puddle.

"I don't know where that's from. I— I don't remember what happened. I don't think I spilled anything, but if I did, I'm sorry. I promise I'll clean it up." Things just kept getting stranger. First the card—now this?

Mary Grace looked at the water under her, confused. The water was not tap water. It was brownish, mucky.

"Don't worry about it, dear. I'm not mad at you. Have you gone outside yet?" she asked, glancing over her.

"No, I just woke up."

Mary Grace didn't feel it was necessary to tell her it was *swamp* water—knowing it would only frighten the girl more than she already was.

"I'll be waiting downstairs," she said as she left the bedroom, shutting the door behind her. It clicked as it latched, followed by the sound of her footsteps as she walked down the hall.

Jane waited a beat, then set the dress on the bed. She pulled out the card once more, looking at it and then at the puddle by the door.

Something was definitely wrong.

Margaret was still in bed when her friend knocked on her door. She didn't feel like getting up today. She wanted to melt into the mattress, hide within the layers of material. She hoped that her silence would trick her friend into thinking she was asleep, giving her a little while more to ignore reality.

But Mary Grace wasn't that merciful. She tried the door and heaved a sigh when she found it locked. "Mar, open up. I know you ain't sleepin'."

"Go away..." she moaned.

"Like I'd listen to you. Open up. I mean it." She knocked again.

Silence.

Mary Grace put her hands on her hips. "If you don't unlock this door, I'll—"

The door swung open, and there Margaret stood, glaring. "If this isn't about Vivian, I don't want to hear it."

"Good morning to you, too." Mary Grace huffed a laugh. "Get dressed. We're going to church."

She squinted her eyes, not knowing whether she was being serious or not. "Excuse me? *We* are going to church?"

"Yes, now hurry. We need to talk—"

"I'm not going *anywhere* today unless it involves looking for Vivi."

Her warm smile faded. "Pray for her when you're there then." A sigh escaped her lips. "I understand that being back must be difficult for you. But I can assure you, it will get easier once you accept every-thing that has happened and just *let go of the past.*" She turned and walked away, deciding that she would tell Margaret about Jane's incident later.

Margaret leaned against the doorframe, unsure how she should feel after that. While she was irritated by her friend's *know-it-all* interruption, she was primarily flustered by the hard truth hidden in what her friend said.

Let go of the past.

It sounded so simple. So easy.

But it wasn't. It never was.

If she wanted to let go, she needed to turn within. She had to reach inside to bring out all of the deep-rooted pain and locate where each strand of trauma led. And, as Mary Grace said, simply *let it go.*

Like returning a fish to the river after taking out the hook.

As Mary Grace's wise mother used to say, *"You shouldn't hold onto things that don't serve you anymore."*

If only Mrs. Abel was still here. She would know what to do.

She always did.

Margaret's mother died while giving birth to her, so Mrs. Abel was her only mother figure while growing up.

Lucille's mother was never around; she was normally found at the local bar or in some club down in New Orleans. And on rare occasions when she *was* home, she'd yell at Lucille and call her names that were too despicable to mention, or she'd sleep for hours on end until she was ready to go out for a drink again. Lucille never met her father, but she's pretty sure she was the product of a fling. A quick love affair, possibly a one-night stand, even. That was her mother, though. Always searching for love in all the wrong places.

Vivian's parents died in a car crash, making her an orphan at only eight-years-old. Mrs. Abel was her godmother, so the woman took her in and raised her as her own.

So, Mrs. Abel was a beloved mother, not just for Mary Grace but for the other girls, too.

Margaret took a deep breath and leaned against the bedroom door, pushing it closed under her weight. After a moment of just breathing, just *being*, she walked over to her dresser and picked out a modest black dress and black flats to match. It looked more like she was dressing for a funeral rather than a Sunday service, but her appearance was the last thing on her mind.

She was downstairs in less than ten minutes. Mary Grace and Lucille were in the kitchen, sitting at the table and drinking coffee. Jane must have still been getting ready upstairs.

Mary Grace looked up at Margaret when she entered. "Well, well," she nodded in approval. "You look great. Never thought you'd be gettin' dressed up for a church service one day, did you?"

"I never thought I'd come back to Belles Parish, either," she sighed, taking a seat next to Lucille at the table.

Lucille was wearing a soft pink sundress that may not be entirely appropriate for church, but that was just Lucille. Nobody expected her to be humble.

"I need to tell you something," Mary Grace said to Margaret, her voice dropping to a hushed whisper. "It's about Jane."

Her face dropped. "What about Jane?"

"She's actin'... different. I think she knows something's up."

"What do you mean?" Lucille whispered, her blue eyes narrowing on Mary Grace.

"This mornin', when I came upstairs, Vivian's door was *wide* open. But the strange thing is, I keep it locked. And the key wasn't even missin'."

"What are you saying?" She shook her head, crossing her arms over her chest. "You think Jane broke in?"

"I don't know for certain, but I think it's possible. But get this—" she took a sip of her coffee—"when I woke her up, there was a puddle of *swamp water* in the middle of her room."

"Swamp water?" Margaret laughed quietly. "What? How do you know if it was swamp water?"

"I think I can tell the difference."

Lucille leaned forward. "Well, what do you think is goin' on?"

Mary Grace shrugged her shoulders, taking another sip. "I don't know."

"But you know *everything*," hissed Margaret with an eyeroll.

"That may be true—but my powers aren't working as they normally do when it comes to Jane. I don't know why," she said before straightening up and saying, "She's comin'."

Margaret sat back in her chair, letting out a deep sigh. Swamp water? In her daughter's room? None of it made sense. Why would Jane break into Vivian's room, and why would there be swamp water?

When Jane entered the kitchen, Mary Grace forced a smile and gasped in awe. "Jane, you look perfect."

The girl smiled, her cheeks turning pink. The dress fit perfectly, soft and flowy around her hips, and the blue complemented her pale skin. She only brought two pairs of shoes— white sneakers and sandals, so she decided on the sandals, hoping it would be appropriate enough for church. "Thanks."

Jane noticed a heavy mood lingering in the kitchen, and she couldn't help but think her presence was the cause of it. What were they talking about before she came in?

"Why do we have to go to church, anyway?" Lucille complained, filling the quiet that settled in the room. Out of everyone in the kitchen, she was the most nervous. She knew the kind of people who went to church—the kind of women. The things they used to say about her when she was growing up still haunted her to this day.

"Because," Mary Grace stood from the table. "It is important to worship the Lord—even during the toughest times. He is the author to our story, y'know."

"Well, I'd like a rewrite," she mumbled back. "But why *do* you go? Wasn't it you who said church was just a building full of stuck-ups and rumors?"

Margaret laughed, remembering that she did once say this.

"Spiritual guidance. And respect. We may not like our stories written for us, but He gave us *life*, nonetheless, and that's a blessing far greater than any gift."

Lucille gave her a look filled with sarcasm and disbelief before sighing, "Well, I'll be."

CHAPTER NINE

RELIGION MADE JANE NERVOUS, let alone a church filled with—as Lucille had so gently put it, *stuck-ups and rumors*. She picked at the hem of her blue dress in the back seat, looking out the window at the boutiques and shops.

She also couldn't stop thinking about last night, about the card she had in her pocket when she awoke and the water on the floor. It was all so frightening and strange, it made her stomach swirl with anxiety.

Gravel crunched beneath their tires as they pulled into the church's parking lot, drawing her attention back to the car.

It was an old church, painted a faded white, with a big iron cross standing tall on top of the steeple. Men and women and children of all ages walked through the entrance, the wooden structure swallowing them softly, effortlessly.

For such a small church, practically the whole town was there.

When Mary Grace parked the car, she turned around and faced her friends. "Now, I don't want any of you to embarrass me. I've worked hard to get some respect 'round here, and I don't need y'all messin' it up."

"We're not kids anymore, Mary Grace," Margaret grumbled in the passenger seat. "I think I'll be fine."

Mary Grace eyed her friend and frowned. "I know *you'll* be fine. When I say *y'all*, I mean Lucille!"

Lucille was applying a fresh layer of red lipstick on her lips when she looked at Mary Grace in the rearview mirror. "Let's just get this over with," she muttered with an overwhelmed look.

The church echoed with loud voices, a cacophony of hushed whispers and rich laughter. It all blended together to make one tune that pushed against the walls and ceiling as if someone were to yell in an empty cave.

Upon entering, the incoherent ringing seized as everyone stopped and stared. All eyes were on them as they walked down the aisle. The people were breathless, amazed, and a little shocked to see the sisters finally together after all these years. Well, almost *all* the sisters.

"Margaret," snapped Lucille, tugging on her friend's sleeve as they made their way up the aisle toward the first pew.

Mary Grace knew everyone expected her to sit hidden in the back row, but she would not settle for that. She wanted to let the townspeople know that she would not cower, no matter how bad the rumors were.

Margaret looked over her shoulder at Lucille and lifted an eyebrow. "Hm?"

Lucille shuddered. "Everyone is staring at us."

"Because," whispered Mary Grace, looking around. "They can't believe you two actually returned to Belles Parish." She noticed a couple sitting directly behind them, boring eyes into their necks as if to say that sitting in the front row was an outrageous verdict.

'Is that—?' the woman behind them thought to herself, staring at Lucille with a disgusted expression. *'It can't be! She came back? No!'*

The man sitting next to the frightened woman stared at Lucille, too. *'Lucille Callaway? My god, she hasn't aged a bit! I wonder if she ever married.'*

Mary Grace laughed to herself when she picked up their thoughts. "John Yancey is glad you're here, Lucille."

"John Yancey?" she gasped, raising her blonde brows and turning around to catch the man's stare.

The last time she saw him was prom night. His girlfriend had caught them kissing under the bleachers. At the time, she didn't know he had a girlfriend. She should have been mad, but it didn't bother her too much. All her life, she has told herself that there were plenty of fish out in the sea. However, she was still trying to catch the right one after all this time. And yet, she hadn't lost hope. At least, not yet.

Mary Grace smirked. "His wife ain't too happy, though."

His wife's eyes I can't believe she actually married that loser," she whispered to Mary Grace.

"Oh, Lucille, be nice—we're in church."

The crowded church began to quiet down when a man carrying a bible walked up on the small stage to the wooden pulpit that stood in the center. He set his bible down carefully and peeled open the cover and then looked up at the people of Belles Parish as he began.

"Happy Sunday, everyone," he said with an underbite smile. Either it was an underbite or the result of missing teeth.

The crowd all greeted him at the same time.

The pastor was an older man, late seventies possibly. He had a square jaw that stuck out and up, and big glasses that sat on the bridge of his nose. The natural light spilling in from the stained-glass windows reflected off his bald head, creating a golden aura around him.

When he spoke, his words came out soft and sweet with a smile, his eyes glistening with genuine warmth.

"Y'all ever read Jeremiah chapter twenty-nine, verse eleven?" he asked the gathered crowd. Everyone nodded and clapped in agreement. "'*For I know the plans I have for you*' declares the Lord, '*plans to prosper you and not harm you, plans to give you a hope and a future*'," he paused, looking around. For a split second, his eyes landed on Jane. "Just a reminder to anyone who needs to hear this. This is where God wants you to be. This is His plan for you, and you must follow it without doubt."

Everyone in the church nodded their heads as if they already knew everything he was saying. Jane wondered how often he had said the same verse before now.

What he said rang in Jane's head a few times. *This is where God wants you to be.* She was beginning to wonder if the pastor's words were some sort of sign—as funny as that sounded.

For the rest of the hour, the pastor talked more of bible verses and Jesus to his faithful listeners. It was a lot for Jane to take in. The pastor quoted various passages from the worn book on the stand, but it was hard to grasp what it all meant, partly because she was too distracted by the gawking eyes of the townspeople. She spotted the three girls from the diner a few pews behind her. Their faces scrunched up when they saw Jane, as if repulsed to see her there.

Margaret couldn't help but follow Jane's gaze to the gawking eyes. She had dealt with the staring eyes her whole life, and she wasn't the least bit surprised the four of them took the spotlight once again. Going to church was like begging to attract gossip. She felt silly for even agreeing to go with Mary Grace. She couldn't comprehend why her friend played along with this *small-town-church-woman* act. But Mary Grace seemed to be really into it, singing with the choir and nodding her head every time the pastor would say something. Despite not understanding how Mary Grace could find God in a church this small and this crowded with people, she was happy for her and even envied her just a little bit. She envied Mary Grace's connection with God in a way she didn't realize she did. After all these years of straying away from any slight spirituality, she could now feel the emptiness it left in her heart as she sat in the hot church. The sudden feeling made her want to cry. She abandoned a part of herself when she left, and her chest ached for that girl she left behind.

Mary Grace reached over Lucille's lap and grabbed Margaret's hand as if reassuring her that everything was okay—or at least was going to be okay.

Sometimes she hated the way Mary Grace could tell when she was overthinking. When she was lost in her own head, her thoughts a tangled web of endless torment.

She pulled back her hand from Mary Grace, keeping her eyes on the pastor. She didn't want to look at her. She didn't trust herself. If she looked over, she was sure her wall would crumble. Mary Grace would be able to see right through her armor, right through her mask, and see her for the scared fool she felt like on the inside.

When the service ended, Margaret felt her shoulders soften. It felt like the longest hour she had ever endured.

Mary Grace spotted Randy Jones and his family heading for the door. She pulled on Lucille's arm once and then led them through the mass of church people.

"Randy," she called out as she followed them outside, hurrying her steps.

Those around gave them a second-look at the name of the parish's sheriff, their gawking eyes only growing more curious when they found the women from the plantation calling him.

"Randy Jones," she called once again, walking down the steps of the white church.

Randy Jones turned around, immediately recognizing that voice. "Mornin', ladies," he smiled with a single nod. He was dressed in simple church attire. A baby-blue button-down shirt and khaki pants. No badge or campaign hat today. The only thing that signified his position in town was the outline of a holster under his shirt at the waist, but almost every man coming out of the church had that same print. Ever since graduating from the police academy, he has never left his house without a gun. He said it felt like something was missing. Like leaving the house without shoes on.

He glanced around the parking lot instinctively. The way he saw it, he was never off from work, even on his days off. He took an oath when joining the law enforcement, *to serve and protect*, and that promise doesn't get days off.

"Any news 'bout Vivi?" Mary Grace questioned as they all stepped out of the way of the stairs. She fanned her face with her hand. A line of sweat had formed across her eyebrows.

"No, nothin' yet."

Bobbie Jo beamed at Jane, her eyes wide, crinkling at the edges.

"Ah-em," his wife coughed, nudging his arm softly. The woman looked just like Bobbie Jo, sharing the same curly hair and slender build. Her eyes were a rich brown, the color of milk chocolate, just a shade lighter than Bobbie Jo's umber eyes.

"Oh, of course." He turned to his wife. "Melissa, this is Lucille and Margaret," he said, and then looked at Jane. "And... *Jane*, right?"

"Yes," Margaret answered.

Melissa then smiled, her smile calm and cheerful. She extended her hand toward Margaret and softly shook her hand. "It's a pleasure to meet y'all. You were Randy's neighbor growin' up, correct?"

It seemed like so long ago that they were neighbors—a different world in itself. She nodded and said, "Yes, I was."

She grabbed Bobbie Jo and gave her a side-hug. "This is my mini me. Bobbie Jo."

"Mom," Bobbie Jo laughed, wiggling out of the hug.

"She told me all about yesterday, and I think it's just wonderful that our girls can be friends," she beamed. Her face lit up with an idea, and she looked at Randy and back at the women. "Hey, why don't y'all come over tonight for dinner? I'd love to talk more."

CHAPTER TEN

IT DIDN'T OCCUR TO HER UNTIL they were halfway home that Mellissa had not brought up Vivian's disappearance. And, though she wouldn't admit it vocally, Lucille was grateful for this. Mellissa didn't speak of Vivian with that sympathetic, sad tone. Didn't make it sound like she was already dead like everyone else in town did. She interacted with them like it was any other day, like there was no reason to worry about Vivian because she'd be back soon.

Mellissa reminded Lucille of Lorraine. She had that motherly presence about her, that gentle disposition which could make anyone feel welcomed and at ease with just a smile.

That gut-wrenching worry returned the second she laid eyes on the Abel Plantation. All the excitement and nerves from the church service cleared and the real reason she was there sunk in once again.

Vivian was gone. The truth was simple and, at the same time, anything but.

She met Mary Grace's eyes in the rearview mirror and concentrated as hard as she could. She hadn't done this in decades, and she wasn't sure if she was even capable of still doing it. Back when they were kids, they'd communicate this way all the time. It was easier with Mary Grace than the other girls because of her telepathic abilities.

She held her breath and tried blocking out every noise in the car, repeating her thought louder.

'Hey.'

Mary Grace gripped the steering wheel, surprised by the alien voice in her head space. She found Lucille's gaze in the mirror and smiled.

She sent a thought back, making sure she was careful. She knew how easy it was to accidentally overpower someone's mind. It was like screaming at the top of your lungs when you were supposed to whisper. *'Didn't think you could still talk.'*

Lucille shut her eyes, grinning like a kid. *'I didn't either.'*

Mary Grace taught her friends how to *talk* with her when they were around twelve years old. It was a talent that she and her mother shared, and it was helpful in crowded places or in situations where talking was restricted. Her mother thought of it as a safety measure rather than anything else.

It took a lot of practice for her friends to learn, a whole summer of practice. They weren't as keen with their minds as she was—but the reason she even wanted to teach them this ability was so that no matter how far apart they were, they'd always be able to talk.

Funny how that played out.

'I want to see Vivian's room.'

Mary Grace hesitated. She parked her car by the side of the house. *'Okay.'*

As they walked into the house, Margaret brushed against Lucille's arm. "You two were awfully quiet," she muttered under her breath. It wasn't difficult to notice Lucille and Mary Grace's back-and-forth stare. "So, what's going on?"

"Nothin'," she said back, walking into the kitchen.

Jane went upstairs, allowing Margaret to raise her voice from a whisper.

"Don't do that."

"What?" She raised an eyebrow, making her way around the kitchen for a glass of water.

"All I'm asking is for you guys to keep me in the loop, okay?"

"Okay, if you must know, I was talkin' with Mary Grace about lookin' around Vivian's bedroom. Is that okay with you?"

"Wait, you can still talk?" She wasn't sure if *she* could or not, but she assumed the latter because of how long it had been since she tried.

"I was surprised too," Mary Grace said upon entering. She grabbed a glass for herself and filled it with water from the faucet. "Wouldn't be a bad idea to practice again. It might come in handy—"

"I already told you. I'm not practicing magic again."

"It doesn't really count as *magic*, does it?" she questioned with an annoyed sigh.

Margaret put her hands on her hips and rolled her eyes. "Reading minds doesn't count as magic? Do you know how ridiculous you sound?"

She almost spit out the water. "*I* sound ridiculous? Try listening to someone who has a wonderful talent and decides not to use it."

"More like wonderful curse," she snapped.

"Why can't you be honest with yourself?" Mary Grace put her cup in the sink, biting her tongue to stop herself from saying anything she would come to regret.

Margaret could feel heat flushing her face. She didn't have time for this. She kept her wall up, telling herself that Mary Grace wouldn't get to her. She raised her chin as she said, "None of us our honest with ourselves. We're all just a bunch of narcissists. We deny our problems and think we know what's best for everyone else."

"Say what you want," Mary Grace huffed, turning around from the sink. She leaned against the counter naturally, her eyes locked on Margaret. "But I saw the way you acted in church. You're scared to death. And why? For what reason, hm?"

She didn't say anything, didn't want to say anything. Any answer of hers would only become fuel to the fire. She chose to let the snappy comments and tension smolder instead by keeping her lips sealed.

Half of her hoped that when she picked up the pillow, the card would be gone. Maybe if it was, she could convince herself she had imagined waking up with it in her pocket. Maybe she could convince herself that it was all in her head—a dream, perhaps.

But the odds were not in Jane's favor today.

After changing out of her church clothes and into something more comfortable, she pulled her short hair back into a ponytail and sat on her bed, eyeing the pillow the whole time.

She moved it to the side and, despite how hard she hoped, there it was. The card.

She picked it up and was suddenly overwhelmed with the impulse to run out onto the porch and toss it over the rail. She had the urge to let the wind carry it away, taking with it all the anxiety she felt.

But she was frozen. Her eyes locked with the card, the question she had that morning returning.

Why did she have this card?

She looked in front of the doorway, at the area where the water had been.

The illustration of the devil smiled up at her in mockery as if it knew something she didn't.

Still clamping the card in her grasp, she began to pace her room, trying to come up with a logical explanation for all of this. She played out every event she could remember from last night, picking apart each detail to find something, anything, that would make sense of all this.

From what she recalled, nothing out of the ordinary happened. She had dinner, went to sleep—

She stopped pacing.

Something from last night she didn't remember before hit her. Snapped in her mind with a flash.

She remembered feeling frightened. As though something terrible was on the brink of impact, she had to prepare herself. Of what, she did not know—but she could remember the fear, that awful, invasive fear that pulsed within her veins.

She looked around the small room, tracing her eyes over the walls and furniture, falling on the stack of books on her nightstand.

The books.

Last night, she saw the books drop from the nightstand.

Yes, she remembered it so clearly now.

They dropped onto the wood floors with a loud crash. Like someone had pushed them off, but no one was there.

She started pacing again as the rest of the night came back to her, gripping the card tighter.

After returning the books to the nightstand, she heard something. No, she heard *someone*. She heard someone walking in the hall. They turned her doorknob, but they didn't come in. They walked away. Jane remembered feeling petrified, but at the same time, eager. Then she had left her room to see who it was.

The rest of the memory was cloudy. She had walked to the end of the hallway and stood in front of the locked room across from her mother's room. It was hard to remember exactly what happened, but one thing was clear.

She had gone inside the locked room. That's where she found the card. The locked room was Vivian's bedroom when she used to live at the plantation.

She froze, sucking in a breath as the memory settled, like dust settling after a dust storm.

She needed more. More answers. More proof.

She slipped the card into the middle of one of the paperbacks on the nightstand and rushed out of the room.

Why had she forgotten everything from last night? It drove her mad. Maybe she was really losing it.

She couldn't go on feeling like she was crazy. There must be an explanation.

She kept repeating this in her head as she proceeded to rush out of the room.

The hall was empty, stretched longer than she remembered. As if the house was messing with her. What did Lucille tell her on the first day here?

'Stick around here long enough, and you'll start believin' in ghosts.'

An icy shiver raced up her spine at the thought of ghosts. It annoyed her how all this talk of ghosts and witches scared her. It shouldn't scare her. She had never been scared of anything in her life—why now?

Logic out ruled the supernatural. She wouldn't stray from reality just because of a stupid card. Especially not here, in a place where the truth was becoming harder and harder to grasp. In a house of confusion and mind tricks.

But it wasn't just the card that made her feel this way, and she didn't want to confess this truth. The card was really one of the lesser important issues in the matter. Her nightmare, this creepy house, the rumors, the secrets—they all played a part.

She was now standing in front of Vivian's bedroom, her hand wrapped around the doorknob.

She wanted answers. Needed answers.

She turned the knob.

It was locked.

Dropping her arm by her side, she took two giant steps back, her eyes fixed on the door.

If it was locked—how did she get in last night? She couldn't remember using a key, and even if she did, where was the key now? She wasn't even sure where to begin looking.

'This just keeps getting weirder,' she thought, standing motionless for another moment before coming to her senses.

If she wanted answers, she had to ask the questions first.

She tried the door again and then turned and started down the hall. She had to talk to Mary Grace—she'd have the answers she was so desperately craving.

She ran her hand over the wooden railing worn with age as she walked down the stairs. Soft jazz music emitted from the record player in the living room, drowning the house with a sweet, lazy tune.

She swept her eyes over the family photos on the blue walls, once again meeting with Vivian's ghostly stare, that déjà vu still there.

When she made it to the bottom of the stairs, her eyes fell on the crystal bowl of caramel-colored candies, and after popping one in her mouth, she walked into the kitchen. The sweet flavor danced along her tongue, a soft smile tugging at her lips. The candy was her father's favorite. It made her miss him.

Lucille was putting a pie dish into the oven when she walked in. She tapped her feet in a little dance while humming the music. She stopped when she saw Jane in the doorway.

"Hey, honey!" Lucille cheered as she closed the oven door. "I'm makin' some peach cobbler to bring over to dinner tonight. You like peach cobbler?"

Jane leaned against the doorframe. "I've never had it." She took a quick glance at the whole room, coming to the conclusion that Mary Grace was not in here. Neither was her mother.

"Never had it?" she gasped, throwing her hands into the air. "My poor, poor child. You're gonna love it." She started dancing again. "You like *Ella Fitzgerald*?"

She shrugged. "I don't know her. Is she related to *F. Scott Fitzgerald*?"

Lucille looked at her, completely flabbergasted. "What?" She sucked in a sharp breath of air.

She wasn't sure what else to say so she shrugged again.

"You know what?" she huffed and then rushed across the kitchen, her high heels going *clink, clink, clink* on the tiles. "Just come with me. I'm disappointed in your mama for not ever showin' you."

Jane followed her into the living room, to the back where the old record player was. Beside it stood a small bookcase lined with vinyl albums.

Lucille searched for a title, tracing her red fingernails across the albums' spines. She let out a quiet sigh when she found the title she was looking for.

A grin pulled at her face as she drew out a dusty record, wiping the cover with her hand. She stopped the vinyl that was already spinning, the jazz music abruptly cutting off.

"Today is the day your whole life is gonna changle, darlin'," she said as she replaced the new vinyl on the round tray. She carefully picked up the needle and placed it on the record as it started to spin. "This," she breathed. "is my *favorite song* in the *whole wide world* by the one and only..." she paused, giving her a wink. "...*Ella Fitzgerald*."

At first, all Jane could hear was a low, staticky noise, like the crackling of a fire as the record spun.

"More commonly known as the *Queen of Jazz*."

Music began to play. A sweet, soft melody of horns and bass and piano. It rang through the room, as gentle as the sunlight pouring from the tall windows surrounding the living room.

A soft voice began to sing, pulling the instruments together. *"Stars shining bright above you..."*

Lucille sway back and forth as if dancing with an imaginary partner, wearing a blissful smile as she closed her eyes.

"Night breezes seem to whisper I love you..."

Jane couldn't help but smile. "She's good," she said, having to raise her voice slightly over the music.

"She's not just *good*," she told her, opening her eyes and letting go of her imaginary dance partner. "She's *amazing*. What kind of music do you like?"

She hesitated for a moment. "Mostly alternative rock. Like *Coldplay* and—"

Lucille dismissed her with a wave of her hand. "You teenagers and your *alternative rock*. Mary Grace's mother listened to nothin' but the best jazz, and she was the one who showed me what good music really is."

Jane's mother never listened to jazz, and the more she thought about it, her mother never really listened to any kind of music at all. Or was that another aspect of her mother that she just didn't know? Another trait she had not yet met? Another version of the person her mother was?

The thought brought her back to why she had come downstairs in the first place. If she wanted answers, she had to ask.

"Do you know where Mary Grace is?"

She turned the volume down and then left the record player, heading for the kitchen again. "Out back. I believe she's grabbin' some rosemary for Randy's wife." She cracked open the oven door and peeked at the dessert. "Is everything okay?" she asked, her back facing Jane.

"Yeah, everything is fine. I just want to ask her something."

CHAPTER ELEVEN

MARY GRACE WAS BESIDE THE BACK DOORS of the big house, cutting small stems of rosemary from a bed of arranged herbs, when she heard Jane walk outside. She wore oversized garden gloves, holding a rusty pruner in her right hand and a wicker basket in her left. She looked over her shoulder at Jane and smiled.

"Hi, Jane," she said in a gentle voice. She pronounced her name with that southern accent Jane was just now getting used to, so *Jane* sounded more like *Jain*. "How are you?"

Jane stared ahead at the circle of angel statues. The angels' faces angled toward the sky, their mouths in a long and twisted frown. They looked different today. More desperate.

The hair on her neck stood.

"Jane?" Mary Grace called again, snapping Jane back to her surroundings.

She looked behind her and found Mary Grace kneeling in front of the herbs.

"You okay?" she asked with concern.

"I'm fine," she answered. But the paleness in her cheeks didn't fade, giving away the lie. Why was she out here again? She shifted her weight from side to side.

Without really thinking the question over, she blurted, "Have these statues always been here?"

Mary Grace went back to work, clipping a stem of rosemary and placing it in the basket. "They were my mother's addition to the garden. They were sculpted to look like my grandmother and my great-aunts. Beatrice Abel was my grandmother's name."

A bird in a nearby tree chirped a repetitive tune, harmonizing with the cicadas and frogs.

"Which one is she?" Each statue looked more miserable than the other, and she had no idea why anyone would want such a sad sculpture of someone.

Mary Grace put down the basket and pointed to the angel closest to Jane. "That one."

She walked closer to it, studying the sad stone face again. "Why do the statues look so sad?" She realized these weren't the questions she came out to ask, but curiosity got the best of her.

"They don't always look that way."

Jane turned around and looked at her aunt, wondering if she had heard her correctly or not. Just as she opened her mouth to ask what she meant, her phone started ringing in her back pocket.

She jumped at the buzzing interruption and pulled out her phone.

Her father was calling. For some reason, she hesitated as she stared at his contact. Like she should call him back later—after Mary Grace explained what she had meant by *they don't always move.*

But Mary Grace had already returned to the bed of herbs.

"Hey, Dad," she said when she hit answer. "How've you been?" She took one last glance at the wailing statues before walking over to the iron table and sitting down.

"I've been okay. I miss you. How's Louisiana?" He sounded tired, which wasn't normal coming from him.

How's Louisiana? It was such a simple question yet she couldn't find the rights words to form a simple answer. She tried not to think about the creepy angels or the card or any of the other strange happenings at the plantation. "It's beautiful. I love it here."

"Hm, that's nice," he mumbled in response. "Is Mom around?"

"No, she's in the house." Jane looked around the garden, the phone suddenly heavy in her hand as she thought about what to say. "Dad, you should see this plantation—it's crazy. I think you'd really like—"

He sighed, "Next time you see her, tell her to call me, okay?"

She paused. "Okay, I will. Are you okay?"

He paused. "I will be when you come home," he said with a forced chuckle. "It's so strange not having you in the apartment. I'm going to be sad when you go to college."

She leaned back in the iron chair and started chewing the inside of her cheek. "I thought you were on a conference trip."

"Oh—well, I just got back today."

She wasn't sure what else to say, so the silence between them grew longer. This was the first conversation she's had with him that felt... *fake*. It was so unlike him.

An uneasy feeling turned in her stomach as her mind began to wander.

"I'm getting another call right now, so I um—I have to go. Tell Mom to call me. I love you, Jane."

She promptly responded, "Love you, too." And when the call ended, she set her phone on the table and replayed the conversation in her head.

Something was off in his voice—that's why she had that bad feeling in her stomach. And then she realized what was bothering her.

He was lying.

Margaret turned off the water faucet and stood in the shower for a moment longer, letting the drops of cold water roll down her face and onto the floor of the tub. She took a deep breath, taking in the scents of lavender soap, and swallowed the knot in the back of her throat.

Since arriving at Belles Parish, she has felt like a tangled mess of raw emotion. Her nerves were spiraling, and it seemed like everything in her life was getting out of control.

Things were okay in New York. Not great, but manageable. She was *Margaret Gardener*. Responsible for designing some of the city's most luxurious hotels and banks and apartments—and even a handful of vacation homes for local celebrities. She was the richest she had been her entire life. She went from living in a broken trailer down in Louisiana to living in a penthouse apartment overlooking Park Avenue. Besides being greatly successful in her architectural business, she was married to *David Gardener*—arguably the best journalist in New York City.

On the surface, her life looked perfect. She was a real-life rags-to-riches story.

But if anyone were to take a closer look, they would find that it was all an illusion. Deep slashes, dense with bitter lies, cut into every aspect of her life.

She had to do her best to keep her chin up so no one would take that closer look. So no one would notice those deep slashes. The ones she has been trying to hide since the day she received them.

Once dressed, she went to check on Jane. She knocked on her bedroom door, but her daughter didn't answer. After knocking again, and still no answer, she opened the door slowly.

The room was empty.

Panic immediately latched onto her, crawling into her skin and flooding her mind with a hundred thoughts.

She was probably downstairs, she assured herself. She shouldn't worry. Not yet.

She bolted out of the bedroom, the sharp smell of dust piercing her head.

She called out for Jane in a trembling voice, and when she didn't get a response, her panic dug itself deeper and deeper.

Her heart beat loudly in her ears as she ran down the hall toward the kitchen. She could hear dishes clashing together and smell baked peaches. If she wasn't in the kitchen, she would search every room in the house. And if she wasn't in the house at all...?

No. She shook her head, ridding herself from going there. From thinking those thoughts.

Jane wasn't missing.

She ran down the stairs and spun around the corner, entering the kitchen. But—

The kitchen was gone.

She was outside, far away from the Abel Plantation and any drop of reality.

Margaret breathed, her head still spinning.

She was standing in front of a dirty white trailer—not in the kitchen at the plantation where she was supposed to be. The yard was littered with junk cars and piles of scrap metal and trash.

Randy's home, she realized.

Her eyes fell on the dark, worn patch of grass in front of the trailer, indicating that Mr. Jones and his Chevy Blazer weren't present. Despite being a grown woman now, she sighed in relief for Randy's sake.

But this isn't real, she thought to herself. *This isn't real.*

She should be back at the plantation, looking for Jane.

How did she get here?

"Hey, Margaret. Wanna beer?" a young boy asked.

Margaret's eyes lifted to the trailer. Randy, the young Randy—the one who was as skinny as a pole and wore his brown hair back in a mullet— sat on the rotten collection of two-by-fours that were nailed together to create some variation of a front porch. "My old man left half a case from last night. Guess he was too tired to get drunk." His voice was croaky and cracked against certain words. He couldn't be older than seventeen.

"Randy Jones! You must be outta your mind!" young Lucille snapped. She was sitting in a plastic lawn chair, filing her nails, and chomping on bubble gum. "If your daddy finds out he's missin' his beer— he'll beat you half to death."

"Shoot..." Randy shook his head as he grinned, waving his hand at her. "He won't know. Heck, he'll probably think *he* drank 'em all."

"I'm not drinkin' any of your daddy's beer," she huffed, rolling her eyes.

Mary Grace was sitting on the roof of a wrecked car with her legs hanging off the side. "I'm with Lucille."

"Me too," a quiet voice to Margaret's right whispered. No surprise, the voice came from Vivian, who was sitting on a large truck tire, nose-deep in a paperback like she always was.

Randy huffed, a playful smirk on his face. "What about you, Mar?"

"This isn't real," she said, finding her voice. "I'm not actually here."

They all stared at Margaret with confusion.

"What?" Mary Grace squinted her eyes. "You okay?"

Margaret inhaled a deep breath, "This. Isn't. Real."

Randy looked around. "What're you talkin' about?"

The pain in her head grew stronger, more intense. She shut her eyes tightly and clenched her fists to bear the affliction. But it just kept growing *stronger, stronger, stronger.* "This is not real! It's only a trick my mind is playing!"

She placed her hands on each side of her head, forcing them against her skull. "This is not real!"

"*Margaret!*" Lucille cried out somewhere far away. Her voice was a mere echo, a distant scream buried under the pain pulsating in her head. *"Margaret, open your eyes! Look at me! Margaret, open your eyes!"*

She did, and she was no longer at Randy's trailer home. She was at the Abel Plantation again, standing in the kitchen in front of Lucille.

Her throat felt closed up, and she realized she was holding her breath. She gasped for air as she fell to her hands and knees. The pain in her head vanished, leaving behind a cold sweat and an achiness that traveled up and down her body.

"Where's…" she struggled to find her voice, taking in deep breaths as if she had never breathed before. She shut her eyes. "Where's Jane?"

"She's out back with Mary Grace," Lucille, the present Lucille, answered without hesitation. She knelt beside her and placed a hand on her shoulder. "Mar, what just happened to you?"

She looked up, tears pooling in her green eyes, and she said softly, "I think I'm falling apart."

CHAPTER TWELVE

MARGARET SAT AT THE KITCHEN TABLE, her eyes resting on the white floor tiles. The vision left her weak. Beat. Embarrassed.

"How long has this been goin' on for?" Lucille asked as she poured her a glass of water.

"Since yesterday. It's strange. It's like I get sucked into this..." she hesitated, "...this different time, and I feel so lost. I've never experienced anything like it before."

She sat across from her and pushed the glass forward. Margaret took the glass with both hands and gulped down the water. "So, it's like your premonitions?" she asked, watching Margaret drink every drop of water.

"Only I don't see the future. Just the past. And these visions feel real. Not like the glimpses I saw as a kid. All my senses are heightened, and because of this, my mind gets... *stuck* in the moment. Like I'm really there."

Lucille just listened, studying her tired eyes as she processed what she was hearing.

"I'm scared that I won't be able to pull my mind back to reality. I don't want to get stuck for good. I'm pretty sure it would put me in a coma," she told her in a whisper, her eyes glossy with tears.

"Hey, hey, don't cry," Lucille pleaded, reaching across to grab her trembling hand. "I am not gonna let you get stuck, okay?"

She let out a soft cry. "When I ran away, I stopped practicing magic. I stopped casting, blocked out the visions—everything. For once, I was a normal human being."

"But you're still a witch, Margaret. You can't deny your roots."

"It doesn't matter." She wiped her eyes with the back of her hand. "What I'm trying to say is that I haven't practiced magic in seventeen damn years. Why is this happening now?"

"Maybe the visions are tryin' to tell you somethin'."

"But the memories are random. If that was the case, I would assume I would be pulled into an important memory—something that contained a lesson or a message or—"

"Maybe the past wants you to accept what has happened." Her words carried a heavy meaning, and Margaret knew what she was referring to.

She paused and clenched her jaw. Lucille's words felt like a punch in her chest, and she found herself angry at her for even bringing it up. "I have accepted what happened," she shot back, her tone flat. She pulled her hand out of Lucille's and dropped it in her lap.

She hated this. Hated the way her friend stared at her right now. Like she was a mess. Like she was weak. Even though seconds prior she was crying, she would not sit and accept stupid pity after everything she has been through.

Lucille noticed the mood shift and tried to soften her words. "You haven't, though. You ran away from who you were, and now that girl you left behind wants you back."

"But I'm not that girl anymore." She never will be again. That girl was weak, she was not.

"That may be true, but that still doesn't give you the right to ignore her and pretend she never existed."

The kitchen went silent for a moment before Mary Grace walked in and gasped. "Did I miss sister-bonding time?" she teased, walking over to the peach cobbler that was cooling off on the counter.

Jane followed Mary Grace into the kitchen, pausing in the doorway.

"This peach cobbler looks amazin', Lucille. I'm surprised you didn't burn it like you always do."

"Mom, are you okay?" Jane asked when she noticed the fresh tears in Margaret's eyes.

Margaret looked over at her and nodded. "Yeah, I'm okay."

'*Another lie,*' Jane noted. How many times did her parents lie to her and she never noticed? "I just got off the phone with Dad. He wants to talk to you."

Margaret almost rolled her eyes but caught herself. Of course, David wanted to talk to her. He was one of the reasons she was falling apart. Not because of the affair, but because she allowed him to stay in her life for so long, knowing exactly the kind of man he was all along. "I'll call him later."

It wasn't hard to miss the irritation in Margaret's voice. Jane wondered if something was really going on between her parents. They never fought, and rarely did they disagree on things. But after hearing the worry in her father's voice and seeing the sudden annoyance on her mother's face, she was beginning to think that maybe something different was going on.

'*If I want answers, I have to ask questions,*' she reminded herself. Why was it so difficult to ask a question? It felt like every time she went to find an answer, she was only met with *more* questions. Like about the statues, her father, her mother, the bedroom upstairs.

Her questions would have to wait because it was already time to leave and head over to the Jones's house.

When they left, a sudden wind picked up. Hot and thick, like the air could drown someone if they breathed too much of it.

Mary Grace turned down a small street right before the diner. *Poppy Ave*, the crooked street sign read.

Well-maintained colonial houses stood on each side of the street, along with the *Belles Parish Library* and a playground. The houses were old, just like everything else in Belles Parish, but they were taken care of. The sidewalks were clean, the green lawns were freshly trimmed, and white picket fences wrapped around each yard like Christmas bows.

"Here we are," Mary Grace said. She nodded to a two-story house that looked like all the other houses on the street, only it was painted a sunflower-yellow. The window shutters were a fresh shade of white, and so was the front porch. The Sheriff's truck was parked in the driveway.

"Well, I'll be," Lucille laughed. "On *Poppy Avenue*. That makes me so proud."

The street was busy. Cars drove by, kids played in the yards and driveways, birds chirped a tiny song with the crickets and cicadas— it sounded like a classic summer afternoon.

Mary Grace pulled behind the truck and shut off the engine.

"So," Margaret said before they got out of the car. "He got his white-picket-fence-house after all." She couldn't help but feel proud of him, proud of how far he has come in life. Of the man he worked so hard to become.

Jane followed the women through the open gate of the picket fence and up the clean walkway to the front porch of the colonial house. Pink and orange lantanas were planted on the front lawn near the door, attracting dozens of fluttering butterflies and fat bumblebees. A running sprinkler was placed on each side of the lawn, along with a concrete birdbath in the corner of the yard. A garden flag stood by the stairs; the words *welcome home* printed in cursive above a smiling ladybug.

The home was the complete opposite of the home Randy grew up in. Instead of empty beer bottles and trash on the porch, there were two pots of bright marigolds placed beside two wooden rocking chairs.

The house was welcoming. It was safe. There were no angry words being screamed, no loud footsteps stumping around inside, no fear, but instead, absolute peace.

Mary Grace held the small basket of rosemary in one hand, reaching her fingers out for the doorbell with the other. She pressed it once and then took a step back.

Mrs. Jones opened the door slowly and smiled at the women. Her smile was wide and genuine and as bright as the flowers planted in the lawn. "Hey, y'all! Welcome to our home. I am so happy you all could make it." She opened the door all the way and took a step to the side. Her hair was pulled back in a low bun, and two curls fell on each side of her freckled face. "Please, come in! Randy is out walking the dog. He should be back any minute."

They stepped inside the house and looked around. The walls were painted a sea-green, a soft contrast against the mahogany wood floors. Family portraits and baby photos of Bobbie Jo were neatly placed around the house like trophies. The staircase was to the right, a small living area to the left, and down a short hallway was the dining room.

The house smelled clean, like fresh paint and laundry.

Mellisa stood at the bottom of the stairs, cupping two open hands around her mouth. "Bobbie Jo, they're here!"

"Okay, be right down!" she answered. Following this came a thud, like something had dropped, then the pattering of footsteps as Bobbie Jo raced downstairs.

She stood awkwardly beside her mother, giving them all a big smile. Bobbie Jo looked like her mother in many ways, but she had that same wild gleam in her eyes that Randy had when he was a boy. That same fire.

"Here," Melissa started, taking the cobbler from Lucille. "I'll show y'all the kitchen."

Just as they turned to follow her, Bobbie Jo softly nudged Jane's arm and asked, "So, have you found any new leads?" She was referring to Vivian's disappearance.

The question made her return to the card and the strange turn of events from last night. Had she found any real leads? No. She couldn't tell her about the memory loss—there was no way Bobbie Jo would take her seriously.

When Jane didn't answer immediately, Bobbie Jo went on, that fire in her eyes ignited by an idea. "I have. Come with me, I want to show you something." She darted back upstairs, leading the way to her bedroom.

"Do you know if Vivian is religious?" Jane asked as she followed her.

Bobbie Jo stopped at her bedroom door and peered at her through a few fallen curls. "To be honest, I don't know. Why?"

What could she say without sounding crazy? And could she even trust her new friend with this information?

She bit her lip and let out a sigh, knowing she had to give her an explanation now. "I found a small picture—well, I think it's a card," she said, doing her best not to sound like she was losing her mind, but even she couldn't wrap her head around what she was saying. "It was in her bedroom. I don't even know how I got in there because the door is supposed to be locked. Anyway." Bobbie Jo raised an eyebrow as she watched her fumble with her own words. "It had a picture on it of... well—well, the devil."

"The *devil*?" She tucked a curly strand of hair behind her ear and squinted her brown eyes at her.

Jane shrugged. "Yeah." She wouldn't tell her about everything else at the plantation—not yet at least. She already sounded crazy enough as it is.

Bobbie Jo looked stunned. She turned back to the bedroom door and pushed it open. "That just don't make no sense," she muttered to herself, hurrying across the floor.

Jane paused at the doorway, looking around her bedroom. Clothes were dispersed randomly on the carpet floor, the bed was unmade, and stacks of books were found in every corner of the room.

Other than the untidiness, the bedroom didn't look like a teenage girl's bedroom.

There was a desk against the back wall that was the heart of the room. Papers and open books lay across the top of it, along with highlighters, sticky notes, and pencils. Above the desk was a pinboard filled with many notes and photographs. The room looked like the kind detectives in movies would have.

As if she could hear Jane's thoughts, Bobbie Jo let out a nervous laugh. "Sorry it's a mess. I've been so busy that I haven't had time to clean." She began picking up articles of clothing and throwing them in the basket beside her closet.

"Don't worry about it. My room looks the same," she said, but that was a lie. Her bedroom in New York was spotless and was almost always organized. But that was just because, growing up, her parents forced her to keep her bedroom clean. Everything had to be clean. Not just her room, but her appearance as well. She had to fit the role of a Gardener and wear her family's reputation like a crown. And that crown was heavy—too heavy. That's one of the reasons she loved it in Belles Parish. She didn't need to worry about appearing a certain way. She could be herself. Not her mother's daughter. Just herself.

Bobbie Jo turned to Jane once she was satisfied with her cleaning. "Back to the card you said you saw. Was it a photograph or a drawing?"

"It was a drawing."

She walked over to her desk and grabbed a sticky note, scribbling something on it. She stuck it on the pinboard next to a picture of Vivian.

'DRAWING OF THE DEVIL??' the note read.

Jane looked at all the things pinned on the board. "So, you like solving mysteries, huh?" She thought about what the girls in the diner had called her. *Detective White Trash*.

Bobbie Jo let out a laugh. "I guess. Ever since I was a little girl, I've wanted to be a detective. Sometimes, I like to sit in my dad's office when he's workin' on a case. I always thought it was so much fun. Not to brag, but," she smirked, crossing her arms over her chest, "in the middle school, my principal's dog was lost, and I found it. It was kind of a big deal. Everyone was lookin', even the police. Took me two days to find the poor thing." Her smile faded then, and she sighed. "But this—" she nodded her head to the pinboard. "—this is different. It's serious, y'know?"

Jane nodded her head, "Yeah, I get that."

She took a long sigh. "Anyway, let's talk about my theories."

Jane sat down at the foot of the bed.

Bobbie Jo leaned against the desk, crossing her arms over her chest. She licked her lips quickly before she began, her gaze narrowed on the floor. "Vivian was— *is* like family to me. Which is why I can't imagine her just *runnin'* away. 'Specially without tellin' me. She's not like that, regardless of what people in town say 'bout her. So, I have *three* theories. First one— her boyfriend kidnapped her." She grabbed a pencil from her desk and pointed it at a sticky note that read, *'DID CODY CARTWRIGHT KIDNAP VIVIAN???'* Next to the small note was a grainy picture of a man with brown hair, a soft grin, and a short beard. He looked friendly but looks alone wouldn't be enough to judge his character that easily.

"Do you know him?" Jane asked, staring at the man in the photo. "I mean, have you met him?"

"No, I haven't. And that's why I think he might be involved with her disappearance."

"Do you know where he lives?"

"Yep, and he's not home. Hasn't been since the night Vivian went missing," she shook her head.

Jane found her eyes, "Sounds sketchy."

"Exactly." She moved the pencil to the photo of Vivian, above the Cody Cartwright note. "Second theory. She *ran away*. I really don't want to believe this, but unfortunately, this kind of thing is common with women like Vivian. She was always quiet, kept to herself. If she was going through a mental crisis, the chances she would have told somebody are slim."

"What's the third theory?"

Bobbie Jo pointed to the new note she just put up. "Third. She was taken by a cult. Or she ran away with one. Obviously, I have no proof to back this one up except for what you said you saw. I'm not sayin' cults are a common thing down here, but religious fanatics? There're more than you'd think."

Jane nodded as she listened. It was a lot of information to take in at one time.

"Do you think you could get me that drawing you were talking about? I'd like to see it for myself."

She chewed her cheek. "Sure."

"And maybe look through her room some more. See what else you can find."

"Well, her room is locked."

Bobbie Jo let out a defeated sigh and leaned against her desk, crossing her legs. "How did you get in there in the first place?"

She shrugged. "Like I said, I can't remember."

She raised an eyebrow and cocked her head to the side, a curl falling in her eyes. "You can't remember?" She paused, shaking her head. "You gotta find the key then. There might be more things in that room—things that could point us in the right direction."

Sneaking around wasn't her strongest suit. She wished she had asked Mary Grace about the room when she had the chance.

But maybe it was a good thing she didn't. Afterall, her mother had the same card. Could it be possible that the women had something to do with Vivian's disappearance? She didn't want to believe this was true. They wouldn't watch everyone in the parish run around like headless chickens while knowing exactly what happened to Vivian. Would they? She didn't know, and that's what terrified her.

"Okay," she finally said. "I'll try to find the key."

CHAPTER THIRTEEN

"HIS NAME IS CODY CARTWRIGHT," Randy told his friends as they sipped the cool, sweet lemonade Melissa made that morning.

They were sitting in the living room as Randy went over the notes he had gathered on Vivian's disappearance. The den was comfortable, a real family room, with an extra-soft cushiony couch, a big recliner chair, and a flat-screen TV above the fireplace.

Melissa was in the kitchen cooking dinner— the smells of chicken-fried steak and collard greens diffusing throughout the house. The three women sat together on the couch, and Randy was comfortably stationed in the recliner chair. His brown labrador stood by his left armrest, and he stroked its head softly as he talked.

The comfort of the room didn't help Margaret much, though. She was still a nervous wreck, picking her nails and gnawing at her bottom lip until she tasted that copper taste of her own blood. She thought she accepted the fact Vivian was missing, but listening to Randy talk made her feel the way she felt when Mary Grace called her that night in New York.

"Are you sure?" Mary Grace asked with concern. "It's just not like her."

He continued to pet the happy dog. "I know—but when my detective and I searched her apartment, it was obvious *someone* was livin' there with her. For a while, looked like. So, we asked around and..." he sighed.

Mary Grace still didn't believe him. "She and I talked almost every day, even when she moved to New Orleans, and she had never once mentioned a lover. She would have—" she paused. "I'm tellin' you, she would have *told* me if she met someone."

"Multiple people said that they knew about their relationship," he told them. "Said they've been livin' together for a while."

"Huh," Lucille exhaled. She took a gulp of lemonade. "Cody Cartwright," she repeated the name. "I will admit, it's not like her to not tell at least *one* of us about this guy."

"We don't need to know every detail about each other's lives," Margaret snapped. Everyone stopped and looked over at her at the end of the couch. She softened her shoulders. "I mean, let's be honest. We barely know anything about each other's lives anymore. The only thing I knew was that you—" she turned to Lucille. "—lived in Georgia while Vivian and Mary Grace were still living together at the plantation. I didn't even know she moved to New Orleans."

Mary Grace nodded her head, knowing that she was right, even though the truth was sad. They all lived separate lives.

Lucille swallowed and said, "I wonder what else she didn't tell us."

The den was quiet for a moment, each of them hoping someone would say something to abolish the silence.

Margaret shifted her weight, crossing a leg over the other as she tried to ignore how much the silence bothered her. "Where is he now?" she asked when a whole minute passed.

Randy took a breath, shaking his head. "Don't know. He left the night she went missin' and hasn't been back. I just got word that some folks up the river saw him at a bar."

Almost out of nowhere, Bobbie Jo swiftly stormed into the den with Jane following, her brown curls bouncing with every step. "When was this?"

Unphased, Randy finished the rest of his glass of lemonade and answered her, "Just last night."

"And why didn't you tell me about this sooner?" she asked with utter disbelief. She leaned against the wall by the door, her arms crossed over her chest. Her confidence and determination was blatant, and she was not afraid to show it.

He shot her a look. "Because I found out *last night*. You were sleeping."

She gave him a look that screamed *'sure'* and dropped it.

Margaret wasn't thrilled with the fact Jane was standing right there, listening, exposed to the possible dangers involved with Vivian's disappearance. She couldn't help but feel like she was somehow putting her in danger. There was real evil in the world, and if that evil took Vivian, she worried it would come after her only daughter next.

"Where up the river?" Lucille questioned from beside Margaret, bringing her back down to the conversation.

"St. Gabriel. A friend of mine saw him. He's an ex-cop—we go *way* back. Real nice old man. He's actually the reason I got my job with the Belles Parish Sheriff's Office. He retired about ten years ago and moved to St. Gabriel to be with his daughter and grandkids."

"Mr. Clark?" Mary Grace asked with a joyful gasp.

"Yup, that's him."

"Oh, I remember that man," Lucille smiled. "There was this one time—when I was about seven or eight, I stole somethin' from that crappy gas station on the West side. I wasn't a thief. It was the only time I had ever stolen. It wasn't anythin' big. I stole a bag of potato chips because I didn't have any food at home. My mother—as wonderful as she was—hadn't been home for days, so I had to take care of myself," she said, shaking her head a little. She stared at the coffee table in front of her as if she was watching the memory play out before her eyes. "I was *real* ashamed when Mr. Clark caught me sneakin' out. But he just looked at me and said, *'I'm givin' you a pass this time, but I better not find you stealin' again, Miss Lucy. You ain't a thief, you a princess'*, and gave me twenty bucks." She pitied that little girl. The one with dirty feet and ripped clothes. The one who was left neglected so many times by a grown woman who chose drugs and alcohol over her own daughter. "Sorry, I'm ramblin'. Back to you, Randy," she giggled, shaking her head to get rid of the cutting memory. "Mr. Clark saw Cody in St. Gabriel."

"Mr. Clark is a good man, that's for sure," Randy answered. "He helped every one of us out one way or another. "I called him last night to tell him what happened to Vivian, when he said he saw Cody at the bar just last night. He said Cody didn't *act* guilty or nothin'. He even stopped and spoke with him for a few minutes. He acted completely normal."

"And how does he know him?" Mary Grace asked.

"He told me that he was good friends with his parents back in the day. He said Cody was a troubled kid growing up, kicked out of schools, fighting all the time, stuff like that. Before Mr. Clark transferred to Belles Parish, he was working in New Orleans. Got a lot of calls for the Cartwright family."

"Great," Mary Grace huffed. "So we're dealing with a violent maniac. Thanks, Vivian," she added, rolling her eyes.

"Eh, I wouldn't go that far. From what Mr. Clark told me, he's a good guy now. His folks just weren't the best parents it sounds like."

She pursed her lips. "Even better. He's got people sympathizing for him."

He knew what she meant. Everyone overlooks the victim with a rocky past. "Anyone who got somethin' to hide won't be found casually having a beer in a local bar."

"Anyone who got somethin' to hide is gonna pretend to be innocent, though," Bobbie Jo said from across the den.

"And you may be right. Cody may be guilty. But as of right now, he's innocent. If we got not proof, we got no case."

Bobbie Jo shrugged. "I know, I know. I just don't trust that guy. I think we need to put out a search warrant for him."

He smiled, laughing softly at her willpower. "I'm afraid that's not how these things work, Bobbie Jo.

"Okay, then, citizen's arrest?"

He looked utterly amused. Just as he was about to open his mouth to respond, his wife walked in.

"There will be no citizen's arrests today. Come on, let's leave work here. It's time to eat." Her smile brightened the room, filling the space with a warmth that flourished from within. Like she was smiling with her heart.

Bobbie Jo nudged Jane's arm as they moved to the dining room and whispered, "No work-talk at the table. Mom's rule."

No one talked about the case the rest of the evening. Not even Randy. But that didn't mean no one was thinking about the case.

Everyone ate in silence, their gazes locked on the plates before them.

Melissa didn't like the quiet. Especially not at the dinner table. It didn't sit right with her. The absence of conversation made her feel like she wasn't doing enough. She cleared her throat. "So, Jane," she started, setting her elbows on the table. "Do you play any sports? I keep tellin' Bobbie Jo she should try out for the softball team before she graduates—"

"High school sports are pointless. It's just a way for a bunch of know-it-all kids to let loose and procrastinate from schoolwork. Plus, I'm pretty sure half the kids at Belles High just get high and sleep with their coaches—"

Melissa slapped the table. "Bobbie Jo, that is *enough*. Sports are great for socializing and learning how to work as a team."

"And why the hell would I want to work as a team with the possibility of being peer pressured and dragged down?" she snapped back, smirking a little.

"Language, please," Randy mumbled between chews.

Bobbie Jo was laughing. "You know I'm right, though! High school sports are a waste of time and energy. There ain't no way I'm giving up my free time to—"

"This wasn't *about* you, so that's enough. I was asking Jane a question," she said, shaking her head. She turned to look at Jane, her smile returning once more.

She scooped up a forkful of collards, and before shoving it in her mouth, she answered, "Um—no, not anymore. I used to play volleyball, but I stopped when I broke my ankle last year."

Melissa sighed. "I'm sorry. That must have been painful."

"Why didn't you try out this year?" Bobbie Jo asked, avoiding her mother's stare.

"Well," Jane tried to contain her smirk. "I wanted to focus more on my grades."

"*Thank you*," she gasped. "You hear that?" She looked at her mother.

Melissa shook her head. "Eat."

They all laughed—but Jane's mind was focused elsewhere. On three things in particular.

Cody Cartwright.

St. Gabriel.

The devil card.

After they finished eating, it was already time for them to go home.

"We should do this more often," Randy had said to the women as they stood on the front porch. "I missed y'all." His eyes became glossy as if all the memories of each and every adventure they shared together rushed back to him.

The sky was a burnt orange with pink rays shooting across like paint strokes. The harsh heat from the day had melted with the sun, leaving only a warm breeze in its place.

Mary Grace hugged him and smiled. "It was nice to be all together—" she stopped midsentence, her words falling into the pit of her stomach.

Melissa stepped forward, understanding the sadness in Mary Grace's eyes. "I'm just so happy my daughter finally has a friend her age."

Bobbie Jo stood beside her mother. She rolled her eyes, crossing her arms over her chest.

Melissa smiled, acting as if she didn't notice her daughter. "She's startin' to worry me, y'know? Cooped up in her *messy* room, studying articles and reading books about crime and murder."

"Mama!" she snapped, putting her hands on her hips. "You make me sound like I'm *crazy*."

Jane couldn't help but smile a little.

"Alright, alright— I'm just teasin'!" She threw her hands up. She walked over to Jane. "But not really," she mumbled and winked an eye before giving her a small hug.

Even though it was Jane's first time hanging out with the Jones family, and she still barely knew Bobbie Jo, she felt as if she had always known them. It was like Bobbie Jo had always been her friend. Like their souls had bonded long before they did.

CHAPTER FOURTEEN

ON THE DRIVE BACK TO THE PLANTATION, Margaret stared down at her phone in her hand, silently counting all of the missed calls from her husband. She knew it wasn't fair to ignore him, but she couldn't bring herself to answer him either. Plus, anything that he needed to tell her could wait until she was back in New York. It wasn't like they could work anything out over the phone. Hearing him, his empty apologies and sorrowful complaints wouldn't fix anything between them. He had fallen out of love with her, and she couldn't really remember the last time she had truly loved *him*. So, who was really in the wrong? Who was the one to blame?

She turned off her phone, the list of missed calls disappearing into a black hole. Her tired and worn reflection stared at her. She could barely recognize the woman in the black mirror. She didn't want to recognize her. She didn't want to know her—the stranger whom she had strayed from time and time again. She flashed her gaze to the windshield.

When Mary Grace turned down the small road where the Abel Plantation hid behind thick walls of green vegetation, Margaret could feel an aching pulse in the back of her skull.

She shut her eyes, the vibrant colors outside suddenly too penetrating to see. But the pain in her head only sharpened.

'Not right now,' she pleaded.

The second the engine was off, Margaret was stumbling out of the passenger door.

The headache felt like metal nails dragging across a chalkboard. She curled both of her fists into balls, her nails digging into her palms, but the pain was a reminder that she could still experience something other than the fire eating her mind.

She turned to the house, forcing her eyes open. Her heart beat loudly with the rhythm of the screaming cicadas.

Something wasn't right. She took in her surroundings.

And that's when she saw that Mary Grace's car, and everyone in it, was gone. An old navy-blue Grand Wagoneer was parked in its place.

"No," she moaned, shaking her head. She tried to snap out of it. Out of whatever time she was in.

The vehicle wasn't old at all. In fact, it was semi-new.

In 1992.

As she stared at it, she began to remember this vehicle. It belonged to Lorraine Abel. But she didn't remember it being so, well, *big*.

She found her reflection on the side of the truck, gasping when she was met with a little girl where her own reflection should have been. She raised her hands and grabbed at the long hair that swayed below her small hips. She looked down at her body, feeling almost sick. Her tongue trailed the inside of her mouth until she felt a gap where her left front tooth should have been.

She was a kid. No older than seven. She couldn't believe it. She knew none of this was *really* happening, but she panicked nonetheless.

Her head still hurt as she looked around. Sun shone on her, excruciatingly bright. She squinted her eyes, looking up at the big white house. The house looked the same as it did thirty years later, which wasn't a surprise. Mary Grace kept everything in precise order from their childhood.

A playful breeze blew through the oaks, and she heard tiny laughs and giggles coming from around the house. It sounded like children. Probably her friends as little kids. Wanting to go back to the present moment, she followed her intuition and the voices to the backyard.

Rubbing her temples, Jane dragged her feet up the porch steps. A strange and sudden migraine burned in the back of her head, pulsing throughout her brain and sending chills down her spine. The migraine felt like the same one she got in the diner with Bobbie Jo.

She was probably dehydrated. That's where she decided the headache was from—lack of water. It wasn't uncommon, especially in a place this hot where sweating was a regular occurrence like breathing. A constant attempt to cool the body off. She needed to get inside and get water.

She noticed her mother walking cautiously around the house, like she was looking for something. That, or she was lost.

"Mom?" she called, pausing on the last step.

Margaret didn't answer but continued walking away, eventually disappearing around the house.

Jane wanted to call out again, but the lingering pain snapped, and her knees buckled beneath her. She fell on her hands and knees, breathless. The pain in her head was radiating. She gritted her teeth against the pain and discomfort. She thought she heard her aunts call out to her and ask if she was okay—but the noises from the frogs and cicadas merged together and created a sort of white noise, drowning out everything else.

She tried to focus only on the sharp breaths that entered and exited her body, hoping it would ease the discomfort building in the back of her head.

She took a deep breath and managed to pull herself up to a standing. Forcing her feet along the porch, she shoved the front door open without a moment's hesitation. She started up the stairs, wanting nothing but the comfort of her bedroom as if the room could numb the pain.

As she meandered down the hallway, the walls seemed to be turning sideways. The walls turned and turned until they were swirling before her like a kaleidoscope. Her balance was lost by the sight of it all. She reached her hands out to feel the walls, reaching for something to keep her steady.

She closed her eyes as another wave of pain crashed against her mind like a rapid wave colliding with a rocky cliff. Her vision blurred, and the only thing she could see was the card with the immoral illustration gawking at her with its evil, red eyes.

The Devil, the cursive writing at the bottom of the card read. It was the card she saw in Vivian's room.

She shut her eyes again and gritted her teeth, trying to get the image out of her head. When she opened her eyes, she glanced down at a vintage doorknob before her. She took a step back and looked around. She was standing at Vivian's bedroom door. She couldn't remember walking there. Without thinking it through, she grabbed the doorknob. It was deathly cold under her palm. She turned it.

The little girl with blonde, curly locks handed a piece of candy to Margaret.

"I know butterscotch ain't your favorite, but I think you should just try it," the girl told her, the candy in between her small fingers.

Margaret reached out and took the candy from her friend. She held it in her hand and leaned back in her chair.

"So why am I here?" Margaret asked out loud, almost laughing again at her high-pitched voice. She looked up at the orange sky, eyeing the silver moon above the trees. "I get it. *I need to accept my past*. But is *this* really necessary?"

Vivian smiled at her friend. "Mar, you're funny."

Margaret looked beside her at Vivian.

"Oh! Oh!" started Mary Grace, clapping her hands together. "Guess what! I asked Mama if she could paint our nails for the fair, and she said yes!"

"What am I supposed to gain from these memories?" Margaret went on. "I don't understand the point of any of this," she wasn't talking directly to the girls but instead to the crescent moon above her. "I am having a *tea party* with my friends—who are kids. *Little kids*. Can anyone explain why I'm going through this?"

"Margaret," tiny Vivian called.

She looked over again, lifting her eyebrows.

Her friend's little face was serious, and a dark glare filled her round eyes. "Margaret, you must find me. And the only way you can do that is to accept your past and tell your daughter the truth. You must find me."

Margaret's eyes widened. She knew this wasn't little Vivian speaking to her anymore. "Vivian?" she grabbed her friend's arm. "Is that you?"

"Close your eyes," the little girl said.

Margaret hesitated, but after a moment, she heaved a sigh and closed her eyes.

"Now, open your eyes and go find your daughter."

She flicked her eyes open. Vivian was gone. The girls were gone. The candy, the teacups, it was all gone. She was sitting on the iron chair completely by herself. The angels surrounding the garden stared down at her. The warm colors of the sunset had vanished, replaced by the velvet night sky and thousands of glittering stars.

The pain in her head was gone, dragged away with the memory like the tide. And like the tide, she knew the pain would return again.

But for now, she had to do what little Vivian told her to do.

She had to find her daughter.

Just like before, the door was locked.

She released her grip from the doorknob as new waves of pain electrocuted her. She fell to the floor, pulling her knees to her chest. She wanted to cry. She wanted to scream. She wanted her mother. Where was she?

Her heart raced, each beat pounding in her ears like a timer on a bomb ready to explode.

"Jane," a soft female voice spoke. It sounded familiar but alien at the same time.

Weak and uncomfortable, she managed to look up at the voice and was instantly overcome by shock.

A woman in a soaked white nightgown stood before her. Her bare feet stood in a puddle of black, muddy water. Her dark hair hung down, covering her face, except for her haunting eyes and blue, quivering lips.

"Jane," she said again, this time in a delicate whisper. "You must remember. You're the only one who can save me."

"What?" Jane shouted. "Who... who are you? What do you want from me?"

"You must remember."

"Remember what? I don't understand—!" With a clap of pain, she remembered the woman. She had seen her before.

It was Vivian.

She licked her lips, her last breath leaving her lungs as she whispered, "You must remember. You're the only one who can save me."

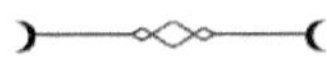

Lucille poured the hot water over the tea bag, filling the mug with a golden liquid. She took a deep breath, the smell of chamomile easing her nerves.

"I don't like this. What if—" she started again.

"Will you just trust me for once in your life?" Mary Grace asked from the kitchen table.

"But what if they need our help? What if they get *stuck* in whatever *dream* they're having, huh? What then, genius?" she muttered before dropping a spoonful of honey into the tea.

"You saw the look on Margaret's face. She was having a vision. We cannot interfere now."

"And what about Jane? Margaret said she doesn't even know about witchcraft—how the hell is she having a vision?"

"All I know," Mary Grace sighed. "Is that we cannot, under any circumstances, interfere with a divine premonition."

"But should we even trust your *gut feelings* anymore? You didn't even know about that Cartwright fella." She pointed the silver spoon at Mary Grace as if she had made a valid point in the argument.

This shut her up. She stared down at her hands intertwined on the table's surface. "I'm still trying to figure that out," she said after a second's hesitation.

The moment was interrupted by a loud thud coming from upstairs.

Lucille dropped the spoon. It clashed against the tiles. "Was that—"

The blood in Mary Grace's face drained as she stood up and finished Lucille's sentence. "—Jane!"

The house was quiet. Not a peaceful silence but a disturbing emptiness. When Margaret ripped open the heavy back doors, a gust of wind blew through the doorway. The air howled as it ran over her, carrying with it a warning.

Her stomach tightened. She stood frozen in the doorway, trying to pick up on any noises—anything that would prove her sudden panic was unnecessary. Foolish, even. But she was only met with the quietness of the big house.

She ran down the hallway, forgetting to shut the doors behind her. The cicadas in the garden grew intense with their hums, deep and almost sardonic, and it creeped into the house, sending echoes of their cries against the walls.

Her heart began to drum in her ears so loudly that she thought it might explode.

Little Vivian told her to find her daughter—and why? Was she warning her? Did something happen to Jane while she was trapped in her stupid vision?

The living room was empty, and so was the kitchen. She began to worry when she couldn't find her friends either. She kicked open each door downstairs, her panic increasing more and more when she found the rooms empty.

She called for Jane while she ran up the stairs to the second floor. When she got to the top of the stairs, her eyes found Mary Grace and Lucille at the end of the hallway, standing in front of Jane.

Her knees felt weak at the sight of them. She should have been relieved to find them—but she was even more scared than when she was looking for them.

Jane was unconscious, *levitating* four feet above the ground. Her short hair hung from her head, and her body looked like she was floating on water. Her muscles were relaxed, and her breathing was steady. Her face looked peaceful, like she was deep in a sweet dream.

But she was levitating. Four feet above the ground with unnatural effortlessness.

Margaret placed a hand over her mouth to hold back a scream, her eyes grew wide with horror. No one moved, no one said a word. They just stared.

Jane was whispering something, far too quiet for them to hear.

Mary Grace looked down at her feet, noticing the puddle of water they were standing in. Another muddy puddle.

"Jane!" Margaret called.

"No, you'll wake her!" hissed Mary Grace in a whisper.

"That is exactly what I'm trying to do."

Mary Grace lifted her hand and hovered it inches above the girl's face like she was trying to feel if a pan on a burner was hot or not. She closed her eyes and pressed her lips together in concentration as she began humming a solid tune like a bee.

"Mary Grace, what are you doing?" she snapped, throwing her arms up.

The woman paused her humming and whispered, "Shhh. I'm tryin' to read her mind. She's dreaming." She kept her eyes closed.

"Wait, what do you mean *trying*?" Lucille said from behind Mary Grace. "Are you tellin' me you can't read her thoughts?"

Mary Grace nodded her head a little. "I can't read or see anythin' inside her head. But I feel a strong... *power*—or energy— radiating from her body. I've never felt anythin' like it before." She began humming again.

Margaret looked at her daughter, a single tear escaping her eye and trinkling down her cheek. "Mary Grace, wake her up," she begged. Her voice came out small and feeble at first, but the more she studied her levitating daughter, the stronger her panic grew, the louder her voice came out.

"Shhh."

"Wake her up, Mary Grace. Right now," she demanded, fear boiling inside her. She couldn't let anything bad happen to her. She *wouldn't*.

"Margaret, please, let me just try to find out what's wrong with her."

She held her breath. "Wrong?!"

"I need you to walk out of the house," she snapped, opening one eye. "I can't hear anythin' but your *screamin'* anxiety."

Margaret huffed, not believing her own ears. "She is my daughter—I am not going anywhere. Wake her up. *Now.*"

Lucille nodded and wrapped her arms around herself as if she was avoiding a chill in the air. "I don't like this. What if she's stuck?"

Mary Grace ignored them. She was confident in her judgement, and she wished her friends would trust her. She hovered her hands over Jane's face, feeling the warmth of the girl's energy touch her fingertips. *What was going on in her head?*

"She's not some puzzle you can figure out," Margaret snapped, pushing her out of the way as she stepped forward. "This ends now." She reached her hand out to touch Jane. She could feel the strong energy Mary Grace was talking about. It made the hairs on her arms stand, but this didn't stop her. She lowered her hand to Jane's shoulder. "Wake up, Jane!"

Mary Grace tried to stop her, saying, "I wouldn't touch her—"

But it was too late.

The moment Margaret's hand met Jane, the air cracked and popped. What felt like a bolt of electricity ran through her veins at the very touch. She yanked her hand back and fell the floor.

As if the air decided *now* was a good time to let her go, gravity returned swiftly, sending Jane to the floor with a loud *thump*. Her eyes immediately shot open and took in her surroundings.

"What... what happened?" she whispered, trying to steady her breathing. Why was she on the floor? Why was everyone looking at her like that?

Margaret started crying. "Are you okay?" She moved to Jane's side and pulled her in her arms.

She didn't have an answer to her mother's question just yet. She scanned her body. Her limbs ached, and her brain felt like it was pounding against her skull.

"Do you remember anything?" Margaret asked another question, giving her a small squeeze before letting her go and looking into her eyes for an answer.

Mary Grace and Lucille stood behind them, giving them space but still silently studying them.

Jane rubbed the back of her head, feeling a fresh goose egg where she must have fallen down. *Was* she okay? She assumed the answer was no, considering she couldn't remember how she got where she was. In the hallway, in front of Vivian's bedroom door. Lying in front of a puddle of water. She felt she was going to throw up.

"Are you okay?"

Jane paused. Didn't her mother already ask this question? She must have been hallucinating. Or dreaming.

"Jane, are you okay?" she asked once again, contradicting Jane's previous thought.

"Did I faint again?" She didn't mean to say this out loud. She knew her question would only scare her mother and her aunts. Her mother's face was so white, she almost asked if *she* was okay.

"What do you mean *again*? This has happened before?" Margaret asked.

Jane thought about it. "I don't know."

"Then why did you say *again*?"

"I think I fainted last night, but I don't know if I really did or not. I woke up this morning, just like this, with no memory of what happened or how I got here." Her voice trembled a little as she spoke.

Mary Grace took a step forward. "You just fainted, darlin'. No need to worry."

Margaret gave Mary Grace a look that said *that's enough.* "How are you feeling?" she questioned, helping her daughter come to a standing.

Her legs were weak under her, knees shaking slightly. "Confused."

Mary Grace knelt by the puddle of water, grazing it with her fingertips. She wasn't surprised when she saw it was indeed the same swamp water she found in Jane's room that very morning.

"You need to rest," Mary Grace said, standing up. "You look exhausted."

Margaret and Mary Grace helped walk her to her bedroom, Lucille following close.

"You just rest, dear," Mary Grace said when she made it to her bed. "I'm going to make you some of my healing tea, and you'll be all better soon," she added before she and Lucille headed for the kitchen.

When they were gone, Jane turned to Margaret, who was sitting at the end of her bed, her face still ghostly white.

She wasn't sure what to say or if she should say anything at all, so she just blurted the first question that popped in her head. "What's healing tea?"

The question pulled Margaret out of her overthinking vortex. Her stomach plummeted. "I know it sounds weird, but I promise it will help you with that headache." She didn't want any of this for Jane. The fainting spells, the levitating, the sharp pain that felt like blades made of ice and fire slicing through her brain.

"Sounds like you've experienced this before."

Margaret looked up from her lap and met Jane's curious gaze. "What?"

"Fainting."

Jane thought she merely fainted from the intensity of the heat, and Margaret had to make sure it stayed that way. That was better than the truth.

"Oh. Yeah. It's more common than not down here."

But something in her tone was off. Just like the phone call with her father.

She pushed the thought away, and turned her attention to what was really important at the moment.

She fainted again. And her memory of what she was doing before she fainted was a messy paint stroke of a distorted unknown that she couldn't reveal, no matter how hard she tried.

The tea was a purplish color and tasted like flowers and dirt. Astonishingly, and fortunately, her foggy headache cured the second the floral fluid ran down her throat.

"Get some rest," Margaret said to her after she took a few sips. She and the other women left Jane alone, closing the door behind them, allowing the silence of the walls to become a shelter from the confusion that lurked.

She didn't want to rest. She wanted to remember what happened before she fainted. She wanted to know why her aunts and her mother looked terrified when she awoke and what they weren't telling her.

There was water again, too. She didn't want to point it out, but she saw Mary Grace looking at it.

Once her worrying quieted just a little, she came to the conclusion that there was something wrong with her. It was obvious before but truly undeniable now. This belief was rooted in her gut, and she would be lying to say she couldn't feel it.

Something was wrong with her—and something was wrong with them. The townspeople could see it. In church, they stared at them like they were aliens. Outcasts.

The three girls called them witches, and they accused them of practicing black magic. It would have sounded comical back in New York, but here, where secrets and mysteries became more common every day, it didn't sound too far off from whatever the truth was.

A chill shot up her spine. She had to stop thinking about what those girls had said. They were just trying to freak her out anyway. Right?

She grabbed her phone from the nightstand and began typing in the search bar "loss of memory after fainting". She watched the loading icon spin in a circle until a pop-up read "no internet connection". She sighed, putting her phone back on the nightstand.

It didn't make sense. It was such a strange mystery, and she couldn't find an explanation that fit the puzzle.

A soft creaking noise from outside her French doors broke her train of thought. It must have been a little before midnight. How was it already so late? She stood up from the bed and stepped out onto the porch. The air outside was still and humid. Up in the velvet black sky, a silver crescent moon cast light on her face and filled her with a sense of comfort.

Not a minute went by before she smelt a strong odor of cigarette smoke. She looked to her right, finding Lucille sitting on a rocking chair and smoking a freshly lit cigarette.

"Hi," was all Jane could find to say at that moment.

Lucille held her pack of cigarettes out to Jane. "Want one?"

She almost laughed. "No, thank you. I don't smoke."

The blonde woman placed the pack next to her, taking a long drag from her cigarette. "I didn't either when I was your age."

Croaking sounds of the insects all around filled the silence between them. Jane walked over to the railing and rested her forearms across it. She looked out at the stretched driveway, thinking about the whole day.

"So, can't sleep?" Lucille asked.

"Nope."

"You know your mama would have a fit if she saw you outta bed." She put out her cigarette and flicked it in the flowerpot next to her. "You better go back to your room."

"I feel fine," Jane sighed. "Confused, but that's it."

"Hmm... well, I still think you should get back to bed—"

She returned her gaze to her aunt. "Lucille, have you ever fainted before?" she asked. Her green eyes darkened with the shadows of the night, and the way they locked with Lucille's made her feel like they were peering into the depths of her soul, reading through every thought and secret that she had locked away.

The woman dropped her eyes to the floorboards as she thought over her answer. She knew Jane couldn't really read her mind, but she still avoided eye contact when she answered with a shake of her head.

Jane took a deep breath as if disappointed Lucille hadn't fainted before. It would have been nice to relate to someone. Maybe she wouldn't feel so scared if she could talk to someone who had fainted just as she did. "Oh. I hadn't either—before today. It's kind of scary, you know? Waking up with no idea where you are or how you got there. No memory of what you were doing," she paused, replaying her mother's worried face searching her own after she woke in the hallway.

Jane turned back to the driveway. She looked so much like her mother under the moonlight. She wore the same expression as Margaret, as if she were battling a thousand emotions trapped behind her hollow eyes. She looked up at the moon and thought about how effortlessly devoted it was. No matter how strange things get for Jane, no matter what happens, the moon will always be there, unaffected. It was comforting to know it would always be there. Watching over her.

"Do you think it's normal? You know, to lose memory?" Jane questioned after a few moments of silence.

The woman shrugged, "Maybe." She wanted so badly to tell the girl what had really happened to her. *'You were levitating, Jane. Just like your mother used to do when she slept.'* But she couldn't. She had to keep her mouth closed. For her own sake.

Jane could not know who she was.

CHAPTER FIFTEEN

HER THOUGHTS WERE SUFFOCATING. No matter how hard she tried, Jane could not go to sleep. After saying goodnight to Lucille, she lay awake in bed, staring up at the crack in the ceiling above her.

An eerie feeling lingered around her. She felt like someone was watching her, waiting for the right time to jump out from the shadows and yell *boo!*

She sat up in bed, ripping the blankets off.

There was no way she would be falling asleep anytime soon.

She needed answers.

But where would she look?

An idea formed in her head, and she felt she had no other choice but to test it. She would sneak downstairs and search for the key to Vivian's room. Mary Grace had to have put the key somewhere. The first place she'd look would be the kitchen. If it wasn't in there, then she'd try the living room. And if it wasn't in the living room... she could see if the internet had anything on how to break an antique lock?

'This is never going to work,' she thought to herself, feeling discouraged.

But trying was better than lying awake. She thought that if she could get into Vivian's room, she could find some answers. She didn't know what answers she was looking for, but there had to be some explanation.

With a deep breath, she quietly crept out of bed. As if the heat from outside seeped into the bones of the old house, the wooden floorboards beneath Jane's bare feet felt warm and humid.

She cracked open her bedroom door, peeking her head out and looking around.

The halls were empty and nearly pitch-black. The natural moonlight streaming through her balcony doors cast soft rays into the hall. After stepping out, she closed the door softly behind her, and the unsettling darkness returned.

'I should have brought a flashlight,' she shook her head as she reached her hands out for the wall in front of her. Slowly, her eyes began to adjust. She could make out the shut bedroom doors and the pictures that lined both sides of the hallway.

As she turned to the right, she caught a faint blur of a figure on her left. She froze, thinking it was her mother coming out of her room, but when she looked, there was no one.

"Jane," a soft voice whispered.

She looked around quickly, trying to find who the voice belonged to. She was the only one in the hall.

"Jane."

The voice was coming from the end of the hall. Not really thinking it over, she followed the voice, being very careful not to make any noise.

She was standing in front of Vivian's door now, and the voice sounded like it was coming from inside the room.

'But this can't be happening, can it? I must be dreaming,' she decided. *'Who's calling my name?'*

Yet deep down, she already knew. The knowing felt like an old memory, dusty and forgotten. But nonetheless, it was still there. And she had to choose to listen to it, or it would go away again.

She had to listen to that tiny voice in the back of her head, that feeling buried in her gut, her banished intuition.

She *knew* who was calling her.

It was Vivian.

It was an enigmatic phenomenon. A strange and unsettling miracle that could not be proven, only believed. She could hear her missing aunt's voice but could not make herself believe it true.

"Jane," the voice repeated as she dragged her feet down the hallway.

She reached her hand for the doorknob, waiting for its brass embrace to meet her palm.

"Jane."

Just as she was about to turn it, a cold hand grabbed her shoulder, yanking her away from Vivian's door.

"Jane!" Margaret hissed in a low whisper that sliced through the eerie silence. She forced her around to look at her. "What on earth are you doing?!" Her hollow cheeks were flushed pink, even noticeable in the darkness.

"Are you even listening to me? Do you know what time it is?" She didn't give her a chance to answer. "It's *four-thirty* in the *morning*."

Jane hesitated, not knowing whether to play dumb or tell her the truth. "I—I don't know what happened. I think I was sleepwalking." She wished she were sleepwalking. If she were, it would be easier to believe that the voice that drew her to the end of the hall was merely a figment of her imagination. Not Vivian's voice, but a weird dream.

"Jesus," she grunted, dropping her gaze to the floor. First the fainting spell, and now this? She could feel her control over everything, even her own *sanity*, slipping through her fingers. "Come on, let's get you back to bed."

She didn't want to go back to bed—she wanted answers. She wanted to know if that was really Vivian she heard in the hall. She wanted to know where that key was.

But it was not the time for answers. They'd come soon enough.

When Jane returned to her bed, Margaret pulled the covers over her and tucked her in the way she used to when she was a little girl.

Margaret looked at her and realized that the little girl was gone, stolen by time. How did the years fly by so fast?

"Mom," Jane started, her voice quiet. "I don't think I was sleepwalking. I don't think I was dreaming at all." She let out a shaky breath, thinking about how to explain this. "I heard someone."

She leaned in slightly. "Who?"

"Vivian." She said her name as if it were a secret.

The blood in her veins ran cold, and her stomach flipped upon hearing her friend's name spoken into the silent air. "What?" she breathed. She blinked a few times, her mind loud with a thousand thoughts.

"I know how crazy it sounds," she uttered back. "But I swear I heard your friend."

Margaret mustered every ounce of her strength to stay calm. She shook her head once and gave her a cool, half-smile. "How do you know it was her—you've never even met her."

"I know, but—"

"Jane, you were dreaming. I was there with you. If someone was in the house, *I* would have heard them."

"But I felt someone else there."

"*Felt*? Sounds like dreaming to me," she mumbled with a forced laugh. "I mean, be honest, Jane. You don't *actually* believe this, do you?"

She frowned and repeated, "I know how crazy it sounds."

"I was there, Jane. There was no one in the hall except us. You were sleepwalking, that's all. Please," she sighed. "Don't freak yourself out. I used to sleepwalk every night when I was pregnant with you. Doctor told me it was from all the stress. He said I should take some time off from work and relax, and then, just like magic, I stopped sleepwalking."

Her daughter thought about it. Sleepwalking sounded like a reasonable explanation. If she was actually asleep, that is.

"Now, let's look at your case. You've left home and your father for the first time in your whole life, you're in an unfamiliar place, and let's be honest, Vivian's disappearance is making everyone under this roof quite stressed to say the least."

There was no use in trying to get her to understand. Margaret made up her mind, and there was no talking her out of it. "You're right."

Margaret stood, satisfied that she had won the argument. "I know. Goodnight, sweet Jane."

Jane rolled onto her side, pretending to be sleepy. "Goodnight."

When Margaret went back to sleep, she didn't have dreams but memories. Only memories. It was like they enjoyed tormenting her. Constantly reminding her of every little thing she can't escape from. Reminding her just how trapped she was in the walls of her life. How stuck she was because of the blood within her.

For some reason, maybe because of her conversation with Jane, her mind wandered back to the first day she ever noticed Jane's natural instinct.

It was springtime. Jane was four years old, and Margaret was watching her play on the playground with a few of her classmates from preschool. The other mothers were there too, talking and making Margaret feel like an outsider. But that was normal. Margaret was an outsider to them. None of them got pregnant at nineteen or ran away from home. They were all raised in a privileged comfort that was so foreign to her. She pretended to fit in, though. It was the only way Jane could have friends.

Jane ran up to her, her pigtails bouncing up and down with every skip and hop. "Mommy!" she called.

The other mothers stopped talking and turned to Jane.

"Yes?" Margaret smiled.

"George wants to go home now." She pointed at a boy on the swings.

The boy's mother leaned forward. "Did he tell you that, sweetie?"

"No," she said, shaking her head. "I heard what he was thinking. He wants to go back home. To Florida. Where his Daddy is. And his friend Nancy."

Margaret knew right away what was happening.

Jane was already developing that inner voice, that higher knowing, that thing some may call telepathy but was more than just reading minds. Deep inside, she felt like a proud parent. Already— at four years old. That's younger than she was. But she knew better than to show this pride or encourage it. The fear she felt for Jane's life was stronger than the pride.

If Jane ever used the powers she had, *they'd* find her. They promised Margaret they would.

And now it was her duty to raise her as a normal human. She would make her think there was no such thing as silly magic. She would raise her to believe that the voice she heard was nothing but her overactive brain.

It was the only way she could keep her safe.

"Jane, why don't you go play?" she smiled, nodding her head toward the playground.

"Okay, Mommy." Jane's small lips turned up into a big smile.

After she skipped away, the boy's mother turned to Margaret.

"Sorry about that," the woman said with an uncomfortable laugh. "I told him not to talk about it because it can be confusing to little ones, but you know how kids are." They both turned and watched their kids. "He's been having a hard time lately. I'm surprised he told her daughter. He won't talk to me anymore."

"Oh?"

"I just divorced my husband and moved here in March from Jacksonville. The change has been difficult."

"Jane, did you hear George's thoughts, or did he tell you about Florida?" Margaret asked her on the ride home.

The girl stared out of the window at the tall buildings of the city. "I listened to his head, Mommy."

"Do you hear other people's thoughts?"

"Sometimes. But sometimes I know what people are about to do— like if they're going to say something or walk away or—"

"How?"

"I dunno," she shrugged her shoulders. "Something just tells me."

"Jane," she took a deep breath, trying to find her stern-parent voice. "Don't do that again. Don't listen to that voice. It's not real. It's bad, Jane. It's not good to hear it, do you understand?" She gripped the steering wheel, her knuckles white.

"Why, Mommy?"

"Jane, listen to me. Don't you *ever* listen to that voice again. It's bad."

"Okay, Mommy."

CHAPTER SIXTEEN

A SHARP, DESPERATE SCREAM PULLED JANE OUT OF HER DREAM. Her own scream, she realized when she snapped awake. Her right hand was clawing at her throat as if she were trying to shut herself up. To stop the screaming.

The second she lifted her eyelids, her gaze found a shadowy figure standing in the corner of the room. Tall and slender. She couldn't catch a glimpse of a face because it was too dark in the corner, but there was just enough light to make out the shape of a woman.

She jolted herself forward, but as soon as she sat up, the figure turned to dust and moved like sand, collapsing into the floorboards.

She sat frozen for a few minutes, wondering if what she saw was real or if she had been dreaming.

It was the same shadow she had seen in the bathroom mirror, the same shadow that followed her throughout the house.

Was it a ghost? She had never experienced anything paranormal before, never even believed in those kinds of things—but she was eager to find *some* explanation, no matter how crazy that explanation may sound.

It was late in the morning. She knew this by the warm glow of golden sunlight beaming through the glass doors. She was surprised no one had woken her yet.

Perhaps after yesterday, they figured it was best if she got as much rest as possible.

She ripped the hot covers off her legs when she realized she was sweating. She eyed the French doors beside her and climbed out of the bed, yearning for fresh air.

A cool, though not cold, gust of wind blew through the room when she opened the doors. This slight relief made a smile tug at her lips.

The second she stepped foot through the doorway and onto the porch, her phone began to ring, drowning out the singing cicadas and chirping birds.

She turned around and went back inside, keeping the doors wide open to invite any cooler air to follow.

She took a quick glance around the room, eyeing the corner once more where she had witnessed the dark figure melt into the floor minutes ago, and then walked over to the nightstand.

Bobbie Jo was calling.

This was a relief. After the somewhat odd call she and her father had, she was hoping she wouldn't find his contact staring back at her.

She couldn't get past the fact that he was lying to her about something, and it bothered her that she couldn't figure out what it was. She trusted her father more than anyone. She had hoped he would be her anchor in this strange and unsettling experience down here—but not even he could offer her that comfort of normality. He was keeping something from her, just like her mother was. Just like Mary Grace and Lucille were.

Bobbie Jo was the only honest person in her life right now.

"What did you find in Vivi's room?" Bobbie Jo spoke fast, her drawl difficult to decipher at first.

Jane took a seat on the edge of the bed. "I couldn't go into her room."

"Why?"

She looked at the corner of the room. "It's complicated."

"What do you mean? Did somethin' happen?"

"Well," she let out a sigh. Where should she even start? How much of the truth should she tell her? "The room was locked. I still haven't found the key. And..." she paused, lowering her voice. "I think I heard someone in the hall with me. I could *feel* them watching me. It freaked me out, so I just went to bed." Not the entire truth, but enough for now. She didn't want to sound any crazier than she already did. And she most certainly did not want to talk about the mysterious shadow that's been stalking her.

Bobbie Jo let out a forceful laugh. "Ooooh, I'm real scared."

Jane shook her head. "I'm not kidding. Someone was watching me."

"Okay, so your mom."

"I don't think so."

"Your aunts?"

"No, I would've seen them."

She was quiet for a moment. "I don't understand what you're tryin' to tell me. Who do you think was out in the hall with you if it wasn't one of them?"

The call was silent for a moment as Jane tried to find the right words, the right amount of truth to tell.

Who did she think she heard last night? Did she really believe it was Vivian—or did she want to believe it was her?

She couldn't prove it was Vivian who she heard last night in the hallway, but she definitely could not deny the lurking shadows.

"Hello?"

She swiped her tongue over her bottom lip. "I don't know who was there last night—but I swear it *sounded* like Vivian."

Now it was Bobbie Jo's turn to become silent. "Did you tell your mother?"

"No. She wouldn't believe me."

"I can see why," Bobbie Jo mumbled under her breath. "Look, if you ask me, it sounds like you're a little paranoid. All that stuff I showed you yesterday must have messed with your head."

"I am not paranoid—" she froze when she heard the floorboards outside her door creak and moan under the pressure of footsteps.

"You still there?"

The creaking noise passed, fading, it seemed, toward the stairs. Jane stood from her bed and rushed out of the room to see who was there.

And there was no one.

"Jane?"

She had her phone pressed to her ear still. Bobbie Jo waited patiently on the other line for an answer, but her exhales became huffs as her irritation grew with the increasing silence.

"Sorry—what were you saying?" Jane pulled her concentration back to the phone call. There was no one in the hall. No reasoning behind the footsteps across her doorway.

Chills began to tickle the hairs on her arms, raising bumps on her skin.

She wasn't going crazy, and she would figure out a way to prove it.

"Hey, I gotta go. Sounds like my dad is havin' a panic attack downstairs. I'll talk to you later, okay?"

She probably felt bad for Jane. Guilty, even, that she tainted her mind and twisted her imagination with Vivian's case.

Jane didn't want her to feel that way. She was tired of everyone treating her like some fragile thing. Just as she was about to say something, to assure Bobbie Jo that she was not losing her mind, the call ended.

'Stop acting like a child and answer your damn phone.'

Margaret read the text message over and over again—as if deciphering what the words meant. As if there was a hidden message.

Though she knew there was no hidden message, and she was indeed acting like a child by not answering any of her soon-to-be-ex-husband's phone calls.

She set her phone down on the iron table and took a look around the courtyard.

There wasn't anything she could do to fix what had happened between her and David. And that was exactly her issue in the matter. She couldn't fix it. She couldn't find a way around it.

David and their broken marriage would still be there when she got home.

No good would come from worrying about it here. She had to find Vivian—that's what mattered. Not her pathetic marriage.

"You okay up there?"

Margaret looked over to her left and found Mary Grace staring back at her. The courtyard was so quiet that she almost forgot her two friends were there.

Mary Grace raised her hand and gestured to her head. "Up there? What are you thinkin'?"

It was a surprise Mary Grace had granted her privacy in the first place. Usually, she wouldn't blink twice before invading someone's headspace. Reading thoughts was her specialty, and because of this, boundaries naturally went out the window.

She squinted her gray eyes softly, searching Margaret's expression for a response.

"Just thinking about Jane," she said, averting her attention from Mary Grace's gaze to the roses around them. It wasn't a lie—she had been worrying about her daughter all morning. She didn't need to tell her about David—he was irrelevant right now.

"You seem upset," Mary Grace noted. She ran her fingers through her long strands of hair.

Margaret reinforced the wall around her heart and lifted her chin. "No shit I'm upset. My daughter's life is in danger."

Lucille frowned, grabbing Margaret's hand from across the table. "You need to tell Jane what she really is."

"She has the magic in her. And it's *strong*. We all felt it. It's stronger than mine, stronger than Lucille's, stronger than Vivian's," Mary Grace let out a sharp breath as she added, "Stronger than yours."

"I don't want to talk about this."

"Well ignorin' it ain't gonna make it disappear," Mary Grace snapped. "What if she ends up misusing it? She already zapped you. Like a bolt of *elec-tri-ci-ty!*"

"I gave up everything to keep her safe. To give her a *normal* and *safe* life that I never had. I gave up my powers, cut out *all* magic—"

Mary Grace shook her head. "And look what good that did you. If you don't face the truth, sooner or later that truth is gonna catch up to you and bite you in the ass."

"Mary Grace, be nice," Lucille whined.

"Stay out of this, Lucille—you ain't any better. For someone who hated their mother, you sure as hell love followin' her footsteps."

Lucille stood from the table, the iron chair grinding against the cobblestones. "You ain't got no rights *judgin'* me so you best shut your mouth now. You are—"

"Sit down," Mary Grace laughed, dismissing her with a wave of her hand. "This is all beside the point."

"And what is the point?" Margaret asked through her teeth.

Mary Grace leaned back in her chair. "The point is… we all need to face reality. These are the cards we have been dealt with. We come from a lineage of powerful women. *We* are powerful women. And we're even more powerful when we're together."

"We need to find Vivian," whispered Lucille as she sat back in her seat, seemingly calmer now. She pulled out a cigarette and a lighter from her bra, casually lighting it. "And I have a feelin' that Jane is gonna be able to help us."

"She told me she heard Vivian last night," Margaret admitted, knowing she would regret telling them this.

Mary Grace gasped. "And you're just now telling us this?"

Margaret sighed. "I just want to keep her safe—"

"Keeping her in the dark is not keeping her safe!"

"I just want to keep her safe from those... those *bastards*. They said they'd find us. They—"

"They're not here anymore, Margaret," Mary Grace said. "No one has seen them since you left. And plus, I put a protection spell on the entire property and on each of us—including Jane. No one who is aimin' to harm her will get anywhere near her. You don't need to worry about her safety anymore. As long as she's with us, she'll be safe. It's Vivian that we need to worry about."

"What if they were the ones who took Vivian? What if it's a trap?"

Mary Grace opened her mouth to reply, but stopped, hearing a distant ringing from inside. The housephone was ringing, bringing with it an urgency that filled her with utter dread.

She jolted up from her chair. Randy was calling. She could feel it in her stomach. She could already hear the panic in his tone.

The backdoors of the white house swung open, and Jane walked out, locking her gaze with Mary Grace, and without hesitation, she said,

"The Sheriff is calling."

CHAPTER SEVENTEEN

152

THEY ALL THOUGHT THE SAME QUESTION.

How did she know? Jane told them Randy was calling with a confidence that was undeniable, proving it was not a lucky guess, it was a statement.

"How does your head feel?" Margaret asked her as Mary Grace picked up the phone. She and Lucille rushed inside when Mary Grace did, and they both stood around Jane, examining her for any signs of anything amiss.

Her face was a little paler than normal, and her pupils weren't fully dilated. She looked like she was about to faint again.

Before she could answer, Mary Grace turned to them. "We need to go. *Now.*" She started running around the house, gathering her keys and a wide-brimmed hat from the coat rack.

"What happened?" Lucille asked, her voice rising. "Mary Grace, what happened?"

But Mary Grace was already out the front door, racing to her car like her life depended on it.

They ran after her.

She unlocked the car and hopped in.

Margaret opened the passenger door. "What the hell happened?"

Her nerves were bouncing all over the place. Like popping kernels. "Randy said her necklace was found in an alligator." She trembled a little as she said this.

Margaret backed away from the car, stunned.

Lucille shrieked, covering her mouth with both hands. "In an *alligator*?!"

"Yes—now let's go! If we leave now, we can see the reptile for ourselves."

It seemed like time was moving fast now, and the world began to spin as Margaret processed everything her friend had said. She looked back at Jane, who was still in her pajamas, standing on the front steps with a look of pure worry painting her face. "Stay here. Grab some water, lie down—just relax. If your head starts to hurt again, *call me*, do you understand?"

"Why can't I go?" she asked, looking back at the house. She didn't want to be left alone after seeing the creeping shadows and hearing the footsteps.

"Because you don't need to go." She and Lucille got into the car, and she rolled down the passenger window, adding, "Call me if your head starts to hurt."

She knew she wouldn't be able to change her mother's mind, so there was no use trying. "Okay," she answered, nodding.

Margaret didn't want to leave her, but she knew it was safer to leave her at the plantation where she was protected under Mary Grace's spell.

Jane watched the car peel down the driveway, leaving a cloud of dust in its wake and leaving her alone at the Abel Plantation for the first time.

She stood in front of the house for a few moments longer, waiting until Mary Grace's green car was completely out of sight.

But the feeling of being alone never came, and she wasn't sure if this was a good thing or not. She was alone now—no one was at the plantation except her, and yet, she felt like eyes were on her. Like the windows were watching her.

She looked over her shoulder, scanning the big house. But as usual, no one was there. The feeling of being watched only grew after two more minutes, and she decided to go inside. Standing in front of the steps made her feel like a sitting duck for some reason.

The floorboards throughout the first floor of the house groaned as she opened the front door, as if the walls were inhaling.

And then the house was quiet, holding its breath as she shut the door behind herself.

The silence finally gave her a moment to reflect on what had happened when the phone rang. Some odd feeling had cast a shadow over her when she heard the phone ringing. And she couldn't explain it or put it into logical words, but she just *knew* who was calling. It was a similar feeling to the odd intuition she had felt in the hallway the night before.

The key. This unexpected time alone would give her a chance to search for the key to Vivian's bedroom, to search for answers and any proof that she wasn't going crazy.

She shook off all thoughts about intuition and started her search in the grand living room, taking in the entire scene from the doorway. There were no shadows, she noted, but that feeling of being watched was still present.

She hesitated only for a mere second with the contemplation of whether or not it was right for her to dig around in Mary Grace's house. But if no one was going to answer her questions, she would have to find them by herself.

She walked over to the bookshelf, tracing her fingertips over the many spines and trying to find a gap in one of the books big enough to hide a key. After no luck there, she turned around to the end table beside the couch.

It was filled with random items: pens, paperclips, bookmarks, a metal lighter, and a photograph of what looked to be her home city.

She moved around the knick-knacks and pulled out the photograph, her curiosity getting the best of her again. It wasn't a photograph—but a postcard.

She flipped it over to read the back.

It was a postcard from New York City, written by her mother.

The date read, *10-21-06*— a day before Jane's first birthday.

The message was hard to understand. She slowly sank onto the couch, reading it again. And again.

And again.

But the words still made her head spin. What did her mother mean by *them*? Who was after her?

She always knew her mother was keeping something from her, but this was different. This was a bigger secret than she wanted to believe.

Did Margaret leave Belles Parish because someone was after her?

What if whoever her mother was talking about was still out there? What if they were still trying to find them?

The phone in the hall started to ring, scaring her so much that she dropped the postcard.

She had to answer it, right? Even though it wasn't her house, it was the right thing to do, wasn't it?

She picked up the postcard and returned it to the drawer.

Maybe she shouldn't pick up the phone. It wasn't her house. Whoever was calling wants to speak with Mary Grace—not her nonbiological niece from up north.

But the ringing didn't stop.

She thought that if she waited a little, the ringing would end, and she could go about her search for the key. But the phone just kept *ringing*.

'*What if it was the Sheriff?*'

The phone screamed, begging her to pick it up.

Whoever was calling *wanted* her to answer. Needed her to answer.

Her forehead prickled with sweat as she sat there and weighed her decisions.

With one swift move, she pushed herself up from the couch. She rushed into the hallway, wrapping her hand around the old telephone.

RINGGG—

"Hello?" she shouted into the phone.

Her chest tightened when there was no answer. It seemed like the heat from outside had found her once again. Sweat rolled down her temples.

She tried again, softening her tone slightly. "Hello?" She pushed the phone closer to her ear, her breathing ragged and forceful.

And just when she thought the call was nothing but a misdial, a woman's voice whispered in her ear.

"*Jane.*"

She held her breath, gripping the phone in her fist. "Who is this?"

She couldn't help but feel frightened by the fact that the caller could recognize her just by the sound of her own voice, and yet, she had no clue who the caller was.

"Who is this?" she asked again after there was no response.

"Jane, you must remember."

Her knees felt weak, her vision beginning to tunnel in front of her. The wallpaper changed, the blue roses turning into a deep sapphire, so dark they looked almost like black spots on the walls.

She shut her eyes, ignoring the hallucinations the best she could. "Vivian?" she said with a gasp.

"You're the only one who can save me, Jane. You must remember," she said, her voice dry and shaky. *"You must* find *me."*

She opened her eyes again, and the hallucinations were more surreal. The now black roses on the walls began to ooze, bleeding streams of ink on the floorboards.

She reached out, though she knew she shouldn't, and touched the black liquid. It was hot and sticky between her fingertips, and when she looked down, she noticed the strange substance was all over the floor.

Muddy water.

It looked like muddy water at her feet, so dark it appeared like ink.

She dropped the phone. It swung back and forth by its curly wire, Vivian's voice still echoing from the speaker.

The water rose, bubbling around her legs.

The last thing she saw before she fainted was her own reflection staring up at her in the murky water—and Vivian was standing right behind her in this reflection, crying.

CHAPTER EIGHTEEN

"Slow down," Margaret hissed as she leaned back in her seat, squeezing the seatbelt strapped across her chest. "I would like to be alive when we look at the alligator."

It was like Mary Grace couldn't hear her. Her eyes were glued to the road ahead, her white knuckles curling around the steering wheel as she hightailed it through town. She ran every yellow light and yielded at every stop sign, racing like her life depended on it. Or, perhaps, Vivian's life.

'Her necklace was in an alligator,' Mary Grace thought to herself, her heart pounding in her ears. If it was really her necklace, it would mean something terrible. It would mean their beloved lost friend could be dead.

They passed the white church on the right, officially leaving downtown Belles Parish and heading into West Belles Parish. Marsh, a couple of abandoned churches, and a few trailer parks were the only things left until you crossed the Mississippi River into the next town.

No one admitted they lived in West Belles Parish, or they'd be painted as poor and trashy.

Margaret grew up on the West side, but since she was always on the plantation, people had forgotten where she really lived. But everyone back then knew where Randy was from, and this made it hard for him growing up. He practically wore his environment, advertising it with a naïve pride. With his mullet and ripped tank-tops and stupid confidence, he could not deny where he came from. True, he might have been a redneck, but he was far from white trash, and that's the misjudgment that was made of him more often than not.

The trailer park had changed over the years, not exactly how the women had remembered it. Most of the trailer homes were destroyed by the hurricane back in '05, and the dirt road was worn with potholes.

"There's Randy's old home," Lucille said, looking to the right at the abandoned trailer covered in mold and moss, the lawn completely taken over by weeds.

Margaret looked to the left of Randy's trailer, her eyes landing on the old double-wide trailer she grew up in. The trailer was untouched by Hurricane Katrina. Empty and cold but still standing the way it had the day she ran away. Seeing it brought tears to Margaret's eyes. She didn't spend much of her childhood there, even though it was her home. She hung around the plantation more because her father was almost always working.

The thought of him made a tender spot in her chest ache.

He was a good man. A hard worker. Everything he did, he did for her. And it pained her to remember that when she left, she left him. As if none of his sacrifices meant anything. All those long days and longer nights at the shipyard in New Orleans, for what? For her to up and leave without a single explanation. She wouldn't ever forgive herself for leaving him that way.

Though his death was labeled a severe heart attack, Mary Grace had told her it was the sadness that truly made his heart stop. She told her this over a phone call fourteen years ago.

Margaret was in the middle of a business meeting when her phone went off. She wouldn't have answered it if she didn't recognize the area code.

She excused herself from the room as she answered the call. "How did you get this number?" she had hissed into her flip-phone, holding it close to her ear.

"I'm sorry—I know I promised I wouldn't ever call you. But I had to tell you."

She ran her hand down her suit, trying to steady her nerves. The office's walls were made of glass, and she could feel everyone's eyes on her. "Tell me what?" She turned around and faced the window wall overlooking the city.

"Your dad is dead."

Her stomach dropped. "No," she pleaded under her breath.

"He died of a heart attack. Last night. I think it was the sadness that made his heart stop. I just wanted you to know. He loved you so much. I'm sorry. Goodbye."

The call ended just like that. Margaret had stared out at the busy city with a blank face, not sure how to feel. She didn't cry. She held in whatever she was feeling and went back to her office and finished the meeting as if Mary Grace had never called.

The tears she held back turned into bitter anger as time went by, adding height to the wall she had built around herself. The wall became a cage over the years, keeping the secrets she held within safe from intruders.

"There it is," Lucille's voice snapped Margaret's attention back to the car.

Margaret ripped her eyes from her old trailer and looked to the right of Randy's deserted home to a nicer trailer.

The Hendersons. They were an older couple in their sixties or seventies. They'd lived there for Randy's entire lives and probably since the trailer park was first built.

Randy's Blazer and a police car were parked in the driveway next to Mr. Henderson's longstanding black F-150.

Mary Grace parked parallel on the street.

They could see Randy and two other men standing around the big oak tree in front of the trailer.

Mary Grace felt like she should say something to her friends in the car— but what was there to say? *Let's cross our fingers it's not Vivi's necklace?*

When they got out of the car, a strange, sticky breeze blew by them. Like the wind was warning them of something.

Mary Grace glanced at the gray, cloudy sky and watched a group of crows fly above them.

"A murder," she said.

Margaret turned to her. "What did you say?"

She pointed up. "A group of crows. A murder. That's what they're called."

"You know what it means when you see crows," Lucille nodded. "Prepare for somethin' unexpected in the near future."

"Can you guys keep your weird bird facts to yourselves?" Margaret sighed as they walked over to the men.

Hanging from the giant oak tree was an eight-foot alligator. The fat reptile was bloody, sliced open from its neck to its bottom.

Next to the creature was a collapsable table covered with guts and other foul things that made the women nauseous.

"Girls!" Mr. Henderson called out, tearing their gazes from the awful scene. He walked out of his trailer and rushed to them, limping side to side with every step.

He hadn't changed one bit.

Mr. Henderson was as tall and thin as a pole, with dark skin, two big ears that stuck out of his trucker cap, and a glass eye that twinkled when he smiled, revealing a mouth full of missing teeth.

"My girls!" he cried, giving each of them a sweaty hug. "You all grown up!" He clapped his long hands together.

"Mary Grace," Randy called from the hanging gator. "Can you come over for a second?"

Mr. Henderson's smile softened and he took a step back. "I'm so sorry 'bout Vivi," he said it like she was already dead, and Mary Grace hated it. It wasn't his fault—but it still made her cheeks turn red.

They walked with Mr. Henderson over to Randy. Two men stood him, a police officer and the detective.

"What are they doing here?" the detective asked Randy. He stood with his arms crossed over his chest with an air of stern professionalism. His hair was black and neatly combed to the side, and his hollow eyes were an icy blue, heavy from either stress or a lack of sleep.

Randy nodded, and when the women had made their way to him, he introduced them to the men. "This is Mary Grace, Lucille, and Margaret. They're friends of Vivian's."

The detective didn't even waste his energy on manners. "And why are they here? This is a crime scene, not a reunion."

Randy flared his nostrils. "Because I called them over." He looked at the women. "This is Detective Dubois. He doesn't always act like an asshole, just to let y'all know."

"Pleasure to meet you, sugar," Lucille said with a playful smirk. "Has anyone ever told you you've got *gorgeous* eyes?"

The detective looked at her, hesitating for a mere second before shaking his head. He walked over to Mr. Henderson, ignoring Lucille's comment completely. "Now, what time did you say you killed the alligator?"

Mr. Henderson thought about it. "Um— it was six-thirty in the mornin', I believe. My grandsons helped me load it on the boat and tie it to the tree. They left about seven-somethin', and I started cleanin' the gator at eight o'clock."

Randy walked over to the table, picking up a plastic zip-lock bag from beside the alligator's insides. The bag contained a delicate silver chain with a heart-shaped locket covered in blood.

"Open it, I want to see it up close," Mary Grace commanded, reaching for the bag.

He pulled back his hand. "Are you insane? I can't touch any evidence without the proper—"

Mary Grace snatched it out of his hand, ripping it open without hesitation. She pulled out the necklace, tossing the bag on the table.

Randy huffed in irritation, shaking his head.

"It's Vivian's, alright," Mary Grace noted, wrapping the blood-stained chain around her fingers. She held up the back side of the locket to Margaret and Lucille, showing them Vivian's initials inscribed in elegant cursive. "This is the necklace her parents got her before they died."

Lucille cussed under her breath.

Margaret felt like she was going to have a panic attack. She remembered seeing the necklace before, multiple times. It was Vivian's only piece of jewelry, and she never took it off. Seeing it now, covered in dark red blood, sent chills up and down Margaret's back.

Lucille slid her finger across the locket, lifting her finger to her mouth.

"No, no, no—!" Randy shouted, sucking in a sharp breath as he watched Lucille lick the blood from her fingertip.

She tasted it, and for a moment, all of them, except for Mary Grace, stared at her in disbelief and disgust.

A *V* formed between Margaret's eyebrows. "What the hell—"

"It's not her blood," Lucille said, a little of the blood visible on the corner of her mouth. "Hey, Randy, got a cigarette?" she asked causally.

Randy automatically pulled one out and handed her a lighter. "Why did you do that?" he asked, concerned but disgusted. "You've got some serious problems."

She took a drag, fanning the smoke away from them as she exhaled. "Well, someone had to make sure it wasn't her blood! Y'all should thank me."

"But— how in the *world* would you know if it was hers or not?"

"I think I'd know if it was human or alligator blood, Randy."

This answer didn't satisfy him, "What? You can't just go around lickin' random blood, Lucille. We got DNA tests for that."

"What—" a voice snapped from behind them. "—are you *doing*?" It was Detective Dubois. He pulled out black latex gloves from his front pocket, quickly putting them on as he walked over.

"Just lookin'," Lucille answered, batting her eyelashes.

"I don't care that you guys are here right now— but you *cannot* touch any evidence," he growled, taking the necklace from Mary Grace.

Lucille looked him up and down and giggled. "Yes, sir," she said sarcastically, giving him a hand salute.

"Now, if you don't mind," he turned to Randy. "I am going back to the office to turn this into the lab so we can find a DNA match."

Randy nodded and gave him a look like he was going to apologize for their actions. "See you there."

He looked back at the women and nodded. "Have a nice day, ladies," he mumbled, glancing over at Lucille one last time, and something about the way she smiled at him made his cheeks blush just a little. He broke their eye contact and walked away.

"Is he single?" Lucille half-jokingly asked them with an exaggerated gasp.

Her friends just rolled their eyes, and they turned their attention to the big alligator in front of them.

Each of them came to the same conclusion. It was obvious yet no one dared to say it.

Vivian was in the swamp.

CHAPTER NINETEEN

"WHERE DID YOU KILL THIS ALLIGATOR?" Mary Grace asked Mr. Henderson after the cop and the detective left with the necklace.

Mr. Henderson scratched the tip of his right ear. "Like I told Randy, I was in the swamp with my grandsons, about a mile away from Lake Maurepas. We was drivin' my old Jon boat—"

"You said a mile from Lake Maurepas?" Lucille put her hands on her hips.

"Yes, 'bout a mile, I think."

Mary Grace thought about it, "Were you headin' towards the lake or into the swamp?"

"I was headin' in the swamp."

The swamp wasn't very far from there, but the swamp itself was a tangled, muddy, wet mess of a forest, so it could've taken hours to drive a boat through. She had no clue why Vivian would have gone into the swamp, but if she did, and something happened to her, her body could be anywhere out there. Swollen with lake water, drifting with the current.

The very thought of such a thing made Mary Grace squirm. She turned to Randy, who was still examining the giant reptile.

"You're sending out a search team, right? Now that we know she was in the swamp?"

He looked over his shoulder, "Already did." Sometimes, he felt like his friend forgot he was the one in charge of this case.

"Good." She nodded curtly.

Lucille pursed her red lips and said, "Vivi never liked the swamp. Why would she go in there?"

"It's obvious someone dragged her in there," Mary Grace sighed, looking at the alligator hanging from the tree and then at Sheriff Jones.

"Unfortunately, it's not obvious until we get more proof," Randy responded. "We shouldn't make any assumptions this early."

Mr. Henderson frowned, "I sure hope she's okay. I've been prayin' for her every night since I got word she disappeared."

Mary Grace put her hand on his shoulder. "Thank you, Mr. Henderson."

His eyes teared up, and he wiped them before any tear could shed.

Randy finally turned away from the alligator, his hands resting on the front of his belt. "Well," he started. "I gotta get back to the office. Thank you, sir, for your time. You were a big help." When he headed for his Blazer, Margaret followed him.

"Randy, wait up," Margaret called after him.

He opened the driver's door, looking at his friend. "Yeah?"

"There were no bones, right?" she asked as he climbed into the truck.

He rolled down the window, closing the door. "No, no bones." His right hand was on the top of the steering wheel, and his left scratched at his walrus mustache.

Margaret was filled with relief. "Good," she muttered, putting her hands in her back pockets. "Thank you for everything, Randy. I'm so thankful that we have you as the Sheriff." The truck came to life, its engine purring loudly over the crickets and cicadas.

"We'll find her, Mar. Don't you worry." He put the truck in reverse, backing out of the driveway.

She watched him drive off and then returned to her friends and Mr. Henderson.

Cicadas screamed under the scorching summer sun. Margaret wiped a line of sweat from her forehead, looking at her two friends, Mr. Henderson, and the dead alligator.

"Would you ladies like to come in for a glass of *ice* tea? My wife should be home in just an hour, and I'm sure she'd love to see you all."

"We would love to, but I'm afraid we can't today. Margaret's daughter is at home by herself, and we'd hate to leave her too long," Mary Grace sighed with a genuine frown. "Please, stop by some time. Don't be a stranger. You still make your ketchup, right? I'd love to buy some."

Mr. Henderson looked sad to hear they had to leave but seemed to understand. "I'll give you a jar when I make some more. Good seein' you girls again."

On the ride home, Margaret stared out of the window at Belles Parish, so many memories flooding her thoughts. She could see herself and her friends as little girls, skipping down the sidewalks, Mrs. Abel walking behind them with a tender smile on her face. She could see them as pre-teens heading to the diner while Mrs. Abel was at church, Randy trailing along. She could see them as teenagers, too, laughing and enjoying their fleeting days of youth.

'God, I hope Vivi's not dead,' she suddenly thought to herself, looking away from the window.

"We need to look in the swamp," Mary Grace told the two of them, disrupting the painful silence in the car.

"I agree," Lucille whispered with a shaky breath. "Can you hear anythin'? I mean, have you heard her thoughts or—?"

"No," Mary Grace shook her head, her fingers closing tight around the steering wheel. "I can't sense a thing. All I know is that she isn't dead. I can still feel her... her *breathin'.*"

Lucille swallowed. "You mean you can't *hear* anymore?"

"I can still hear, just not if it involves Vivi."

"Which means," Margaret spoke for the first time since they got in the car. "Someone is guarding her, right? That or she's found a spell to block you out."

"Vivi wouldn't put a spell on me."

"Who do you think *kidnapped* her?" Lucille said it as if the words tasted bad in her mouth.

Mary Grace raised her eyebrows, "I'm not sure. An evil witch. A dark entity. A—" she lowered her voice. "—*demon*."

This was too much for Margaret to hear right now. She didn't want to hear any more of this. She needed to get out of the car.

An *evil witch*? A *demon*? It was fairytale stuff, or at least, it should have been. She couldn't bear to hear this conversation come from a bunch of grown women in their mid-thirties. It sounded delusional. Fictional. And yet, with everything she had been through, she knew that they were real. All of it was. The witches, dark entities, demons.

She inhaled a sharp breath when her next thought crossed her mind. "What if it was *them*?"

They knew very well who she meant.

"What would *they* want from Vivi?" Mary Grace scrunched up her face. "It just doesn't make sense—"

"What would *anyone* want from Vivi? She's the sweetest person in the world. She wouldn't hurt a bug if her life depended on it," Margaret shook her head. "Don't you get it? *None* of this makes sense."

"But I haven't seen any of them since the year you left town."

Margaret shut her eyes, blocking out that year from reentering her mind. The twisted recollections it carried burned in her memory, trying so hard to be seen. "That doesn't mean they ever left."

Jane's eyes opened to an angel made of concrete standing above her, its face staring at her with a desperate expression.

She inhaled a sharp breath, bringing her knees to her chest. She swallowed as she looked around, her thoughts jumbled.

She had fainted *again*— this time waking up in the courtyard. She closed her eyes, trying her best to remember what she was doing before she woke up— but all she could remember was finding that postcard in the living room.

She glanced up, eyes narrowing on the angel above her. Something looked wrong with it today. She didn't know how that was possible, but it seemed as though something had changed. The angel's left arm was extended out to the side, its index finger pointing towards the backdoors of the big house. She could have sworn both of its arms were down the last time she saw it.

She stared at the eerie statue, following its extended arm in the direction it was pointed.

The moment her eyes landed at the backdoors of the white house, the doors opened wide, and Mary Grace rushed outside. The woman put her hand to her chest and sighed in relief when she saw Jane.

"Jane," she gasped, fanning her face with her other hand. "What—what are you doin' out here, darlin'?"

She quickly stood up, brushing grass and dirt off of herself. *'I was just asking myself the same question,'* she wanted to say but instead replied, "I was just looking around."

Mary Grace raised an eyebrow.

Margaret stepped out of the house behind Mary Grace, the same panicked expression on her face. "Jane? Are you okay?"

Jane bit her lip, "Yes? Should I not be?"

"Why aren't you wearing shoes?" her mother asked, her eyes widening at Jane's bare feet.

She looked at her feet, trying not to seem surprised at the mud caked all over. Where did she go when she blacked out? She bent forward and traced her fingers on her ankle. The mud was still wet.

"I don't know, I just didn't want to wear shoes." She stood back up and shrugged her shoulders, rubbing the mud between her fingers.

The mud on her feet stopped a little above her ankles. She had walked *through* mud. But where? What made her even more confused was that she couldn't recall seeing any puddles nearby.

Mary Grace hesitated. "Come on inside, dear. I need to show you something." She rushed back into the house, Margaret nodding once before following.

Jane glanced back at the angel one last time before going in behind them. She stopped before entering the house, looking down at her dirty feet.

"Don't mind the mud, darlin'. I gotta clean the floors anyway," Mary Grace said from down the hall as if she had read Jane's mind.

Mary Grace and Margaret were standing at the end of the hallway in front of the house phone. Margaret's face was scrunched up, looking back and forth between the phone and Jane.

"What's wrong—" Jane had begun to ask, but her question was soon answered when she made it to them.

The phone was hanging by its curly wire, hovering an inch above the floor. The base mounted on the wall looked as if it had caught on fire. The plastic was black and burnt, and a smokey gray ring circled the base on the wallpaper. It *had* caught on fire.

"What the hell?" the words slipped out of Jane's mouth, shaky and almost inaudible. Just then, a memory flashed in her mind. The memory itched, scratching behind her eyes as a foggy cloud evaporated, letting her finally see the truth.

She was on the phone before she blacked out. She remembered being scared but couldn't remember why exactly. Who was on the other line? Why would she have picked up the phone? She couldn't remember the phone catching on fire. All she could remember was the *feeling* she had when she was talking on the phone.

Chills ran up her spine, raising goosebumps on her arms. She took a small step backward, hearing a faint voice in her memory. Who was on the phone?

Mary Grace looked over. "Do you know how this happened?"

"How would she know what happened?" Margaret snapped back.

Jane didn't hesitate, "I don't know what happened."

Margaret gave her friend a look that read, *'See?'*

But Mary Grace didn't give up that easily. "Anyone call while we were out?" She picked up the dangling handset, turned it over, and examined the black speaker.

"No," she answered a little too quickly. "Not that I know of."

After an awkward pause, the woman dropped the phone and clasped her hands together. "Well," she said with a smile. "You go upstairs and clean up. I am fixin' a late lunch. Have you ever had *étouffée*?"

"No, I haven't." She didn't know why, but it bothered her how suddenly Mary Grace dropped the conversation about the burnt phone.

"You're gonna love it."

As Jane washed the mud from her feet in the shower, she watched the brown water swirl down the drain and disappear into the veins of the house.

'Where did I go?' she thought, shaking her head. She couldn't get Mary Grace's judging eyes out of her head. It was like the woman knew something had happened and wanted Jane to confess it. But she wouldn't. She *couldn't*. Not when she wasn't a hundred-percent sure what had happened herself.

She shut her eyes, reaching back into her memory. But all she could remember was finding the postcard in the living room, answering the phone, and waking up in the courtyard.

The postcard. She had almost forgotten the message her mother wrote. *'I can't let them find us.'*

So many questions tugged on Jane's conscience.

A ring sounded from her back pocket. The noise made her jump, almost falling into the tub. She pulled out her phone, staring at the caller's name.

'Dad,' it read with a picture of them making a silly face at the camera. She didn't want to answer his call. Not now. But after five seconds of staring at their picture, guilt bloomed in the pit of her stomach, giving her no choice.

"Hey, Dad," she said, turning the water off.

"Hey, how are you?" He sounded just as tired as he did during their last phone call, maybe even more so.

She bit her lip, "Fine."

"Is everything all right? Your mom hasn't called me back yet."

"Yeah, everything is all right. Mom's just really busy, you know, looking for Vivian and everything."

"Right," he let out a deep breath. "I'm sorry you're stuck there. I know it's really stressful with your mom's friends. I've been told they can be a little *intense*. If you want me to come get you, I can see if there are any plane tickets available—"

She dried her feet with a towel. "No, no—it's okay, really. I like it here."

He paused, "Huh."

"Is everything all right with you?"

"It will be—once you guys come back. I just need to talk to your mom."

Downstairs in the kitchen, Mary Grace and Lucille worked as a team as they made étouffée. Margaret watched them, leaning back against the fridge.

"What was Jane thinking when you showed her the phone?" Margaret asked, crossing her arms over her chest.

Mary Grace sighed, stirring the gravy in the saucepan. "She was on the phone with someone."

Lucille saw the phone when she first entered the house, but she just figured it was something Mary Grace had done. She looked over her shoulder at Margaret, her eyes wide. "Say what?"

Margaret sucked her teeth, frowning slightly. "Who was she on the phone with?"

Mary Grace shrugged. "I can't tell."

"What else happened when we were gone?" she questioned. "I feel like I can't leave her alone anymore without something happening."

"At least she didn't get hurt," she said, lifting her eyes from the saucepan to Margaret's worried face. "She noticed the angels out back have changed. She asked me about them yesterday—she's curious."

Margaret started to chew a hangnail on her finger, a habit she hadn't done since she left Belles Parish seventeen years ago. "Why are they changing *now*?"

Lucille stopped mincing the vegetables.

Mary Grace locked eyes with Margaret, and, lowering her voice, said, "Trouble is on its way, Margaret."

Jane walked in a second too early. "Trouble? What trouble?"

They all looked at the girl, frozen in their places. It appears Mary Grace's senses were weakening.

"Nothing, Jane," Margaret said, trying her best to hide her panic with a tight smile.

Jane looked into her mother's eyes, picking up on the lie instantly.

So many secrets.

Sitting down at the table, Jane tapped her fingernails against the surface as she thought. She decided to tell Margaret about her phone call with her dad later. "So, was it really Vivian's necklace?"

Margaret sat down in the chair across from her. "Well," she swallowed. She hated having to tell Jane about the case, but because Vivi herself might be contacting her, Margaret thought it was only right to tell her the truth now. Not the entire truth, though—not yet. "Yes."

Jane's eyes widened. The natural blush in her cheeks faded, leaving her ghostly white. "Does that mean—" she bit her lip. "Is she dead?" She couldn't help but think about the voice she heard last night, the voice she believed belonged to Vivian Banks. Was that who she was on the phone with?

Lucille sucked in a breath as she said, "Heavens, no! It just means she was probably in the swamp." She said it with so much hope that it made Jane think Lucille was trying to convince herself of this.

"And that's all Randy found," Margaret said simply, as if finding Vivi's necklace in an alligator wasn't that big of a deal. "They're running a DNA test on it now, just to make sure the blood on it isn't hers."

"There was blood?" Jane gasped.

"Lots, dear," Mary Grace commented with a sigh. "The necklace was in an alligator's stomach."

She stopped tapping her fingernails and froze. "Oh." And then, she looked up at her mother again. "If she was in the swamp, we should check there, right? Maybe she's stuck somewhere?"

"Randy has a search team for that," Margaret told her.

"But shouldn't we help?" Jane was shocked. Were they supposed to just sit back and watch?

"We don't really need to," she said, shaking her head slightly. "He's got enough help right now."

Jane wanted to call Bobbie Jo and tell her about the news that minute, even though she was sure she already knew, her father being the sheriff and all.

She felt like they were getting close to finding Vivian. She wanted to search the swamp, but from the sound of Margaret's tone, she made the assumption that they weren't going to.

Thinking of the swamp made her think back to the mud that was on her feet when she woke up by the fountain, and this made her wonder how far the swamp was from the plantation.

CHAPTER TWENTY

A LIGHT PITTER-PATTER OF RAIN FELL on the roof while they ate étouffée and drank iced tea. When Mary Grace heard the rain, she nodded her head and said to herself, "It's going to be a long rain."

And it was.

The nighttime sky clouded over while a hard rain greeted Belles Parish with gusts of aggressive winds that howled and screamed around the town and throughout the Abel Plantation.

"Do you think this is a hurricane?" Margaret had asked in a shout as she and Mary Grace stood on the front porch later that night, sharp wind and rain blowing on them without mercy.

Mary Grace shook her head. "No. This rain is just a warning." Her hair thrashed behind her with the wind, going one way then the other.

"What?" It was hard to hear Mary Grace's gentle voice over the loud storm. "A warning?"

"Yes," she sighed, looking out at the gray metallic rain that fell in a crash on the plantation's ground. Puddles of water formed along the driveway and in the green grass, drowning the earth.

Margaret thought about it. She crossed her arms over her chest, trying to bear the hard rain. "What is it warning us about? To buy some umbrellas next time?"

She gazed out in deep thought, her face detached as if the truth hurt to hold in. "It's warning us that there will be troubles in the near future. Troubles like we have never had," she looked at her friend and frowned. "And no one will see 'em coming."

Margaret's face softened as she saw the seriousness in the woman's expression. "Not even you?" Her eyebrows furrowed, her green eyes dense with concern.

"Not even me."

What could possibly be coming that her wise friend would not know?

Thunder *boomed* in the distance. Margaret flinched. She sucked in a sharp breath, her heart pounding against her chest.

"Whatever it is," started Margaret. "Whatever is... *in the near future*—we'll be okay. I know we will."

Mary Grace inhaled a deep breath, then exhaled it out slowly. "I don't know. I can't see it. I can't hear it. It's just... quiet. I really don't know."

Margaret put her hand on her friend's back. "Maybe your sight will clear up soon?"

"It's a shame you've disconnected *your* sight."

Margaret shook her head, "C'mon, let's get back inside. I'm soaking wet."

When they stepped inside the house, Mary Grace sighed and shook her head slightly. "I cannot see what's coming, but I have a *strong* feelin' it involves your daughter."

Margaret clenched her jaw. "I hope not."

But as much as she didn't want to, part of her believed Mary Grace. It was hard *not* to believe her friend. Mary Grace had the strongest intuition out of all of them, and most of her assumptions were always proven correct. But she had to doubt Mary Grace's hunch— for her daughter. If anything were to happen to Jane, Margaret wouldn't be able to live with herself. She had to keep Jane safe.

Safe and hidden.

It was still storming when night fell. Jane sat on the floor of the living room and read one of the books Mary Grace left her. Lucille sat on the couch in front of her, going through an old magazine she found tucked in the bookcase across the room. She had put another Ella Fitzgerald record on, and the old jazz music sounded almost eerie with the loud storm outside.

They jumped as a round of thunder clapped. Rain fell louder against the roof of the old house, almost as if it were knocking eagerly to come in.

After the wave of thunder seized, the gray sky snapped white as a bolt of lightning cut across the plantation.

The lights in the house turned off, and the jazz music stopped.

"Jesus," gasped Lucille, trying to adjust to the darkness in the room. "Guess we lost power."

Mary Grace walked into the room, a candle in each hand. "Power went out," she said, as if they hadn't already noticed. She set the candles on the coffee table between them. "I figured you might need some light in here."

Jane closed her book and placed it on the table, staring down at the two flames in front of her. It made her feel uneasy, the way Mary Grace brought in the lit candles not even ten seconds after the power went out.

"How does she always know?" she questioned when Mary Grace left. Lucille looked puzzled, so she went on. "I mean, how does she know when things are about to happen?"

Lucille scrunched up her face. "I guess I've never really noticed."

"What? No way. You've never noticed the way Mary Grace just *knows things*?" She pushed a strand of her bob behind her ears.

She tried to look clueless. "What do you mean, *knows things*?"

Jane laughed a little. "Seriously?"

"I guess..." Lucille thought carefully over her next words. "...she has a strong intuition?"

"Intuition?" Jane repeated, squinting her eyes as she inched forward.

"Like an inner voice?" Lucille was worried she had said too much.

Jane frowned a little. "I know what intuition is—I just—" she sighed. "I don't know, maybe I'm going crazy." The candle's light cast a golden shadow on Jane's pale face, darkening her green eyes to a muddy hazel. She looked so concerned, so serious. As if she *had* to understand. As if understanding would fill in the missing piece of a puzzle. Maybe she *was* trying to find pieces to a puzzle. Subconsciously. Lucille pitied the girl. It must be terrible to not know what was happening, to not be told what was really going on. She was totally and fully cut off from the truth.

"Sometimes, I feel like she can read my mind," Jane said under her breath.

Suddenly, Lucille needed a cigarette. Immediately.

She stood up and grabbed her pack of cigarettes and lighter from the coffee table. "I'll be right back, darlin'."

Jane nodded and moved from the floor to the couch after she left. She felt even more confused by what Lucille had told her. *'Inner voice?'* She knew what *intuition* meant, but she had never heard of an *inner voice*. She had always thought intuition was simply an obvious prediction or a lucky guess. Was there more to it? What did Lucille mean by an *inner voice*?

"Hey," Margaret said from the dark doorway, snapping Jane out of a daze.

At first, the room was too dark to see her. A flash of lightning struck, shining a white light on Margaret for just a moment, and the room went dark, her figure disappearing into the shadows again.

She walked over to the table, the candle's light illuminating her sharp features. She took a seat next to Jane on the couch and pulled her lips upward into a half smile. "How are you doing?" she asked just before another round of thunder sounded.

The storm was hovering over them like ghosts trying to scare their victims.

Jane thought about the question. "I'm okay," she said after a long pause. "What about you?"

Margaret didn't hesitate. "I'm fine." She shifted her gaze to the flame in front of them. The fire danced in the reflection of her green eyes. She looked like a different person in the dark. Jane could see all the weight her mother carried by the way the shadows painted her. What else is her mother hiding from her?

"Mom," she began. "Is everything alright with you and Dad?"

Margaret stared at the flame, calm yet utterly thunderstruck. She forced her eyes to meet her daughter's again as she answered. "We're fine."

Jane hesitated. "He called again. He doesn't sound fine."

Her brow furrowed as she dropped her eyes.

"Why haven't you called him back?"

"Because I don't have anything to say to him," she muttered, shaking her head. "Look, your father and I are—" she stopped and huffed. "We had a small argument before we left, and I think we just need some time to…" She lost her thought when she saw the concern in Jane's eyes.

"To what?"

"I love your father, you know that, right?" she questioned, trying her best to smile. "But, right now, I just need a break from him. I think it's best if I wait until I get back to talk to him." Surely, that would satisfy her daughter's eager curiosity. But Jane squinted her eyes a little and leaned forward slightly as if she were a psychologist listening to a patient, eager to extract more answers.

"What was the argument about?"

Margaret pressed her lips together and frowned. "That's something between me and your father. When we get back, we're all going to sit down for a family meeting, and you can ask all the questions you'd like. But tonight, I'm tired," she forced a laugh and then stood up, looking down at her daughter. "Good night, sweet Jane." She smiled softly before walking out.

Jane focused on the dancing tendrils of the flames.

Lucille never returned, leaving their conversation about Mary Grace's *'inner voice'* unfinished. And when Jane thought about it, Mary Grace never finished their conversation about the statues, either. Every time a certain topic was brought up, both women would get the same look in their eyes, and they'd stop talking. It bothered her to no end. Her aunts were keeping something important from her, and so was her mother—and she was determined to find out what it was soon enough.

The storm raged on outside. Mary Grace and Lucille went to their rooms without saying goodnight. She wasn't close to being tired, but being alone in the dark living room made her feel scared.

She blew out the candles before leaving the room, letting the shadows of the night take over completely.

Rain pattered against the windows like a thousand tiny fingers tapping on the glass.

As she headed for the stairs, she caught something in the corner of her eye. A small object above the front door.

A skeleton key. It hung by a thin string from a nail directly beside the coat rack.

She rushed over to it, reaching her arm up as high as she could.

Jane grabbed the big key and studied its intricate design. The metal was cold and heavy in her palm.

She walked by the key several times during her search earlier that day, but not once did she see it. It was right there the whole time.

A round of thunder shook the house, telling Jane it was time to leave before one of the women saw her.

CHAPTER TWENTY-ONE

THERE WERE NO FOOTSTEPS, or none that Jane could hear over the rain—which she hoped meant everyone in the house was asleep. She crept down the hallway, holding her breath.

This was the night she was going to sneak into Vivi's room. In her hands, she held a skeleton key that she was sure would unlock Vivian's bedroom door. She wasn't going to mess this chance up.

Like downstairs, the second story of the house was pitch black, but she could make out just enough not to run into the walls.

Thunder cracked the sky, causing the key to slip from her grasp and fall to the floor with a thud. But the noise was completely silenced by the summer storm. No one in the house would hear her.

Before she knew it, she was standing in front of Vivian's bedroom. She slipped the key into the lock, and it clicked as she turned it to the left.

She pushed the door open, her hungry eyes scanning the bedroom. Half-expecting to find someone, her heart jumped up to the base of her throat. She felt eyes on her, like someone *was* in there.

As she stepped across the doorway, lightning flashed from the windows on the back wall, brightening the entire room for a split second. When it went dark again, she stopped, waiting for her eyes to readjust to the darkness.

The air in the room was cold, lacking any warmth. Goosebumps spread across her arms, and a shiver ran down her spine. The whole house was muggy and humid—but not this bedroom.

Jane padded across the bedroom to the vanity desk, the sound of the pattering rain intensifying as she neared the glass windows. She knew she had been in the room before, but it felt like it was her first time.

She pried open the desk drawers, pushing her way through the clutter. She didn't know what she was trying to find. All she knew was that she wanted answers. Answers to questions she didn't know she was asking. She wanted to find something that would prove she wasn't going crazy. Something that made sense of all the secrets and mysteries that lived within these old walls of the Abel Plantation. That's when she spotted the deck of cards. Intricately designed like the sinister one in her room, they were all different. She sighed in relief as she picked them up, but she wasn't sure why she was relieved. The cards terrified her. It meant that those girls at the diner might be right. That the town's rumors might be right. She didn't know what she would do if the rumors were true.

Her fingers trembled as she held the cards before her. She whipped around, moving fast for the door. The bedroom was creepy.

White lightning flashed for a split second. Out of the corner of her eye, she saw a figure standing across the room. A boom of thunder sounded, making her jump and trip. The cards flew across the room as she fell on her hands and knees.

She looked to her left, where she saw the person, but there was no one.

She crawled over to the cards in a panic, picking them up.

When she stood, lightning lit up the room once again, and she could see that slender shadow from the corner of her eye. She almost screamed when she turned around and found that, still, no one was there.

Wind roared as rain beat against the window. The storm seemed to intensify as her panic increased.

She raced out of the room, holding the cards close to her chest with one hand, locking the door shut with the other, trapping in whatever strange shadow she saw.

Jane stuck the key in the front pocket of her pajama shorts, hurrying down the hall. She lifted her eyes straight ahead, finding another figure right in front of her.

She ran smack into the figure, almost falling backward, but the figure caught her by her free hand just before she hit the ground.

It was too dark to see her face, but she could tell just by the high-pitched southern drawl that it was Lucille. "What are ya doin' in Vivian's bedroom?" she quickly whispered.

Jane inhaled a sharp breath, realizing she had been holding her breath since she ran out of Vivian's room. "I—um—"

"And what're ya doin' with Vivian's stuff?" Lucille's eyes dropped down to the cards in Jane's hands. "Do ya even *know* what those are?"

"I—"

A round of thunder went off, interrupting her.

Lucille wrapped her robe around herself, crossing her arms tightly. "Jane, I think you and I need to talk."

"*Please*, don't tell—"

"I ain't gonna tell your mama. Don't you worry 'bout that."

She swallowed, feeling a mixture of guilt and relief.

"Come on. I'll make you some chicory, and we'll talk about this."

Lucille lit a candlestick she found tucked in one of the cabinets by the sink and placed it on the kitchen table before Jane and the stack of mysterious cards.

Jane chewed the inside of her cheek. Her hands were shaking, and her heart drummed loudly in her ears. She locked her gaze on the cards in front of her.

As Lucille made the chicory, she worked quickly yet quietly.

A minute later, the smell of fresh coffee steeped through the air. The smell of it relaxed Jane's unsettling nerves.

Lucille set a mug in front of Jane, and the girl immediately grabbed the warm cup, stopping her hands from shaking anymore.

"I figured it's far too late to drink coffee, even though you're already *wide awake.* Now—" she started, but was cut off by another voice from behind Jane.

"Mhmm, chicory smells good, Lucille." It was Mary Grace. She was wearing a black nightgown trimmed with lace and cotton slippers. She smiled at the ladies, walking over to the pot of black liquid. As she poured herself a mug, Lucille huffed.

"What are you doin' up? I thought you were asleep."

"Same reason you're up," she said, turning around to face them, a mug in her hands. "I heard noises—*someone* sneakin' 'round upstairs."

Lightning flashed outside, illuminating the kitchen. Mary Grace's eyes glowed, locked with Jane's, and then the light vanished, encasing them with darkness once more.

"Let me explain—"

"No need to apologize, darlin'," Mary Grace whispered. She stepped closer to the candlelight. "It's okay to be curious. But when you add trespass*ing* in the mix—that's when things turn from *okay* to *bad* real quick."

"I wasn't trespassing!" she gasped, her voice low. "I was... I was—"

"Waitin' until everyone was asleep to explore a locked room?" Mary Grace interrupted, shaking her head. She sat down in front of Jane beside Lucille.

Jane stuttered, "Well, I didn't think you'd let me in there if I asked, so I..." She frowned. "Look, I'm sorry, okay? I realize how immature I sound by saying this, but I didn't think it would be that big of a deal. I wasn't going to mess anything up. All I wanted was..." she stopped, sighing at how foolish she sounded.

Lucille leaned forward. "All you wanted was—what? Vivian's deck? Why?"

"I'd like to know this, too," Mary Grace took a small sip of the warm, chalky chicory, watching Jane over the lip of the mug.

"I went into her room before. On Saturday night. It wasn't locked so—" Her eyes dropped to the mug in her hands, ashamed.

"Wasn't locked?" Mary Grace hissed in a whisper. "That door is *always* locked. For a reason, y'know. I don't like nosy teenagers roamin' through my best friend's stuff."

"It wasn't locked, I promise! I can't remember why I went in there. That night is a little blurry. I think I heard something—or… I don't know. But when I woke up the next morning, I couldn't remember anything. And then I found one of the cards in my bed." The card that haunted her, mocked her. The one that got her into all this mess. The same one that she first saw on her mother's desk back in New York.

"It says *the devil*. The card is in my room right now. I can get it if you don't believe me." She pictured the thick cursive words in her head. "That's why I went back into her room tonight, though. I wanted to find answers. I don't know who exactly Vivian was—but the cards might have something to do with why she's missing."

Mary Grace lifted an eyebrow. "What do you mean?"

"This might sound crazy—but what if Vivian was in a cult? What if she was a Satanist?"

Lucille choked, laughing under her breath. Mary Grace nudged her.

"It's not nice to laugh," she whispered. She looked back at Jane, who stared at them with furrowed eyebrows.

Were they Satanists, too? Were they in the same cult as Vivi? Is that why they were laughing at her? Because she figured it all out so easily? Was her mother in whatever cult the three of them were in, too? She had to be, since she had the same illustration back home.

"Dear," Mary Grace started, taking another sip. "The Devil card is not satanic. It's just a Major Arcana card. I promise you, Vivian wasn't a satanist."

"What does a *major arcana card* mean?" Jane shot back, keeping her voice in a whisper.

The women exchanged looks.

"Well—" Lucille started.

"It's—" Mary Grace cut her off.

Lucille huffed, "Let me try to explain."

Mary Grace took another sip, rolling her eyes. "Fine."

"You see, Jane, there are twenty-two Major Arcana cards in a tarot deck."

"Tarot?"

Mary Grace thought about it. "Tarot cards are a sort of *guidance*. They help you gain insight from your past, present, and future."

"I don't understand," Jane said, squinting her eyes at the cards in her hands.

The storm outside had slowed, and the only thing remaining was a soft *drip-drop* from the rain.

"They're used as a tool for fortune-telling," Lucille tried again, but Jane looked even more lost.

"Fortune-telling? Was Vivian a fortune-teller?"

Mary Grace was the first to laugh this time. "No, dear. She never liked reading other people's tarot."

"Reading?" Jane paused. "Never mind. How do cards tell your future? That sounds like stuff in kids' stories." She was no longer scared. She wanted answers. The cards didn't make sense to her, but for some reason, they fascinated her nonetheless.

"Well, I personally believe a greater power is guiding me *through* the cards," Mary Grace answered.

"Greater power?"

"Yes, dear," she nodded. "Like God, or the Universe—or something we can't understand simply because it's not for us *to* understand. The cards can answer questions and help you understand something that's happening a little more. They're just a form of guidance. To help you. It can't solve all your problems or grant you wishes—but it might help you see things a little clearer or prepare you for what is yet to come."

Jane chewed her lip as she listened.

"Tarot cards," Lucille chimed in. "are something you either believe in or you don't. There's no real explanation to how they work."

"But if they're not evil, then why is there a card of the devil?"

Mary Grace didn't hesitate, "Each card has a meaning. Each card symbolizes something. Think about the Devil. He was an angel once but was cast out of Heaven because he was greedy. He gave in to his temptations and selfishness. So, that card represents *greediness, fear, overabundance, obsession, overcontrol*— you get the idea."

She started to, but still, she didn't fully understand.

Lucille reached over the table and took the cards from her. She pulled out a random card, flipping it forward to show Jane. This card was a picture of a big gold sun, sunflowers, and a white horse underneath. The cursive writing on the bottom of the card read, *The Sun*. "This card means *strength, happiness, good fortune, and joy*. It's a good card to get." She started shuffling the deck.

"Do all of you... *read* cards?"

"Yes. I've been reading cards since I could remember," Mary Grace told her.

She wanted to ask if Margaret read cards, too, but she figured she knew the answer to that since she had seen tarot cards in her mother's room already. But why would Margaret want to read tarot? It didn't seem like her.

"There's no real way of explaining what the cards do unless we just show you," Lucille said, looking over at Mary Grace. She handed her the cards, nodding her head. "Go on," she told her friend.

Jane inched forward.

Mary Grace pulled the top card from the deck, placing it in front of the girl. The card was a picture of a heart with three swords sticking out of it and blood dripping from the blades. *III of Swords*, the bottom read. "Your past," she muttered. She flipped over another one. This one was of a creepy, hunched-over grim reaper with a wicked smile standing on a pile of bones. It read *Death*. "Your present."

Jane gasped, "What does that mean?"

She ignored her, flipping the next one. It was a picture of three gold cups floating in the sky, gold rays wrapping around them. It read, *III of Cups*. "And your future."

"What does it all mean?"

Mary Grace looked down at the cards, pointing to the first one. "Three of Swords—your past. In your recent past, it says you were depressed." She paused.

"I was not. What does Death mean?"

"Jane, just listen, or I won't be able to tell you."

She pressed her lips together, impatient.

"You probably felt like nothing you said or did seemed to matter. You felt voiceless, lifeless. Like you were just a breathing machine walking around. Doing what your parents expected of you. Getting good grades, staying out of trouble, never asking for anything."

Mary Grace's words stung, and the girl felt somewhat insulted. But she was also utterly shocked. Even though she would never admit it, there was truth in her words.

"Now," She pointed to the card in the middle. "Death— your present. It says you are currently *changin'*. You're transforming into a new version of yourself. Your old self is *dyin'*, and with death comes *birth*. You're being *reborn*, in a way, into the young woman you are made to be."

She lifted her chin slightly.

"And lastly, Three of Cups—your future. In your future, there will be a celebration. A sense of community and belonging. You will accomplish something great. You will get past your current state of change."

"What will I accomplish?" Jane leaned forward, eyeing the three cards.

Mary Grace smiled thinly, "That is for you to find out, my dear."

Lucille exchanged a look filled with curiosity with Mary Grace and then smiled tenderly at Jane. "So, do you understand what tarot is now?"

She sighed, chewing the inside of her cheek.

Mary Grace picked up the cards, shuffling them in the stack. "Jane," she started, her rounded chin lifted with pride. "I want you to have these cards. I think Vivi would want you to have them as well. But please, do not go around calling people *Satanists*. Just because you don't understand something someone else does, does not mean you get to label them."

"I'm sorry," Jane said, realizing how critical she had sounded.

"But most importantly," Lucille told her. "Do *not* tell your mother we told you about this."

"Why not?" She thought of the card her mother had.

The women looked at each other.

Mary Grace sighed. "We can't tell you. Not tonight. She just wants to keep you safe."

Jane's mind was crowded with nagging thoughts that deprived her of sleep. She lay awake in her room, her eyes open, just silently gazing at the ceiling, her mind running wild with questions.

She thought she would feel better after finding the cards and talking to her aunts. But what bothered her now was how they told her not to tell her mother. She felt like she was drowning from all the secrets in the house.

The next morning, the storm left just as suddenly as it came. The gray clouds parted, and a baby-blue sky appeared with golden sunshine that set off the birds into cheerful and chipper songs. The only things that the rain left behind at the plantation were a few puddles of water and a spongy lawn.

CHAPTER TWENTY-TWO

CICADAS BEGAN HUMMING THEIR DEEP melody throughout the grounds of the Abel Plantation when the night brightened into morning.

Jane had grown to love the sound of the critters and creatures down in the south.

People always said to move away from the city for some peace and quiet. You may be able to find some peace in the bayou, but you are never going to find silence. The bugs and animals are too proud and busy to hush.

It was a constant cycle of life down in the south. Things were being born, things were dying, things were hunting, things were being hunted. It was an everlasting flow of chaos. A chaos so loud yet so blissfully tranquil to the human ear.

Jane was rocking in the rocking chair outside of her room, listening to the hums and chirps and rustles. She could feel her breath move steadily in and out of her lungs.

So much was going on around her, not just with the creatures hidden under the giant oaks in the morning light but also with everything in her life.

She felt divided from the women in the house. They were all keeping something from her, and every time she thought she was getting closer to finding out what it was, she ran into more secrets.

She needed someone to talk to about all this. And she couldn't turn to Lucille or Mary Grace because they were keeping just as many secrets from her as Margaret was.

She grabbed her phone from the coffee table next to her. There was really only one person she could trust right now.

The phone rang only two times before Bobbie Jo answered. "Hey, what's up?"

"I went into Vivian's room last night."

She let out an excited gasp. "And?"

The glass door at the far end of the porch opened, and Margaret stepped out, smiling when she saw Jane.

"Do you want to go to the diner?" she asked Bobbie Jo, giving her mom a small smile. "I'm going a little stir-crazy here."

Bobbie Jo understood the change of tone. "Yeah, sure. I'll pick ya up in thirty minutes. Sound good?"

"Sounds good."

She lowered the phone and looked at Margaret.

Margaret was not thrilled with the idea that Jane was leaving the house, but because she felt bad for dragging her into the mess of Vivian's disappearance, she allowed her to go. She was glad Jane was making friends here. Most of the kids back in New York didn't talk to her. Either they were criminals-to-be, or they were stuck-up rich kids. Jane had a few friends, sure, but not good ones. Most of them were classmates who only hung around her whenever they needed help on an exam. They weren't true friends. Not like the friends Margaret grew up with.

Margaret always felt lucky growing up with a group of girls she'd considered sisters. She understood not a lot of people got that lucky, which was one of the reasons she felt obligated to come back home when she heard Vivi had gone missing. Throughout their childhood, they grew to understand that you stick with your best friends no matter what. That's what makes them *best* friends. Staying by their side through the good days and the bad ones. Helping them out when they need an extra hand. Listening to them when they need advice. And standing up for them. Always.

Margaret sat in the rocking chair next to her and grabbed her hand, looking into her eyes. "You okay?"

The question was sincere and gave Jane whiplash at first. She tried to find the right words. "Yeah. Why?"

"Nothing. I'm just worried for you, that's all."

"Why are you worried?"

Margaret let go of her hand and looked out the driveway. "You know why. Since we came here, you've fainted, heard voices—" she huffed, shaking her head.

Jane didn't say anything, just studying her mother's pale face. She tried to imagine all the secrets that hid behind those gray-green eyes.

"Look," Margaret moved her eyes to Jane. "If there's anything you want to talk about—anything that's bothering you, you can tell me. I'll listen. I know it seems like I don't care because I'm always working, but I do care, and I'm always here for you."

Jane hesitated, not sure what to say to that. She didn't want to talk. She wanted answers.

"I just wanted to tell you that. We live under the same roof, but I feel like we don't even talk anymore. You're growing up so fast, too. Only one more year until you graduate school and move on to the next chapter of your life."

Owls hooted in the distance.

"Anyway, you should get dressed now," Margaret sighed, standing up from the chair.

Jane thought about the tarot cards, about the one she saw on Margaret's desk. She wanted to ask her about it, but when she opened her mouth to speak, Lucille and Mary Grace popped into her head. They made her promise she wouldn't tell, and for some reason, she felt she had to keep that promise. She wanted to ask her mother about the cards and all the other strange secrets hiding around every corner of the plantation, but first, she had to ask her aunts *why* she couldn't talk to Margaret.

After Jane changed out of her pajamas, a loud, worn-out engine sound rolled down the driveway. A small horn beeped, as if trying to shout over the loud chuckling of the motor.

She looked through the glass doors and found an old white VW Beetle racing down the long driveway, flying over every bump in the road as it honked an ugly cry for attention. She could see a head of brown curls bouncing around and Bobbie Jo's wide grin.

Putting her phone in her back pocket, Jane rushed out of her bedroom and through the house.

"What on *earth* is that noise?" Mary Grace asked from the kitchen. She and Lucille were sitting at the table discussing their plan for the day when Jane stuck her head in the kitchen and told them she was grabbing breakfast with Bobbie Jo. They looked a little worried at first. Like they weren't sure if they should let her go. With everything they told her last night, it made them nervous.

"Are you gonna tell her about..." Lucille had whispered before Jane left. She didn't need to finish her question. Jane knew what her aunts were worried about before Lucille even asked.

"I may," Jane answered plainly, trying to keep her answers simple and quiet. She could hear Margaret coming down the stairs.

"Say whatever you want 'bout us—but don't you go spreadin' rumors," Mary Grace snapped, her warm smile vanishing.

"I'm not going to spread rumors," she shook her head. "But I'm not keeping any secrets either. I still don't understand why I can't tell my mom—"

Mary Grace took a deep breath. "If you trust Bobbie Jo not to tell the whole parish we're... what did you call Vivi? A Satanist?" she laughed under her breath. "If you trust the girl not to tell everyone we are *Satanists*, then I do too."

The horn of Bobbie Jo's Bug cried out again.

The minute Jane stepped outside, the hot air stuck to her skin. She swiped the back of her hand across her forehead to get rid of the sweat already pooling at her hairline.

The white Bug was parked in front of the steps, and Jane could see Bobbie Jo in the driver's seat, waving at her with excitement. She beeped the whiny horn three times. She stuck her arm through the open window and smacked the side of the car.

"Hey, Jane! How ya like my car?" she asked with a squeal.

Jane moved her gaze from the old white Bug to the grinning girl. "*This* is your car?" she gasped. "This is so cool."

Bobbie Jo blushed, "Ain't she the cutest, though?" she nodded her head to the passenger side. "Hop in. We don't got AC, but we do we have music."

She walked over to the other side of the car, opening the squeaky door. The car seats were tan leather, smelled brand new, and the carpets were the same color as the leather. The dashboard was the only thing that looked out of place. It was black with cracks and scratches, and the radio was smaller than a smartphone.

"Ain't she cute? I just got it back from the shop. It's a *1974* Super Beetle. I just did a lot of work on it. New seats, new carpet, fresh paint job—everything is basically restored *except* the dash. Daddy says he's gonna get that fixed up before school starts."

Jane slid into the passenger seat, shutting the door with an unintentional slam. "I wish I had something like this. This is so cool." She had her license, but owning a car wasn't something her parents ever discussed with her. Because she lived in such a big city, it was easier to walk than drive.

"Thanks. I saw this beauty for sale on the side of the road on our way to New Orleans last year," she told her. The car jerked to a roll when she put the gear in drive. "I told my Daddy, I said, *That's my first car.* Can you believe they were selling this thing for only *$500*? Of course, we had to put a motor in it and replace the bumpers and brakes and redo the inside—but it was all worth it, don't you think?"

Jane didn't know much about cars, but still, she smiled and nodded her head in agreement.

Bobbie Jo turned the radio on, pushing a button that spat out a cassette tape on the top of the radio's face. She pulled it out, flipped it over, and slid it back in.

"You have cassette tapes?" Jane asked over the loud, bubbling noise of the engine.

She laughed, shrugging her shoulders. "They're my dad's. He gave me all his tapes after he replaced his truck's radio."

Music started to play; warm, rhythmic guitars harmonizing through the old speakers.

"Greatest band in history," Bobbie Jo said matter-of-factly.

Jane raised an eyebrow.

She looked at her and gasped. "Don't tell me you don't—" She stopped herself and shook her head. "It's fine. You get a pass because you're a *northerner*." She said *northerner* like it was a disease Jane carried. "This is *Free Bird* by *Lynyrd Skynyrd*. Greatest song ever known to man."

Once they were on the beaten road, Bobbie Jo reached her hand out and touched the summer wind. The sky was a brilliant blue, like the shade of Lucille's eyes. The blue above made the trees and grass look lively and vibrant. It was a beautiful day, a classic example of summertime.

A waft of mud and swamp blew through the car, and for the first time, Jane realized she didn't mind it.

The old Beetle flew twenty miles above the posted speed limit, launching over every pothole in the road. Jane assumed Bobbie Jo didn't need to worry about getting pulled over, being the Sheriff's daughter.

They arrived in the main downtown strip before the first song ended. Bobbie Jo parked parallel in front of the diner, and as soon as she killed the engine, she grabbed a tote bag from behind her seat and jumped out of the small car, running towards the diner.

The gold bell chimed above Jane when she pulled open the door. The smell of pancakes and warm syrup overcame them the moment they stepped through the doorway. It was like the smell was painted on the walls.

No one was eating at the diner that morning except for an older couple sitting in a booth near the back.

With a confidence Jane could never obtain, Bobbie Jo marched straight to the bar and slapped her hand on the countertop, grinning, "Mornin' Jim!"

Jane remembered the old man from the last time she came. His face lit up when he saw the girls, and Jane smiled.

"Ga' mornin', girls. What can I get y'all this mornin'?" he asked with his big, toothless grin.

"I'll have the usual," Bobbie Jo smirked.

With a nod, Jane said, "I'll get what she's getting."

"The usual, huh?" he scratched his bald head and laughed. "Comin' right up."

When he walked away, Bobbie Jo set her tote bag in front of her, pulling out her phone, a notepad, and a pen. She squinted her eyes at Jane, making the freckles on her nose and across her cheeks scrunch together.

"So—tell me *everythin'*," she leaned closer to Jane, her big brown eyes growing wide with excitement, like they were talking girl-talk about boys and drama. "You said you heard *Vivi* in the house? With you?"

Jane looked around the diner before answering. "I don't know."

"Now you *don't* know?" She rolled her eyes. "Did you hear her or not?"

Jane paused, shifting her weight on the stool. "Look, I've never met her, Bobbie Jo. To say I heard someone I've never heard speak before sounds... impossible. So, I'd rather just say I don't know."

Her gaze was locked on Jane, searching her expression for answers. "But you *did* hear someone, didn't you?"

Jane pressed her lips together in a firm line and nodded once.

"Okay," she replied, talking more to herself than to Jane. She looked down at her notepad, her face painted with deep concentration.

"There's something strange going on at the plantation. I don't know exactly what yet, but I know my mother and aunts are keeping something from me. Hearing Vivian calling my name isn't the only peculiar thing that's happened. I fainted and woke up with no memory of what I was doing before. This happened two times—I think. I might have fainted more, and I just can't remember. I don't know what's wrong with me. I've been forgetting so much lately. It feels like I'm literally going insane. It's like I'm being gaslit or something."

Bobbie Jo furrowed her eyebrows as she listened, her lips slightly parted in apprehension.

She took a deep breath, thinking about the postcard, the burnt house phone, the tarot cards, and the long discussion with her aunts that followed.

"I snuck into Vivian's room last night and found more of those drawings like the one I was telling you about." As she went on, her voice lowered. "They're—um," she looked around again. "They're tarot cards."

Bobbie Jo suddenly looked sick. She blinked a few times as she processed Jane's words. "So... all the rumors are true? About the witchcraft, about them—"

"No, the rumors aren't true. Lucille caught me as I was leaving Vivian's room, and she and Mary Grace told me what tarot is."

"I know what tarot is. It's what *witches* use."

She shook her head. "They told me that the deck of cards is used as a like—like a *guide*. A small prediction of the future."

"Sounds like witchcraft to me." She couldn't believe it—the rumors were true. She had trusted Mary Grace and Vivian and even treated them like her own aunts.

Jane hesitated. "I don't know."

"Maybe they've been keeping a secret. A dark secret. And maybe they've just been *tryin'* to fit in this whole time."

"A dark secret?" Jane knew there were secrets floating around the plantation. So many it was overwhelming.

Her face was serious. "You know what I mean."

"I don't know..."

"C'mon, Jane—listen to yourself. Tarot cards? Vivian went missing, and you said it yourself that something strange is going on at the Abel Plantation. Witch—" she looked around. "—craft."

"Maybe it is. But I know they're not satanists."

"What—they're *Christian* witches?"

Jane's head was beginning to hurt. As if to save Jane from Bobbie Jo's gawking eyes and penetrating questions, Jim came out of the back kitchen with their breakfasts. Jane was no longer hungry, though, but relieved to focus on something other than *witchcraft*.

Before shoving a huge bite of French toast in her mouth, Bobbie Jo said, "I want to see the cards."

CHAPTER TWENTY-THREE

"DID YOU GUYS HEAR anything last night?" Margaret asked her two friends as they all sat in the rocking chairs on the front porch, just talking and sipping coffee. It was a lovely day, the kind of day that was made for kids to bike around town, climb trees, and take a boat out on the water. She could feel the nostalgia of her adventurous childhood creep up on her.

Mary Grace answered first. "No," the answer was too quick. Too suspiciously quick.

Lucille approached the topic smoothly. "I did. I think a branch fell on the roof or somethin' like that. That was an *awful* storm last night, wasn't it?"

Margaret nodded her head, but she could detect that something was off in the way Mary Grace answered. Her thoughts returned to her daughter, and her heart stiffened with fear. "I'm worried about Jane."

Mary Grace hummed in agreement and raised her mug to her lips as she said, "She's bound to find out what we are, Mar. You know I try not to eavesdrop on everyone's thoughts, but I did hear somethin' 'bout witchcraft last night."

"Damn it," she sucked her teeth, her hands tightening around the mug.

"Maybe it's not such a bad thing, Margaret," Lucille said in an optimistic tone. "I mean, maybe this is God's plan."

She rolled her eyes and said through clenched teeth, "Why would *God* plan this? Do you know what's going to happen— if this *is* His plan? Huh?"

Lucille sighed.

"Nothin' that isn't already gonna happen," snapped Mary Grace, cutting her eyes at Margaret. "You can't protect her from this. She will find out what she is, what *you* are, and then you'll have to tell her the truth— the *whole* truth."

Margaret stared at her friend, fear seeping into her.

The porch fell silent, and only the crickets and frogs and cicadas talked around them.

Mary Grace let out a sigh. "Everything will be okay. Jane's going to be okay, and we'll get Vivian back."

After a moment of silence, Margaret sighed and said, "I'm sorry—"

The two women turned their gaze to their Margaret, leaning in slightly.

She bit her lip, finding the words harder to spit out than she expected. She tried again, "I'm sorry about what I did." The truth tasted bitter, more bitter than the black coffee she washed the words down with.

Mary Grace started to shake her head, but Margaret went on.

"No, what I did was awful. I was rude and selfish. I thought I could just run away from my problems—but you know what? Doesn't matter how fast you run, they'll catch up eventually. And they'll cause even more problems along the way." Tears pooled in the corners of her eyes. She wiped them away with the back of her hand.

Lucille frowned, "Don't feel bad about it, hon. You did what you thought was right to keep poor Jane safe."

"Still, it wasn't fair. I should have at least called you all once in a while or—I don't know. It was just selfish. If Jane did that to me, I'd be so worried every day. I wouldn't know if she was dead or in trouble or needed my help—"

"But I did know, Margaret," Mary Grace smiled. "I always knew you were okay. Not just because of my gift but because you are quite the fighter."

Lucille nodded, "Yeah, I always knew you were okay, too. I'm sorry I wasn't ever here, either. I spent the last fifteen years searchin' for love in all the wrong places. I was lookin' for a love that didn't exist." Tears pooled in her eyes. "But the love I needed was right here all along."

Mary Grace nodded slowly, a pleased smile on her round face. "I am glad to hear you both finally grew up. Took you long enough." She chuckled and stood from the rocking chair, raising her mug to her lips and consuming the last drop of coffee. "Well, let's get dressed now, ladies. I think we oughta take a trip down to Lake Maurepas."

Margaret pushed her eyebrows together. "I thought we agreed to let the detectives do their job."

"We did," Mary Grace nodded, and before walking away, added, "But we are also gonna check for things they might've missed."

The women arrived at the boat ramp a little after ten thirty. None of them thought about eating breakfast, so they were all running on a cup or two of black coffee, with the heavy feeling of dread knotted at the bottom of their stomachs caused by the fear of what they might find and the fear of not finding anything at all. The boat ramp was empty, which was unusual for a Friday morning. The lack of eyewitnesses made Margaret uncomfortable. If there were a kidnapper or killer hiding in the swamp, the women would surely disappear as Vivian had.

"Should we call Randy up here?" Margaret asked Mary Grace as they stepped out of the cold A/C of the car and into the hot, muggy parking lot.

Puddles of muddy water from the recent storm drowned half of the whole gravel lot. A mosquito flew in Margaret's face, and she swatted it away with an annoyed huff. The bugs became worse the closer you were to the swamp. They were more aggressive. Hungrier. Gnats and mosquitoes and other ruthless insects swarmed around Mary Grace's car, desperate.

Mary Grace smacked a mosquito on her left hand and looked around the boat ramp. She hadn't been there for a long time, but it looked the way it had years ago, which made her sad for some reason. "Let's look around on our own today." She said it in a way that told the women more. She wanted them to use their gifts to look for Vivian. That's why she didn't call Randy. He didn't know about their gifts.

"What about protection? Don't you think what we're doing is kind of stupid? Our friend recently disappeared, and we're by ourselves in the *middle* of nowhere with no way to defend ourselves if—if there's a serial killer out here," Margaret said through her teeth.

Lucille held up her smartphone. "And there's no cell service."

Mary Grace squinted her eyes at her friends. "What do you mean *no way to defend ourselves*? You know very well we can defend ourselves. But as for cell service, who cares?" She walked away, heading in the direction of the small office ahead of them.

Lucille and Margaret exchanged looks, then rolled their eyes and followed her.

The lake didn't look refreshing in the slightest. Green slime covered most of the water's service as it always did. That water certainly wasn't the kind to swim in. It was filled with alligators and leeches.

"I haven't been here in *ages*," Lucille said to Margaret. "Remember when Randy used to take us fishin' here every Sunday? I miss watchin' him fish. He was *so* bad at it, but he had so much determination that it was worth keepin' him company."

Margaret thought back to those long, hot summer Sundays as a teenager. Randy would pick the girls up in his old pickup truck and just fish all day, talking about the most random topics and plans for the future.

"I miss watching him fish, too."

"They're closed," Mary Grace called from the office's porch. "There's a note that says *be back in ten minutes*."

"Maybe we should come back?" Margaret suggested, wiping the beads of sweat forming above her top lip. She felt like she was melting under the sun.

Mary Grace walked down the porch steps, shaking her head. "No, not worth it. We'll just wait here until they come back. C'mon, let's walk around and play detectives while we wait."

The wicked sun beat down on the three women as they walked the crooked dock on the lake and looked out.

"How are we supposed to find anything on the dock?" Margaret asked, throwing her hands up.

"Do *you* have a boat for us, Margaret?" Mary Grace snapped.

"Maybe if we had *planned* this in advance, I would have rented one," she shot back and rolled her eyes.

"Oh, everything must be planned out for you, doesn't it? You always have to keep a tight schedule, boss everyone 'round—"

"Girls!" Lucille hissed, stomping her feet. "Please, I can *barely* stand this humidity—I don't need to hear y'alls' bickering too."

Mary Grace and Margaret went silent.

Lucille looked behind her shoulder at the tangled mess of woods that surrounded the parking lot like walls. She walked off the dock, heading in the direction of the woods behind the office shack. Her friends followed her without questioning where she was going.

They knew.

The woods eventually turned into the Maurepas Swamp Wildlife Management Area, where true swamp is found as far as the eye could see. Of course, the women didn't want to go into the swamp. It was too dangerous, too easy to get lost out there among the Spanish moss-covered bald cypress trees. The swamp wasn't their territory. It was the home for creatures that nightmares were made of.

Margaret came to an abrupt stop. Mary Grace almost ran into the back of her.

"Lucille, wait!" Mary Grace called, walking around to face Margaret.

Margaret's eyes were wide with a strange sort of shock, but she wasn't focused on anything. She was in a daze, a sort of dream.

"What's wrong?" Lucille asked, turning back.

"She's having another episode." She waved her hand in front of Margaret's face, but the woman didn't flinch. She just stood frozen with her eyelids stuck open. Her pupils dilated big and then shrank.

"What do we do?" Lucille queried once she made it beside Mary Grace.

Margaret turned her head to the right as though staring at something.

"Nothing. We do nothing but wait for her to go through it. Whatever memory she's in right now, she needs to go through it."

Still in a hypnotic-like daze, Margaret strolled back toward the lake.

She looked like she was sleepwalking—and in a way, she was. She stepped onto the dock and just stood there staring at the water, her breathing steady.

A loud, lifted truck with shiny rims entered the parking lot and pulled up next to the office building.

A young man jumped down from the truck and noticed the three women on the dock. He thought they looked strange and a little out of place.

The pretty woman in the tall heels whipped around when he closed his truck door. She elbowed the shorter woman with long hair and said something to her as she pointed in the boy's direction.

He sighed to himself, figuring they were just tourists who got lost and needed help getting back to the interstate. He grabbed the office key from his back pocket, slipped it in the lock, and stepped inside.

"You think we should just leave her here?" Lucille asked Mary Grace, her hands on her hips.

She pursed her lips. "I don't think she'll run away if that's what you're askin'. Let's go talk to the kid. She'll be fine."

After leaving the diner, Bobbie Jo and Jane headed back to the plantation.

The Sheriff's daughter was determined to see these cards for herself. She didn't want to believe Vivi and the other women were witches, but what else was she supposed to believe? She grew up hearing all the terrible stories about them, but was told by her father to ignore the mean rumors. Did he know about this? Had he been lying to her?

When Bobbie Jo turned the old Bug down the driveway, Jane immediately noticed the green car was gone. She guessed that Lucille had left to run errands, but as they got closer, it seemed as though the entire house was empty.

"You think they left?" asked Bobbie Jo as they got out of the car. She pulled back her curly hair in a ponytail. A few stubborn curls stuck out on the sides.

Jane looked up at the big house, searching for any signs of her mother and aunts. "I don't know." She walked up the porch steps, relieved yet nervous to find the door unlocked.

The house was quiet—an empty quiet. She looked down the hall, "Hello?"

No answer.

Bobbie Jo stepped in behind her, closing the door. "Maybe they went out grocery shopping," she suggested, looking in the living room.

"That's not like them to leave without telling me. Especially not my mom," she muttered, walking into the kitchen to search for clues.

Bobbie Jo walked over to the bowl of butterscotch candy in front of the stairs. She quickly grabbed a piece, tossed it in her mouth, and hurried into the kitchen after Jane.

She stood by the small table with a sheet of paper in her hand. "They left a note," she told Bobbie Jo.

"What's it say?" Being her nosy self, she walked up to her and read it over her shoulder.

"Says that they needed to shop for groceries, and they'll be back soon," Jane answered, even though Bobbie Jo was reading it as well.

Bobbie Jo smirked. "Told you."

Jane set the letter down. Something didn't feel right.

"You know," Bobbie Jo started, pacing around the kitchen. "I haven't been in this house in years. Hasn't changed a bit, though," she said, sucking on the candy.

Jane turned from the table and the suspicious letter, looking over at her friend. "Ready to see the cards?"

Bobbie Jo swallowed but lifted her chin slightly.

"What happened to the housephone?" Bobbie Jo gasped when they passed by the burnt phone dangling from the wall.

Jane shrugged her shoulders, walking up the stairs. "Can't remember, but I think it was my fault. I fainted right after talking to someone, and I don't know who it was or what happened."

"Jeez," she shuddered, eyeing the phone as she climbed the stairs behind Jane.

Once they made it to the second floor, Bobbie Jo shivered and rubbed the fresh goosebumps on her arms. "It's kinda cold up here, isn't it?"

"Sometimes it's like this. Randomly cold in some areas of the house, and hot and humid in other areas."

"No offense, but this house gives me the creeps." She looked over her shoulder down the hall.

Jane laughed under her breath. "No offense taken." When she made it to her room, she grabbed the doorknob but hesitated to push it open. She knew it was too late to turn back, but still, she wondered if she should go on. She was still frightened of the cards and didn't want to see them again. She couldn't wrap her head around how they worked, let alone explain to someone else how they worked. She shut her eyes tightly, and as she opened them, she pushed the door wide open.

Bobbie Jo stood in the doorway and watched the girl walk to the dresser against the wall. She opened the top drawer, pulling out the deck of cards.

"Here they are." She took a seat on the floor, crossing her legs. Bobbie Jo joined her. Carefully, she spread out the cards and searched through them until she found the one she was looking for.

The card didn't seem so evil now that she knew what it was. It's funny how quickly perception can change once a mystery is resolved.

Bobbie Jo sucked in a breath, "Oh my— that's a sure sign Vivian was in some cult or—"

"No, she wasn't. And she wasn't a satanist, either. Mary Grace and Lucille told me. The Devil card represents something, just like..." she trailed off, digging through the deck until she pulled out a random card that read, *The Lovers*, "this card means something. Each card symbolizes *something*, and it's not all evil."

She didn't get it. She scrunched up her freckled nose, tilting her head to the side. "What do they do?"

"Foreshadow the future. And Mary Grace and Lucille told me they also used the cards, and they made it sound like it was—was a secret."

She stood up and began pacing the room as her thoughts started forming. "So, I was right, then. Vivi is a witch. And so is Mary Grace and Lucille and... and your mom."

"Maybe," Jane admitted. "Maybe they're all witches." Somewhere in the back of her mind, she had always thought this, but hearing herself say it out loud made her somewhat believe it.

"This is crazy! Witches? Like *real* witches."

She sighed, looking at the cards. "We don't know this for a fact, though."

Bobbie Jo shook her head, "I can't believe this."

"Believe me, I understand how crazy this all sounds. Ever since I got here, *strange* things keep happening."

Bobbie Jo stopped pacing.

"And, I've been having these nightmares that I can't remember—and I wake up feeling like I'm having a panic attack. And now, I'm blacking out during the day."

"And you're hearing voices." Bobbie Jo laughed, almost out in mockery.

She rubbed her lips together in thought, "And I'm seeing things. I know how crazy it sounds."

"Everythin' you're sayin' sounds crazy!"

Jane ignored her, "There has to be a reason all this stuff is happening."

"And the reason is... is *witchcraft*?"

"I don't know."

"You said you *see things*, too? What do you see?"

She hesitated, shaking her head. "I don't want to tell you—"

"Jane, I don't give a crap. You already are crazy. Just tell me." She put her hands on her hips, stomping a foot.

"I keep seeing shadows. Like figures in the corner of my eye. And, the concrete statues outside moved."

Her lips parted, and she let out a quick gasp, her eyes wide with disbelief. "The statues?" She felt like she should run. Run out of the house as fast as she could, jump in her car, and not look back. But she didn't. As crazy as Jane sounded, Bobbie Jo didn't want to leave just yet. She had to hear more of what Jane had to say about all this.

"Yep." Jane nodded, her cheeks turning red. She said too much. She could tell by the way Bobbie Jo's mouth hung open. "I don't understand what's going on here. I'm just as shocked and confused as you are. I just—" She grabbed the cards off the floor, putting them in a neat stack. "I needed to tell someone. My aunts won't answer my questions, and they told me not to tell my mom. They're all hiding something from me. I don't know if it's witchcraft or something worse—but there is something, and I'm going to find out what it is."

Bobbie Jo looked shaken. "This is a lot to take in," she let out a sigh. "You sound paranoid, Jane."

"I'm not paranoid." She stood up. "And I'm not crazy. At least, I don't think I am."

"You're under a lot of stress—"

"I am not paranoid," she snapped, running her hand through her hair. "There is something going on with my mom and aunts that they aren't telling me about."

She scoffed. "That they're *witches*?"

Just then, she remembered something from the night she first went into Vivian's bedroom. A journal. She remembered the cursive writing on the first page. *Vivian's Spell Journal*. She didn't understand why she was just now remembering this notebook, but she was grateful that she did. Maybe Bobbie Jo would believe her if she saw it with her own eyes. "I need to get something from Vivian's room." She walked past Bobbie Jo, racing down the hallway to the stairs.

Bobbie Jo chased after her. "What exactly are you getting?" she asked, not entirely sure if she wanted to hear that answer.

"Vivian's journal," she answered, storming down the stairs. "She has a spell journal. I just remembered now. The key is hanging by the front—" she stopped when she made it to the front door.

The key was gone.

CHAPTER TWENTY-FOUR

SEVENTEEN-YEAR-OLD RANDY JONES sat on the end of the dock, his worn cowboy boots hovering an inch over the silky water and a fishing pole comfortably in his hands. Beside him, there was a faded green plastic tackle box and a soda bottle. 90s country hits blasted from a portable stereo behind him. He wore a red trucker's hat that made his messy mullet stick out in weird ways. With a cigarette hanging from the corner of his mouth, he sang along with the radio—messing up the lyrics and going off-key.

Margaret watched her old friend, a smile tugging at her lips. He was young. Even though he was a year older than the girls, he always looked a year younger with his skinny arms and legs. This was the last summer he spent with the girls. His father died that winter, making poor Randy an orphan. He tried to fend for himself for a little while, but he somehow fell into the habits of his father, and it nearly killed him. He left Belles Parish the next summer and moved in with his great-aunt in Georgia.

She looked down to her right at her three other friends. Lucille and Mary Grace were talking about going back to school, and Vivian was reading, as she usually was.

She recognized the book, remembering the day Vivi bought it. The four girls were out shopping in New Orleans when Vivian insisted on going into a small hoodoo store, called *Madam Louise's Shop*, hidden in an alleyway in the French Quarter.

It was the first time any of them had gone into a store like that. Hoodoo was different than the magic they grew up with. Because it was so foreign, the girls decided it was best if they didn't shop there often. Magic was a dangerous thing to play with. If they weren't careful, magic could turn on them. Hoodoo leaned a little too close to black magic for the girls' comfort, and they didn't want to mess around with the shadow side. That was a conjure they stayed far away from.

But still, Vivi had an interest in the shop that none of the girls had. And now that Margaret remembered this, she worried. What if Vivian went back to that shop—even though she agreed with the girls she wouldn't? What if she was attracted to that kind of magic? What if she played with *black magic?*

Vivian shut the book, snapping Margaret out of her thoughts. "You catch anythin' yet, Randy?" she asked, looking behind Margaret. "I'm gettin' hot."

Randy snorted, "Vivi, I *just* put the darn hook in. You gotta be patient. Fishin' takes time."

Vivian sighed, looking out at the lake.

Margaret took a seat next to her. "What are you reading?"

She held up the book for Margaret to see. "Same book. I'm almost finished."

Margaret nodded, staring at her hands in her lap. "Where did you go?" she asked under her breath.

Like a carpet being rolled out, a layer of gray clouds lay over the blue sky. A sharp wind wailed around the friends, brushing through the Spanish moss and dodging the cypress trees that stood sporadically in the lake.

Margaret didn't remember this part of the memory. The memory was altered. She looked down at her friends, but they didn't seem to notice the storm moving in around them.

Vivian's face suddenly changed. Her thin lips pulled down in a long, unnatural frown, and her eyes became glossy with fresh tears. "I just wanted to protect you all," she whispered, her words soft against the rough wind. "I tried so hard to—" she stopped midsentence.

"Tried so hard to what?" This wasn't the sixteen-year-old Vivi anymore. This was present-day Vivi. She could tell by the sudden, horrified look on her pale face. Like she was in pain. As if she was about to scream out in anger like a banshee or melt into tears. But what scared Margaret the most was that she didn't do either. She was holding in whatever pain she felt inside.

Her eyebrows lifted and pressed together in a *V*. "Tell your daughter the truth, Margaret," she pleaded in a whisper, the words slow and drawn out like one long moan hitting different tones.

Margaret couldn't respond. She didn't understand. Why was Jane involved in this? And what did she mean by *I just wanted to protect you all*? She looked out at the muddy lake and let out a shaky breath between her lips.

As if someone flipped a button, the wind stopped all at once.

The country music cut off.

She looked over at her friends but found an empty dock instead.

They were all gone.

The memory was gone.

In the office, Lucille tapped her nails on the desk. Her patience was running thin, and it took everything inside of her not to start yelling at the kid. "Her name was Vivian Banks."

The boy heaved a sigh, not acknowledging her, just staring at the two women with a blank face.

"She's about as tall as me, has dark hair, skinny as a pole, real quiet and shy—"

He rolled his eyes. "Like I told the police, lady, *I* haven't seen her."

"She could have been with someone, perhaps?" Lucille suggested, her voice rising. "Do you maybe recall a scary-lookin' *murderer* or *psychopath* and a helpless woman walkin' round here?!"

He huffed. "Ma'am, I'm gonna have to ask you to leave if you keep *screaming* at me."

"Don't give me an attitude, boy—"

Mary Grace grabbed her friend's arm, giving her an assuring nod. She looked at the kid and smiled. "I understand you are miserable. But it's not our problem that you drink too many energy drinks and scare away girls." She took a deep breath, keeping her voice calm. "Do you know a man named Cody Cartwright?"

The boy looked shocked by her insult. It took him a moment to even hear her question. He squinted his eyes at her. "Yeah, I know Cody. He stops by now and then. How's he involved with this?"

"He's the woman's boyfriend. Do you know when the last time he came in here was?"

He sighed again, then turned to the computer on the desk. "Hold on," he mumbled, typing with annoyance.

Lucille looked at Mary Grace, raising her eyebrow.

"Says he came in here five days ago and bought some bait. It was on Thursday—I don't work Thursdays." He lifted his eyes from the screen. "Keith Richards works then. He's working tomorrow if y'all just wanted to come back and—"

Mary Grace shook her head, "Do your cameras work here?"

"Nah, they've never worked. My boss just put them up there to scare off vandals."

"Do you know where Cody might be now?" Lucille asked, but he just stared at her as if he didn't understand, so she kept going, "You talk to him? Have his number, maybe?"

"Bro, why would I have his number? I only know him because he sells shrimp and stuff."

Lucille's left eye twitched, her cheeks turning red. "Do you know if he works for a company? Or does he just sell shrimp as a side hustle?"

"He works for a company. Who sells shrimp as a side hustle?"

Lucille clenched her fists.

"Well, darlin', do you remember what company?" Mary Grace questioned, rolling her eyes slightly. The kid's attitude was starting to get to her, too.

He thought about it, biting his bottom lip in concentration. "Um..."

They leaned forward.

"Oh—I remember. It's called the Fish 'n Shrimp Company," he mumbled and shrugged his shoulders.

"Fish 'n Shrimp Company," Lucille repeated. "Easy enough to remember."

They thanked the young man and left the office. As they stepped outside, they both scanned the area for Margaret, finding her sitting on the dock, staring thoughtfully down at the water. When they got closer, they noticed she was crying. Not crying— sobbing. Her shoulders shook violently with every breath. She didn't acknowledge her two friends when they made it to her.

Mary Grace knelt, putting her arm around Margaret and giving her a small hug.

"I miss her," Margaret cried, resting her head on Mary Grace's shoulder.

Lucille sighed. They both knew who she meant. "What memory did you have?" Lucille asked, her heart feeling as heavy as the hot humidity. It was one thing to be sad herself, but to see Margaret—the least emotional sister—crying like this, made her feel awful.

Margaret either couldn't answer or didn't want to. She instead burst into another round of tears.

"We're gonna find her, darlin'," Mary Grace stroked the back of her head.

She looked up at her friends, tears rolling down her cheeks. "What if we don't? What if something bad happened to her? What if we never find her?"

Lucille shook her head, putting her hands on her hips. "No. You can't say that, Margaret. *I* can't hear you say that. I need you to stay calm. You're the stable one, remember? If you fall, we'll all fall. Please, don't give up now. Please."

She used the back of her hand to wipe away the tears, then took a deep breath. "Didn't you always say *what is meant to be will be*? What if we're never meant to find Vivi? If we were, don't you think we would have found her by now?"

A moment of silence passed before Mary Grace spoke, "You may be right, Margaret. We might never find her. It's quite hard and damn near impossible to look for someone when you aren't lookin', is it not?" She sat straight, looking out at the lake. "You were not only the most stable out of us—but also the most sensible. Of course, it makes perfect sense we will never find her. If we aren't trying to find her—if we don't believe we'll find her—surely, we won't ever find her, right?"

"I don't understand what you mean," Margaret sniffled.

Mary Grace rose to her feet, offering her hand to Margaret. Warily, her friend took it, and together, they all stood on the dock, gazing at the swampy lake.

"You're right—we'll never find her like this. What we need to do is start *looking*. Not just waiting for what the detectives might find—but try finding her on our own." She nodded, as if making up her mind. "And that is exactly what we are gonna do. Starting now. You know as well as I do that we don't really need help from higher authority. We *know* things that those men with badges don't. I think you've forgotten, Margaret, just how strong our gifts are."

Margaret dropped her eyes to her feet. "How strong they *were*, you mean."

"No, they're still just as strong as when we were young. Even after the years of blocking them out and—" she eyed Lucille "—drowning them with alcohol, they are still there. Why do you think you keep having those past visions, huh? Your gifts are still here. Maybe a little rusty, but with practice, they'll strengthen again."

"I don't want to practice magic again, Mary Grace. I told you—"

"You do want to find Vivian, right?" Mary Grace snapped with a huff. "We need our magic, Margaret."

Lucille grabbed Margaret's hand, her blue eyes pooling with fresh tears, "We got our first clue. Vivi's boyfriend worked for a fishin' company called Fish 'n Shrimp."

"Where is it?"

"We don't know." Mary Grace raised her chin a little. "But that's what we're about to find out." She turned quickly, marching off the dock to the car. "Let's go, ladies."

CHAPTER TWENTY-FIVE

THE KEY WAS GONE. Hidden, Jane suspected. Mary Grace must have found it and locked it away during last night's hushed conversation with her aunts in the dimly lit kitchen. A perfect setting for such an opportunity.

As she searched through the living room, she came across her mother's postcard. She moved it aside and kept looking, not wanting to read those inky words again. Her mother's note scared her. According to the postcard written sixteen years ago, there were people out there trying to find Margaret, Jane, and perhaps even her father. Who were they? Or what Jane wanted to know more— *what did they want?*

Bobbie Jo stood in the doorway of the living room, watching Jane as she frantically looked around for the key.

"*Now* do you see what I'm talking about?" Jane asked, moving over to the bookcase to look there. "She wouldn't have hidden the key if she wasn't trying to hide something. They don't want me going in there because they don't want me finding out the truth about what's happening here."

Bobbie Jo raised an eyebrow. "We could always pick the lock."

Jane looked over her shoulder at Bobbie Jo. "You know how to do that?"

"I mean, who doesn't?" she giggled, her cheeks turning pink.

"*I* don't," Jane laughed with her. "Alright, let's go upstairs. I think Mary Grace probably flushed the key down the drain."

Walking out of the living room, a loud slam sounded from the back of the house. Bobbie Jo jumped a little and almost tripped over her shoelaces. Unfazed by the noise, Jane began walking toward the back of the house to see what the cause was.

"Um—what the heck was that?" Bobbie Jo asked, her words thick with twang and almost too quick to understand.

Jane looked around. Nothing looked out of place. "Not sure," she answered, then narrowed her focus on the big doors that opened to the backyard.

"Sounded like someone slammed the doors." She whipped around fast as if trying to catch someone sneaking up on them. No one was there, though, and that frightened her even more. "You think the house is haunted?"

Jane looked over at Bobbie Jo and laughed. "Haunted?"

"Don't say it like that—ten minutes ago, we were talking about *witchcraft*. If your aunts are witches, then I wouldn't be surprised if this place was haunted."

She opened the heavy doors and was instantly greeted by a hot breeze and the smell of sweet grass. Half-expecting to find someone waiting outside, she looked around but found nothing except the four gloomy concrete angels.

With caution, Bobbie Jo walked down the steps of the house. She studied the garden, searching for anyone or anything that may have caused the doors to open and shut. There had to be some sensible explanation. The doors couldn't have opened and slammed shut by themselves. She walked around the water fountain like a detective, her eyes running over everything in the garden. Finally, with a discouraged sigh, she put her hands on her hips and turned around to Jane, who was staring up at one of the statues.

"This is freaking me out," Bobbie Jo said, shaking her head.

"Welcome to my world," Jane muttered under her breath, still looking up.

"I don't understand. What made the doors slam?"

She shrugged her shoulders. "Maybe the house is haunted. Maybe there are ghosts messing with us." Though she was serious about this, Bobbie Jo said this with a laugh.

She walked over to her and looked up at the statue. "So, you said you saw these statues *move*?" Now that she was really looking at the statue, she saw just how creepy they looked. The one she was looking at had a long face with a theatrical frown that was wide open in a desperate scream.

"I haven't *seen* them move, but every time I come out here, they change in some way. Today, this one is closing its eyes. Yesterday, they were open. And Mary Grace told me they don't always look like this—whatever that means."

Because Bobbie Jo looked like she was about ready to scream, Jane decided it was best if they left the statues and went back into the house.

In the kitchen, Bobbie Jo held the glass of iced sweet tea tightly to keep her hands from shaking. Cold sweat from condensation dripped down the outside of the cup, running over her small fingers.

"So, the rumors were true," she stuttered, her eyes locked with Jane sitting across her at the kitchen table.

She shook her head, sighing to herself. "No, we can't make that assumption yet. We would sound crazy to claim such a thing." She bit her lip. "But, yes, maybe."

Bobbie Jo shifted her weight. "Alright."

"Remember, you can't—"

"I'm not gonna tell anyone," Bobbie Jo vowed as she nodded her head and then washed the words down with the sugary drink.

"We have to figure out what's really happening here."

The front door swung open, and the four women rushed into the house.

"It says the company is still in business and will be open from nine to—" Margaret stopped her sentence midway when she noticed the girls sitting in the kitchen. She put her phone in her back pocket, forcing a smile on her lips. "Oh! Hello, girls." Lucille and Mary Grace walked into the kitchen after her.

"What company?" Jane asked, squinting her eyes.

Mary Grace was pouring herself a glass of water by the sink when she answered, "A fishing company, dear."

Bobbie Jo, now slightly terrified that the women may be real witches, tried to be as quiet as she could in hopes they wouldn't notice her. But Mary Grace looked over at her before chugging down a glass of water.

"I wasn't expectin' to see you here, Bobbie Jo. Stayin' for dinner?"

She stood slowly from the table, setting her glass down carefully. "No, thanks, Mary Grace. I should be gettin' home now," she laughed nervously.

Mary Grace could feel the nerves bouncing off the Jones girl. "Don't be shy—stay for dinner."

Somehow, maybe under a spell or something, Bobbie Jo ended up staying.

"So, why are you guys looking into a fishing company?" Jane asked later that afternoon as they ate dinner. Rays of burnt orange light shot through the oak trees outside, filling the kitchen with a warm glow.

Margaret licked her lips, trying to decide if she should share the information with her daughter and Randy's daughter. She gave a quick glance at her friends for guidance, and they stared back at her just as clueless. She looked at Jane and Bobbie Jo across the table. "Vivian has a boyfriend named Cody. He—um..." She looked back at her friends.

"We found out where he works," Mary Grace finished for her. "The *Fish 'n Shrimp Company*. It's in Greenville."

Bobbie Jo straightened up, setting her fork down beside her plate. This was news.

"Have you told Mr. Jones?" Jane questioned.

Margaret nodded. "We called him on the way back."

"Back from the grocery store?" she raised an eyebrow, sarcasm written in her manner.

Bobbie Jo bit her bottom lip to keep herself from laughing.

"Okay, fine. We weren't grocery shopping." She pauses, bracing for Jane's response. "We were at the lake."

"But you said you weren't going to go there," she said, mainly hurt that they hadn't taken her with them. She was the one who suggested that they explore the lake in the first place.

"Well, we changed our minds."

"Why didn't you just tell me the truth, then? Why lie about grocery shopping?"

Margaret huffed, rolling her eyes, "Because, Jane. I don't need to tell you everything I do." The words were shot out as quick and violent as a gunfire.

Too annoyed to say anything, she went back to eating what was left on her plate. The table fell silent and stayed that way for the rest of the dinner.

After thanking Mary Grace for cooking, Bobbie Jo said her goodbyes, desperate to leave the haunted house.

Jane walked her outside. During the awkward silence of dinner, Jane had been brainstorming an idea, and the minute the two girls stepped outside, she blurted it out.

They'd go to the fishing company and try to find Vivi's boyfriend themselves. She knew her mother wouldn't help her—or even approve of this decision—so she decided she wouldn't tell her until it was all over. She'd say she was going over to Bobbie Jo's house for the day.

She thought it was time to take matters into her own hands. If her mother and aunts weren't going to be honest with Jane, she would find out what they were hiding.

Bobbie Jo sat in the driver's seat with her window down, staring up at Jane with a stunned look on her freckled face. She couldn't tell if Jane was being serious or not. After a minute had passed, Bobbie Jo shook her head. "Jane, it's all the way in Greenville." She was always up for an adventure, but that was just too far. Her parents didn't even let her go to New Orleans by herself. "That's three hours away. There's no way—"

Jane sighed, crossing her arms over her chest. "Do you want to find Vivian or not?" She caught sight of the moon rising above the tree line.

She dropped her gaze to the steering wheel. "Well... my dad is probably sending the boys out there first thing tomorrow morning."

"Then we'll get there before they do."

Bobbie Jo heaved a breath and started playing with the ends of her curls. "Look, I'm not scared or anythin', but this doesn't sound smart."

"If you don't want to come with me, then don't. I'll go by myself, I don't care." She said it with so much confidence that even she believed her own words. But the truth was, she needed Bobbie Jo to go with her. Besides not having a car, she needed someone to go with her in case anything went wrong.

She started her Bug, shaking her head to herself. "Alright, alright. I'll pick you up tomorrow mornin', six o'clock," she shouted over the chuckling engine.

Jane smiled and took a step back as she watched the old car fly down the driveway, leaving a cloud of dust behind.

CHAPTER TWENTY-SIX

JANE WAS ANXIOUS for the morning to come. She told her mother Bobbie Jo was picking her up for a girls' day. She had never told such a lie before, but to her surprise, Margaret didn't suspect anything. She said Bobbie Jo's mother was going to take them shopping. Margaret made her promise that she would be back before the sun set.

It felt sort of good. To get back at her mom for that day. A lie for a lie.

Jane awoke from her regular nightmare to the darkness of the night. She grabbed her phone off the nightstand and flinched from the bright screen.

3:00 AM, the time read. She got out of bed and stepped onto the porch. There were only three more hours left until her alarm was going to go off, but she felt too scared to fall back asleep.

It was quiet outside, peacefully quiet. She took a deep breath to settle her nerves. Goosebumps danced on her arms and legs, and her hands shook. It wasn't even close to being cold outside, though. Her shaking hands and sudden chills were caused by the recent scare from her vanishing nightmare.

What was she dreaming of? Why couldn't she remember it?

A voice spoke up from behind her, making her jump. "Good mornin', Jane. Three a.m. worries?" It was Lucille. She sat in the rocking chair by her bedroom door, smoking a freshly lit cigarette and staring wistfully out at the tunnel-like driveway.

Jane sat down in the chair next to Lucille. "No, just a nightmare."

"Ah," she sighed. "About what?"

"I don't know."

Lucille made a surprised face. "You don't know?"

"Nope. I can't remember. It's like, every night I wake up scared, but I don't know why."

"Have you told your mama about this?"

Jane shook her head, "It's not that important." She gazed up at the moon. The waning phase had begun. "What's worrying you tonight, Lucille?"

"Tonight, I'm worried about…" she thought about it. "Well, I don't know. I guess a lot of things." It was probably best if she didn't tell Jane about her worries. Jane already knew about tarot cards. If Lucille wasn't careful, she would end up telling her everything.

They sat in silence for a moment. Frogs croaked around the house as if they, too, were talking.

"Lucille, do you know where the key to Vivian's room is?" Jane asked, not thinking over the question.

Lucille took a long drag before asking back, "Why?"

"I was just wondering."

"Look—I get you're curious, but you just can't go through her stuff. You might see somethin' you ain't supposed to see." She regretted saying those words the minute they slipped out. She slipped the cigarette between her lips.

"What am I not supposed to see?"

"No—nothing," she stuttered.

"You guys are hiding something, aren't you? What is it?" She leaned forward, her green eyes locked on Lucille's.

An owl in the distance laughed at Lucille's speechlessness. Ashing her cigarette nervously, she thought of how to answer.

Every second that passed proved that Jane's assumptions were correct. They were all hiding something from her.

Out of irritation, she gave up waiting for Lucille's answer. She pushed herself up from the rocking chair and, without looking back or saying goodnight, returned to her room. She fell on her bed and closed her eyes.

She would find out what they were hiding from her soon enough. Their secrets would be exposed, and she would know the truth. About them. About Vivian. About herself.

It felt like only a few moments passed before golden sunlight fluttered in from the sheer curtains.

Heavily sleep-deprived, Jane got ready for the long day ahead, changing into a pair of jean shorts and a white tank. She pulled her hair back with a clip and then slid on her white sneakers, hurrying downstairs.

The house was still quiet. She rushed into the kitchen, eyeing the bowl of fresh apples on the counter beside the sink. She didn't even notice Mary Grace at the table until she spoke.

"Good mornin', Jane," she said, lifting her eyes from the daily newspaper in front of her. She took a sip of coffee, setting down the mug carefully. "Where are you off to this early?"

Jane froze, the apple inches away from her mouth. "Bobbie Jo is picking me up. We're going shopping."

She narrowed her gray eyes on her. She could see there was something off with the girl this morning. She looked almost nervous. Before she could figure out why, the noisy engine of Bobbie Jo's old car signaled outside.

Jane bit into the apple, racing for the front door. "Will you tell my mom I said bye?"

Before Mary Grace could answer, Jane was out of the house. The heavy door closed with quite a loud slam, making the woman jump a little and spill a splash of her coffee on the newspaper.

Something was up. Mary Grace didn't want to intrude on whatever Jane was doing, but the girl's strange and quick behavior made her nervous. She wasn't going to Bobbie Jo's house, *that* she was sure of. She had a plan, and Mary Grace wanted to know what it was, but also wanted to leave the girl's mind alone. She let it go for the moment and finished her coffee.

"The seafood market had another location in New Orleans, but it closed down last year," said Bobbie Jo as they left the plantation. Just like Jane, Bobbie Jo was too nervous to fall asleep last night and, instead, stayed up doing research. "There was no specific reason it closed. My guess is the rent was too high. Greenville is a cheap area, which is probably why the owner kept that location and shut the other one down."

Jane checked her phone and sighed in relief when she saw she had no messages from her mother. She was worried that her mother would figure out what she was really doing.

"Who's the owner?" Jane asked, rolling down her window. A gust of warm air stormed through the open hole.

Bobbie Jo rolled her window down too, holding her arm out. It was still early enough that the breeze felt somewhat cool. "Some man named Colter. I couldn't find a last name—or anythin' else about him. It's a small business, though, so we might be able to talk to him. On his *very outdated* website, it said there were three fishermen, including Colter."

Jane repeated the name in her head so she wouldn't forget. "Who's the third fisherman?"

"Don't know." Her stomach was in a knot, and she felt like she was going to throw up. "My parents are gonna kill me if they find out what I'm doin'," she muttered.

Jane knew her parents would be just as upset. This was the first time she had ever done something like this. It was crazy, really. Immature and reckless. Two teenage girls driving three hours away to speak with a man who could have potentially kidnapped or even *murdered* someone. And if anything went wrong, it would be all Jane's fault.

They drove by an old sign on the side of the road that read, *Thanks for Visiting Belles Parish, Come Back Soon!* in a chunky cursive font.

"Do you like living in a small town?" Jane asked after five minutes of silence.

Bobbie Jo looked in her rearview mirror, wondering if she could still see Belles Parish's welcome sign. It was a strange feeling—to leave her hometown. It was like a weight being lifted off her shoulders. The feeling made her sigh with relief and, at the same time, left her feeling empty. Like something was missing.

"I guess I hadn't really thought about it before," she finally answered, bringing her focus back to the swampy backroad. "I think I would like it more if my dad wasn't the Sheriff. Everyone avoids me. They all think I'm gonna snitch on them." Then she laughed a light cackle, as if remembering something. "One time, when I was gettin' out of school, I saw this dumb football player— he's like the team's favorite, *and* he used to date Charlotte, so that should explain *everythin'*—he and a few of his buddies were smokin' marijuana under the bleachers. Idiots, right? Anyone *dumb* enough to smoke on school grounds, thinkin' they wouldn't get caught, are plain fools. So, anyway, I just minded my own and kept walking, but this idiot thought I cared enough to tell my dad, so he ran up to me and *begged* me not to tell. I said I wouldn't, but that idiot didn't believe me!"

Jane giggled, "What happened?"

"That week, he followed me around, pretendin' to be interested in me. He left flowers at my locker, notes on my desk—it was *embarrassin'*. And he did all this just so I wouldn't tell, and he wouldn't be kicked off the team. Why would I even tell my dad that? Even if I did, my dad has other things to worry about."

"When did he stop?"

"Ha! The minute my boyfriend found out another boy was buyin' me flowers."

They both shared a laugh, and then Bobbie Jo let out a sigh. "I miss him—my boyfriend. He went up North with his family for the summer. His parents are what you can call *snowbirds*. But anyway," she paused, looking over at Jane. "Do you like it here?"

"Yeah, I do."

Bobbie Jo fanned her face with her hand, rolling her eyes dramatically. "Wait until August. If you still like this place after bein' in the heat of August, then I'll believe you."

She laughed, then wondered if she would be able to come back in August. It made her sad to think of leaving Belles Parish and going back to the crowded city.

Bobbie Jo turned on the radio, hitting play on the tape. Lynyrd Skynyrd began to play softly under the loud rumble of the engine. She turned up the volume, a wide smile painting her freckled face. It was moments like these that fueled Bobbie Jo's heart. Driving down backroads through the swamp with the windows rolled down and listening to music. For a split second, her worry faded and was replaced by a blissful feeling of adventure.

Jane smiled, too, sitting back in her seat, ready for the long drive ahead.

They drove in the deep swamps of Louisiana through small zones of poverty and scattered trailers and shacks on the brink of abandonment. The towns on this side of the swamp felt forgotten.

After an hour straight of driving down the deserted two-lane back road, they passed by a small gas station that didn't look to be in use. Rusty antique vehicles were left in front of the store, and tall weeds that nearly towered over cars had forced their way through cracks in the concrete parking lot, long since neglected. Crushed cans and cigarette butts were scattered throughout the premises.

A girl, maybe six or seven years old, dressed in a torn, mud-stained princess costume, was crouched barefoot on top of a picnic table near the side of the building, staring out at the street like a feral animal.

"You gotta wonder where her parents are," Bobbie Jo said as they passed the gas station. "If she has any."

That was the last thing they saw for miles. As Jane stared through the windshield, a layer of drowsiness came over her, and after some time passed, she fell into a heavy sleep, letting her nightmare return once again.

)———◇◇◇———(

The smell of blueberry muffins and scrambled eggs filled the plantation house. When Margaret walked into the kitchen, she scanned the room quickly and frowned, then turned to Mary Grace. Her friend was standing in front of the stove.

"Jane left already?" Margaret questioned, crossing her arms over her chest. Without saying goodbye? That wasn't like her.

"Yep. She told me to tell you that she said goodbye."

Lucille came in shortly after Margaret, looking around with a puzzled face. "Where's Jane?"

"She left," Mary Grace answered without hesitation. They all felt something was off, but no one wanted to admit it yet.

Lucille sat down at the table and chewed the inside of her cheek. "Margaret, I think," she looked over at Mary Grace and then back at Margaret.

Margaret was leaning against the counter beside Mary Grace. She lifted her chin. "What is it, Lucille?"

Lucille pressed her lips together for a moment as she thought over her words carefully. "I think it's time you tell Jane the truth. She already knows—"

"Knows what?" Margaret snapped.

Mary Grace looked at Margaret. "She knows we're hiding something."

"And what if Vivi is really trying to talk to Jane? What then?" Lucille asked, her blue eyes widening. "She told me she's having nightmares, Margaret."

"What nightmares?"

"She said she doesn't remember them. She's going to figure out what we are."

Margaret sighed a deep breath. "*What* we are?"

"You know what she means," Mary Grace said as she pulled out the tray of muffins and placed them on the stove beside the pan of eggs. "We're not normal. And neither is she."

"Jane, wake up—we're here."

Jane's eyes flicked open, and she gasped for air like she had forgotten to breathe. Her hands were gripping the seat belt strap across her chest, and her heart pounded in her ears.

The little car hit a pothole in the middle of the road, practically launching into the air.

Bobbie Jo laughed and then looked over at Jane. "Oh, finally, you're awake. We made it to Greenville."

She breathed slowly, trying to calm her nerves.

"You okay?" Bobbie Jo asked when she noticed the scared look on Jane's face.

Jane swallowed, finding her voice. "Yeah. I just had a nightmare."

"'Bout what?"

Jane looked out of the window. The so-called 'town' was more of an organized mess of wrecked cars, weathered houses, and vandalized buildings.

"I don't know. I can't remember," she mumbled, irritated at herself for not remembering again. She could feel the nightmare was so close, the aftermath of it a dense swarm in the pit of her stomach. Pure terror boiled in her veins.

Bobbie Jo raised an eyebrow as if she didn't believe her, but she let it go. "You know, you talk a lot in your sleep. It was creepy."

Jane straightened in her seat, releasing her grip on the strap across her chest. Her eyes were wide with keen curiosity. "What was I saying?"

She lifted her eyes from the road ahead of her and met Jane's intense stare. "You said somethin' 'bout *dreams 'n visions will show the way*—or *show* you *the way*. You just kept whispering that over and over—"

"I said dreams and visions will show you the way?" She gasped. The words felt familiar to her ears. She had heard these words before. Many times before. Goosebumps rose on her arms as she processed the eight words.

What if the nightmare she had every night was more than just a dream?

What if it was a message?

She answered with a confident nod of her head as they passed by a confused homeless man pushing an empty shopping cart on the overgrown sidewalk. "When we get to the boat ramp, let's stick together."

"This place looks like a ghost town," commented Jane, gazing out of the window.

"Wasn't always like this. The whole town lost everything after Hurricane Katrina hit. A lot of people lost their homes—their jobs— it was pretty bad." She turned down a dead-end, a clearing for the Mississippi River visible at the end of the street.

A feeling fired up inside of Jane—maybe of excitement or worry, she wasn't sure quite yet.

"Whoa," gasped Bobbie Jo, and as Jane was about to ask what she saw, she pointed to the sky ahead of them.

A murmuration of birds swarmed in wild, intricate ways that looked like an illusion. They flew together and formed a solid, black blanket that stretched across the sky, rippling and twisting before finally breaking apart. The birds scattered like sparks of a firework.

"Here we are," she said as she turned the wheel, entering a small gravel parking lot.

Fish 'n Shrimp was a shack-like building on the side of the river with a boat ramp beside it. Two ragged boats were stationed by the dock. An old bungalow house sat tucked away behind the shack, along with a white truck that was parked next to the house. Jane guessed the house belonged to the owner of the fishing company, judging by the crab traps and buckets piled in the truck's bed.

"This looks sketchy," Jane said as Bobbie Jo pulled into a parking space by the front door.

When Bobbie Jo cut off the engine, they sat in the car for two solid minutes, soaking in the silence and trepidation.

"I can't believe we're doin' this," Bobbie Jo commented, staring at the shack before them. She pulled out a small vanilla folder from the backseat, opening it in her lap. "I printed these before I left. Figured we could leave a few." Inside the folder was a thin stack of missing person posters of Vivian Banks. The woman looked so happy in the picture, so gentle and sweet. Bobbie Jo couldn't imagine anyone hurting her, and it made her heart heavy remembering that she was gone.

Jane nodded, then closed her eyes, taking a deep breath before she opened the door and stepped into the all-too-familiar humid air.

Bobbie Jo sucked in a sharp breath. "What're you doin'?" she hissed in a whisper. But it was too late for doubts. Too late to turn back. Bobbie Jo grabbed a poster and jumped out of the car, standing frozen like a deer in the headlights. It took a second to pull herself together.

The idea of finding Vivian's boyfriend *sounded* like a good idea—but now that they were miles away from Belles Parish at a secluded shack in the middle of nowhere with a potential criminal somewhere nearby, it was hard not to have second thoughts.

The phone in Jane's back pocket began to vibrate. She pulled it out, looking down at her mother's contact photo. She turned it off, slipping it away, and returned her gaze to the shack. "Come on, let's go."

CHAPTER TWENTY-SEVEN

MARGARET LOWERED THE phone from her ear, cursing under her breath.

"You're probably overthinkin'," Lucille chuckled nervously, watching her worried friend pace around the living room.

Mary Grace was sitting next to Lucille on the couch, pretending she wasn't also worried. She knew from the beginning that Jane was up to something but mustered the strength to trust the girl—hoping that whatever she was doing, she'd be smart doing it.

Margaret heaved a sigh. "No, I'm not. Something isn't right. She always answers my calls."

"She's seventeen," Lucille smirked. "Having some girl time isn't gonna kill her. Remember what you were doin' at seventeen?"

"Jumpin' off railroad bridges and runnin' from the cops," Mary Grace answered, forcing out a little laugh.

"And *you*," Margaret pointed her finger at Mary Grace, a fiery look glowing in her gray eyes. "You've been acting awfully strange since Jane left. You know something, don't you?"

Although hesitating, Mary Grace nodded.

"Oh, you *do*. I knew it. What is Jane really doing?"

Mary Grace rolled her eyes. "She's with Bobbie Jo!"

"I didn't ask who she is with. I asked what she is doing."

Lucille looked at Mary Grace, then back at Margaret. She, too, could see that Mary Grace was keeping something from them.

"I don't know—and I'm not gonna intrude her mind. She is spendin' time with Bobbie Jo. At her house."

The old clock on the back wall seemed to tick louder as the silence crept in.

"So," Margaret pressed her lips together in a firm line, narrowing her eyes. "What you're telling me is, if you call Mellissa right now, she'll tell you that Jane and Bobbie Jo are at the house?"

Mary Grace hesitated.

"Where is she?" Margaret asked her, her voice rising. A mother's intuition was never wrong. She threw up her hands. "Where is my daughter?!"

When Jane pushed open the creaky door to the seafood market, an instant aroma of dead fish and salty sweat greeted the girls.

Like the avid true crime fanatic Bobbie Jo was, the curly-haired girl immediately took in her surroundings, scanning the room for exits, hiding places, and possible traps.

The river shack was exactly how the girls expected it to be. There were a few large coolers filled with various frozen fish and shellfish and a wooden counter against the back wall with knives and tools.

To their immediate right was the register. Packs of cigarettes, lighters, and a stack of maps were displayed. Behind the quite dusty counter was a man deep in a fishing magazine. He was sitting back in an armless computer chair, his dirty cowboy boots resting on the countertop. They couldn't see his face from the way he held the magazine up. At that moment, they thought it was Cody.

Jane thought of what to say, but Bobbie Jo spoke first.

"Excuse me."

The man lowered the magazine, squinting his eyes at the girls.

It wasn't Cody.

He had a narrow face, long with high cheekbones, and crow's feet by his hollow, green eyes. His skin was tan and worn by the many years underneath the ruthless sun. But what stuck out the most to the girls was the deep scar that stretched down the left side of his face. He was nearing forty but looked older from life's pains and hard work.

"Can I help you ladies with somethin'?" When he talked, his voice was scratchy and coated with a thick southern inflection. He looked at Bobbie Jo and then at Jane, his face lighting up with sudden bewilderment.

Jane stared back at him. "We're looking for Cody Cartwright. Is he here?"

His mossy-jade eyes grew wide. "Cody? Yeah—yeah, he's out back. 'Bout to take the boat out to pick up our crab pots."

"You Colter?" Bobbie Jo asked, studying the man's face. He was strange. Very spacey and confused, as though mentally preoccupied with a conversation with someone else.

He shifted his gaze from Jane to Bobbie Jo. "Yes, ma'am."

She nodded her head. "It's nice to meet ya. You got a nice business here, sir." She set down one of the flyers, sort of smacking the paper on the counter. "Have you seen this woman 'round here? She's our aunt."

The man gazed down at the paper, an unreadable emotion washing over his face. His mouth was open, but no words came out. He looked like he recognized Vivian, and for a moment, Bobbie Jo and Jane thought he was going to be a lead—but he swallowed and blinked, shaking his head. "No, sorry. Haven't seen her," he answered, looking back up at the girls. "I'll tape this to the door for y'all. Who should I call if one of my customers know anything?"

"Belles Parish Sheriff's Office," Bobbie Jo answered.

"Alright, will do," he looked at Jane again, raising his eyebrows. "You said you're lookin' for Cody? You best go now. He's leavin' soon."

Jane took a step back. "Thanks," she said, nudging Bobbie Jo's arm as a signal for them to leave.

They raced out of the shack, heading for the dock.

"He was *weird*, wasn't he?" Bobbie Jo asked under her breath.

They turned the corner, stepping on the dock. "Yeah, he was—" She stopped midsentence when she spotted a man working in a center console boat about two yards down the dock.

The boat was tied to the cast iron cleats on the wooden pilings, swaying back and forth with the water. The man kneeled over the open engine in the back, prying and working on it with a wrench. He was dressed in a stained white T-shirt, worn jean shorts, and a pair of once-white sneakers stained from the muddy waters of the river. A red baseball hat covered his umber-brown hair except for a few determined locks that stuck out on the sides.

'There he is,' Bobbie Jo thought, letting out a small gasp between her lips.

Jane could hardly breathe herself.

He was right there in front of them—Cody Cartwright. Vivian's secret boyfriend. A possible killer.

A million things ran through Bobbie Jo's head during that moment. She started to have realistic worries, like how they were going to protect themselves and what they would do if he tried kidnapping them.

But Jane could see the man was harmless from the minute she looked at him in the eyes. Maybe it was the way he appeared or the way he whistled with the seagulls as he worked. Whatever it was, she could tell he hadn't hurt Vivi. But this guess alone wouldn't be enough assurance.

"Cody Jameson Cartwright?" Bobbie Jo called out, catching the man's attention instantly.

He snapped his head up, narrowing his gaze at the girls on the dock, the sunlight in his eyes.

"Yeah?" He scratched his prickly beard with his free hand.

"We have a few questions about Vivian," said Jane quickly, ripping off the band-aid.

He set down the wrench and stood up, scrunching his dark eyebrows together. "Who are y'all?" he asked, wiping his hands on his shirt.

"I'm Bobbie Jo." She leaned over the dock to shake his hand.

He cautiously accepted the gesture and then looked over at Jane.

"My name is Jane." Unlike Bobbie Jo, she didn't reach over to shake his hand, not trusting her balance enough.

"So, how do y'all know Vivian exactly?" he asked, taking off his hat and running his hand through his sweaty hair.

"That's not important right now," Bobbie Jo answered first, her voice dripping in sudden confidence. Jane could hear her inner policeman fire up. "Let's talk about Vivian first. When was the last time you spoke to her?"

He put his hat back on and knelt over the engine. Any friendliness he had vanished in an instant as he began working again. He grabbed a small tin can of chewing tobacco from his back pocket, putting a pinch-full of the stuff in the side of his mouth. "She put you up to this?" he asked in irritation as he fiddled with the machine.

The girls stood still on the dock, watching him.

"What do you mean?" Jane questioned.

He shook his head, turning the wrench. He bit his bottom lip and grunted as he worked on whatever he was working on.

"What do you mean?" she tried again, her voice louder this time.

He stopped, looking up at the girls. "Listen, ladies, I don't have time for this. I'm working. So, you can tell Vivian that I'm not ready to go back and that if she wants to talk to me, she can come here herself."

"You don't know what happened to her, do you?" Bobbie Jo interrupted, taking a step forward.

Her question took him by surprise. He put down the wrench on the floor of the boat, then stood back up, directing his full attention to the girls now when he saw they were both serious.

"She's missing," Jane told him, crossing her arms over her chest.

His reaction was enough for Bobbie Jo to realize this man was innocent, too. His brown eyes were wide with a sort of confusion and disbelief. His lips parted slightly as he sucked back a breath.

"What?" He looked like someone had told him the world was going to end.

Jane sighed, dropping her eyes to the wood boards. "When was the last you spoke to her?"

He took his hat off again, this time balling it up in his fists. The vein on his left temple surfaced, and he locked his jaw, spitting out the words, "Is this a joke?"

Bobbie Jo growled. Instead of running back to the car, she whipped out her phone and held the screen up to Cody.

It was a picture of Vivian Banks—beautiful Vivi with her dark hair and shadowed eyes. Above her head were the big, red words *MISSING PERSON*.

He stared at the picture, more shock hitting him.

"Look it up yourself if you still don't believe us. *Missing persons in Louisiana*. I bet she's one of the first ones up there," Bobbie Jo muttered, putting her phone down. "My dad is the Sheriff of Belles Parish—this ain't a joke. Vivian is like family to me."

He swiped his tongue over his bottom lip, thinking. "This is all my fault. I need to find her. Now." He started to climb out of the boat, but Bobbie Jo took a step in front of him, blocking his way.

"No, not yet."

He looked up at her, shocked. "What—"

"Look, the cops are gonna come after you. Like—soon. They think you might be involved. I know the inside scoop. Right now, they don't know what happened to Vivi. All they know is that her *mysterious boyfriend* went missin' the same time she disappeared," Bobbie Jo told him.

"Well, thank you—but I'll just tell them I didn't do anything."

"You think they're gonna believe you? With your record?"

He raised an eyebrow.

"Three robberies before the age of eighteen, a couple bar fights, and a DUI?" she reported, rolling her eyes. "You're all they got right now. You're the answer to the problem. Hell—they might just throw you behind bars to keep the town at bay. No one wants crime in our town, trust me. And they'll do anythin' to sweep it under the rug."

He shook his head, his brown eyes growing wide. "She doesn't even live there, though. I don't understand—"

She went on, "Do you know the penalty for first-degree murder? *Prison for life* or *punishable by death*. The cops ain't gonna let a *class two felon* like yourself just get away. No. They're gonna catch you. And like I said—they'll do anythin' to keep the townspeople at bay."

"Whoa, whoa, whoa," he held up his hands. "I am not a criminal!"

"True, but they don't care 'bout that. I know what's going on in the office. My dad's the Sheriff, for cryin' out loud! And they just want to solve this case quickly."

Jane knew scaring him wasn't the best option, but what else could they do to get him to talk?

He shook his head again. "I don't believe this. What happened to Vivian?"

"We're hopin' you could tell us that," Bobbie Jo tucked her hands in her back pockets, looking around. "We don't have much time. Can you tell us about the last time you spoke to Vivi?"

He swallowed, still processing everything she just said.

Jane hesitated, "We're going to find Vivian and prove that you're innocent—but you need to trust us."

Running the back of his hand across his brow, he sighed, "How am I supposed to trust two kids?"

Bobbie Jo's cheeks turned red, and she sucked her teeth. "Okay. I can run back to Belles Parish right now and tell them I found the *murderer* of Vivian Frances Banks if that's how it's gonna be."

He thought about it, "No, no. I'll answer your questions. But after, I'm leavin' to find her, okay?" He loved her. Even now, regardless of what he might have done or said before she went missing, they could see that he truly loved her.

"The last time I spoke to her was about a week ago. We got into an argument. She kicked me out of the apartment, and I've been staying at my boss's house since then," he said, almost like he was in pain. Like the words burned his throat. He fidgeted with his hat in his hands.

The girls exchanged a look.

"What was the argument about?" Jane pressed.

He scratched his chin again and put his hat back on. "I don't even know what it was about anymore. I told her I wanted us to move—and she didn't like that. I went to a bar and woke up the next morning on a bench a few blocks away. When I walked back to our house, she had thrown all my stuff out on the street. She wouldn't answer the door. Or her phone. So, I got pissed and left New Orleans." He looked down at his feet.

"What if she didn't answer the door because she wasn't there? What if that was the night she went missing?" Jane thought out loud, looking over at Bobbie Jo.

Bobbie Jo nodded, turning back to Cody. "How long have you dated Vivi?"

"About a year now. I've been living with her for the past six months. The company closed in New Orleans and moved here, and my boss offered to co-sign with me on the ownership, but she didn't want to leave New Orleans. After she kicked me out, I drove my boat up the river, and I've been here since."

A seagull perched on top of the boat cried out.

"Was she actin' at all different leading up to y'all's argument?" Bobbie Jo wiped the beads of sweat from her eyes. A soft wind blew through the dock, relieving them for a minute from the sun's burning heat.

"No, not at all. She was pretty happy. When I first met her, she suffered from some bad depression. Vivian is just a sensitive person. Things affect her differently than they do to others. When we started dating, she got better. Happier. She kept me out of trouble, and I kept her out of the dark."

A boat drove by, sending wake to the dock. The boat rocked, but Cody was unfazed. His brown eyes looked out at the water in contemplation.

"If anyone hurt her," he muttered, still looking out. "I *will* become a murderer."

"Tell us more about Vivi," Jane started, bringing his focus back. "Did she have any friends in New Orleans? Any coworkers you remember? Strange neighbors?"

"No. She was an introvert. She hated people."

"Did she tell you anything about her past? Maybe something that's stuck out?"

He shook his head. "No. She told me where she grew up and shared a few memories she has with her old friends—but nothing strange or anything."

'Which means she never told him anything about being a witch,' Jane noted. She would assume Vivian would have told her

boyfriend this, the man she trusted enough to live with. Maybe the rumors of witchcraft were just rumors, after all?

"How about the *morning* before your argument? Remember what happened?"

"We got breakfast at a local café and talked about our plans for the weekend. Nothing else happened. I went to work, and she went to work. That's all."

"What were y'alls' plans?" Bobbie Jo asked. Her phone started ringing, making her jump a little. She turned it off.

He sighed out of irritation. Every second that passed was another second Vivian was still missing. "We were gonna take my boat out on the river and eat lunch like we did every Sunday."

"Where does she work?" asked Jane.

"She works at a plant nursery on Decatur Street."

A blare of urgent sirens in the distance pierced the air, sending a horrifying sensation running through the two girls.

Cody's eyes lit up with shock as the noise came closer. "What's that?" he shouted, more to himself than to the girls.

But Jane answered anyway, "They're here." She had hoped they wouldn't get caught, but she wasn't the least bit surprised.

"You set me up?" Cody asked in a sort of yell, his gaze locked with Jane.

She shook her head, stuttering, "No—no. You need to get out of here. *Now*. Go up the river and hide!"

"The hell I will!" he huffed, his face turning red. "I ain't runnin' from the cops when I didn't do anythin' wrong."

Bobbie Jo rolled her eyes. "Fine. You wanna spend the next few days in the Belles Parish Sheriff's Office in questioning?"

He clenched his jaw. The screaming siren was closer now, flying down the street toward them. "If that's what I have to do to get my Vivi back." He said it with so much determination—like no one would be able to change his mind.

The sirens were in the parking lot now, and they could see Randy Jones's cream-colored Blazer followed by a single cop car.

The vehicles slammed to a stop, dust clouding around them.

A cop and the detective got out of the car, holding a gun before them. Randy jumped out of his truck, his face in a panic.

"CODY CARTWRIGHT, GET OUT OF THE BOAT NOW," Randy shouted, his voice echoing across the river, disrupting a flock of birds nearby. He stomped towards the dock, his face red with anger. The accessories on his belt jingled and clinked as he walked.

He pulled out his gun, switching the safety off and pulling down the hammer with a click.

Cody wiped his hands down his shirt and straightened his hat before hopping out of the boat and standing beside the girls. He held his hands up, knowing there was nothing he could do now.

"If you get any closer to those girls, I will shoot!"

Cody didn't move an inch.

The girls looked at each other.

"Girls, get in the truck!" Randy shouted, not lifting his eyes from Cody. A bead of sweat rolled down the side of his face and dropped on his shoulder.

Bobbie Jo took a step closer to Cody. "Daddy, you don't have to arrest him. We know he's innocent—"

His face turned even more red. "Bobbie Jo, step away from him and GET IN THE TRUCK." He didn't have to repeat himself again. The girls hurried over to him.

"Now," Randy said to Cody, "turn around 'n put your hands on the back of your head!"

The detective and the cop ran to the girls, asking if they were hurt.

Cody sighed, turning around slowly.

"We're fine—he's innocent, Detective Dubois," Bobbie Jo told the detective, her eyes filled with sheer worry. Her body shook with adrenaline.

He ignored the girls and looked over his shoulder at the cop. "Check the shack for anyone else."

The cop nodded once and ran off.

Randy marched over to Cody, pulling out the handcuffs from off his belt. "Cody Cartwright, you are being arrested for—"

"For what?" he laughed out without humor. "I was mindin' my business before those girls came and told me about Vivian."

Randy didn't respond. He grabbed Cody's hand and locked the handcuff on tight. "You have the right to remain silent. Anything you say can and will be used against you in a court of law—"

"Goddammit, I didn't do anything!" he shouted as the other handcuff was locked on.

Randy continued, using the Miranda Rights to calm his temper and not beat the fisherman up right then and there until he confessed what happened to Vivian Banks. "If you cannot afford an attorney, one will be provided for you." He yanked Cody toward the vehicles. "Do you understand each of these rights I have explained to you?" he barked.

"Really?" he huffed as Randy slammed Cody face-first on the side of the passenger door.

The cop ran out of the shack. "No one is here," he said to the Sheriff and the detective.

The girls looked at each other, both thinking the same thing.

Colter was gone.

He ran from the cops.

Why?

The officer opened the back door for Randy, and Randy shoved the fisherman in with force.

"I didn't do anything!" Cody repeated as he fell back onto the seat.

Before closing the door, Randy narrowed his eyes on Cody and mumbled, "That's what they all say."

Randy turned to Detective Dubois and the cop, out of breath. "Take him back to the office. I'll meet you there after I take the girls home."

CHAPTER TWENTY-EIGHT

"THEY'RE WITH ME NOW. Safe and sound," Randy told Margaret on the phone. He was racing through Greenville, his police lights on.

He was mad. And disappointed. He expected his daughter would know better. But they found Cody Cartwright, and now he didn't know if he should yell at Bobbie Jo for doing such a stupid thing or feel proud that she had found him on her own.

"Yeah, we got him." There was a pause. "No, no one else was there." Another pause. "Alright, I'll see you in a few. Bye." He dropped his phone on the dashboard, and then looked over at the girls.

He cleared his throat. "Now," he began, narrowing his eyes at Bobbie Jo, who sat awkwardly between her father and Jane. "What in the *world* were you thinkin'?!"

Jane bounced her knee up and down, trying to think of the right thing to say. "It was my idea, sir—"

He rolled his eyes, "Save it for your mother. I wanna know why *my* daughter was stupid enough to drive three hours away from home to talk to a suspect—*without tellin' me first.*"

All Bobbie Jo could say was, "What—what about my car?" The car was the least of her worries, but she was too stunned to answer him. They talked to Cody, and the owner left when the cops came. Colter was hiding something.

Jane knew this, too. She couldn't stop chewing the inside of her cheek.

"*Your* car? As long as I'm payin' the bills, that's *my car.* You're suspended from drivin'. I'll have it towed back, but you can forget about it for now."

"For how long?!"

"For as long as I want!"

Tears filled the corners of her eyes, and her chin began to quiver.

Jane finally realized just how bad this entire idea of hers really was.

"We'll talk 'bout this at home with your mother. You worried her sick! Why would you do such a thing?"

Bobbie Jo didn't say anything—couldn't say anything. Her emotions had got the best of her. She didn't want to cry in front of Jane, but she couldn't help the few tears that slipped out of the sides of her eyes, silently rolling down her face.

Jane could only imagine how furious her own mother was right now. Just waiting in anger for her to arrive, her fury growing with every second that passed.

But even though the girls were in trouble now—they both knew it was worth it. It had to be done.

Trying not to think about what waited for her at the plantation, Jane thought of the facts she had gathered today.

She talks in her sleep. Vivian Banks suffered from depression, worked at a nursery, and had lunch on the river every Sunday with Cody. Cody, the mysterious fisherman who had been a possible suspect, was madly in love with the woman. And the other fisherman, Colter, wasn't there when the cops arrived.

The drive back was quicker than the drive there. Randy slammed on the brakes when he pulled up to the plantation.

Jane opened the door and jumped out, relieved to be out of the tight space. She felt like she could finally breathe again. "I'm sorry again. I didn't mean to cause—"

The man huffed and shook his head. "It's alright, Jane. But you gotta understand, you're still a kid. I've hired grown adults to find Vivian. It's not your responsibility to investigate this case."

"But—"

"I know you're concerned about Vivian. But don't worry about it, okay? I'm gonna find her."

"We were only trying to help," Jane uttered, dropping her eyes to her shoes.

He tapped his thumb against the top of the steering wheel. "And I understand that—but again, it's not your place."

She held her tongue.

"Promise me, Jane, you're gonna leave the investigating to me and my detective," he had said before leaving.

She met his gaze again, lifting her chin slightly as she responded with a sigh, "I wish I could, but I can't make that promise, sir." She looked over at Bobbie Jo and frowned. "I'm sorry."

Bobbie Jo gave her a nod, signifying it was okay.

She shut the door and turned to the big house, readying herself to face her mother with a deep breath.

As she walked inside, she noticed how the temperature was off. The air was colder, as if they had turned up the A/C to full blast. The extreme heat from outside and the cold air between the walls produced a condensation that she could feel on her upper lip. It was like the house had cold sweats.

The minute she closed the heavy door shut, her mother's voice called out her name from the living room.

"Jane? Jane?" Almost in an instant, her mother came flying towards the door, her face ghostly pale and her eyes filled with relieved tears that streamed down her cheekbones. She crashed into her daughter, giving her the biggest hug she had ever given her. She held her in her arms for a long time, just softly crying on her shoulder.

"Mom?" She tried freeing herself from Margaret's strong grip, barely being able to breathe.

Her mother let her go, her face dropping into a serious frown. "What were you thinking?!" she yelled, throwing her arms up. "You could have gotten yourself killed!"

Jane was ready to bear the strict criticism she was sure her mother had.

"Why would you do that?!"

She looked into her mother's panicked eyes, realizing how senseless this was. If her mother had done what she had done, she would have told Jane it was none of her business.

She found Cody Cartwright—shouldn't her mother be excited?

Instead of answering, she walked into the kitchen.

"Excuse me?" Margaret growled, chasing after her. "Are you even listening to me? I can't believe you thought it was a good idea to drive *hours* away—" she put her hands on her sharp hips. "—to find a man you've never met! I thought *my* daughter would surely be smart enough to know better."

Jane filled a glass of water and turned around to face her mother as she drank. She just realized then that her aunts weren't there. "How did you figure out what I was doing?" she asked, lowering the glass.

Margaret could feel a headache start to come on. She closed her eyes tightly, then opened them, focusing back on her daughter. "That is not relevant right now. I want to know why you chose to—"

Jane set the glass down on the counter with an unintentional force. "Since when do *you* care about what I do?" she asked back, her voice raising in pitch. She had tried to remain calm, but her irritation was growing stronger. The argument was quickly turning in a different direction. "You *never* care about what I do."

The pain in her temples increased with her daughter's tone. She shook her head slightly, ignoring the headache. She couldn't allow it to distract her. "That is not true. Just because I have to work, doesn't mean I don't care about you."

"Really, Mom?" She rolled her eyes. "You are *always* working—which is ironic, really, since you own the company and hired people to work for you."

She shut her eyes again, breathing.

An anger inside of her grew, an old anger that she's kept contained most of her childhood. "You know what I think? I think you built a wall around yourself that you can freely hide behind. You call it *working*, I think it's hiding. You hide behind Gardener Builds so that you don't have to face *yourself*." She frowned, holding back tears. "And now you want to criticize *me* because *you* can't trust *me*. But you can't trust *anyone*. You'll never be happy because you can't even trust *yourself*."

Like fingernails on a chalkboard, a screeching sort of pain burst in the back of Margaret's head. The room was spinning. Her knees started to shake.

Jane stopped talking, noticing the change in her mother's face.

Margaret's legs collapsed underneath her, sending her crashing to the floor.

"Mom?!" Jane cried out, immediately dropping beside her.

Mary Grace and Lucille came running into the kitchen like bulls in a China shop. No doubt they both were eavesdropping on the other side of the wall the whole time.

"It's happening again!" Lucille gasped in terror.

Jane shook her mother, then looked up at Lucille, her eyebrows pushed together. "What's happening?"

Not a word was spoken between the father and daughter on the ride home. The silence made the ride worse, though. Bobbie Jo would much rather hear his disapproval in words than to hear it in his silence. When the truck pulled into the driveway, the Sheriff turned his head to his daughter, who sat silently with a guilty look in her eyes. He tried not to feel upset. He knew he would do the same thing if he was in her place. They were so much alike, and that's what frustrated him the most.

What he said next surprised Bobbie Jo. She wasn't sure if she heard him correctly at first. "You're still grounded—but good job today. That was real brave of you."

She turned her head to her left, her eyes suddenly pooling with tears again. "Thank you."

He nodded his head, his eyes locked on the road ahead of them. "I'm proud of you, kid—but don't let your mama know I said that."

She smiled a little.

"I want you to stop worryin' about this case. I don't care if you hang out with Jane, but leave the case alone, you hear me?"

She looked away, out the window at the Spanish moss hanging heavy on trees lining the road and didn't say anything else.

"Okay," she said, only because she knew she had to say something.

"Don't leave the house. Your mama will be home soon. Stay put," he told her before driving to the office.

The detective and officer had just pulled up to the office when Randy's Blazar came flying in. Speed limits didn't matter to the Sheriff, and no cop in Belles Parish would dare pull him over.

When Detective Dubois got out of the police car, he looked at Randy, who was already marching towards them. The officer stepped aside, getting out of the Sheriff's way.

"Feels good we're finally getting somewhere with this case, doesn't it?" the detective asked as Randy opened the backdoor of the police car, revealing the sad fisherman.

Cody stared down at his lap, the metal handcuffs cutting into his wrists. He couldn't believe this. The detective's words echoed in his head. He said 'the case' as if it wasn't Vivian he was talking about.

Vivian Banks. His Vivi. Gone. Disappeared. The truth stung, and the pain never went away. Only lingered in a tender spot in his chest.

The knot in his stomach overpowered every emotion, and this awful feeling was of pure guilt and regret. The worst feeling of them all. If he didn't find Vivian, this feeling would eat him piece by piece until it consumed him completely.

He regretted so much. He regretted the way he acted the last time he saw her. He regretted drinking so much that night instead of talking to her. He regretted leaving. He regretted not trying harder.

He couldn't remember much from that night, but he could picture her face vividly. She stood in the small living room by the set table, a look of pure disappointment on her tired face. Her dark brown eyes were hazy with a sort of undoubtable sadness.

Two plates of dinner were placed neatly on the table, along with silverware and glasses of water. The dinner she had made grew colder the more they argued. He was too distracted by the anger inside of him that he was oblivious to the hurt in her eyes when he stormed out of their townhouse.

Randy grabbed Cody's forearm and pulled him out of the car, the memory of that night disappearing in an instant.

People on the sidewalk near them stopped and stared with a sort of disbelief.

The Sheriff had caught the "bad guy"—or at least they hoped he had.

Cody looked up at the staring people and quickly dropped his eyes to the sidewalk. He still couldn't believe this was happening. None of this felt real. From the moment the girls told him about Vivian, he lost his grip on reality, and everything happening now felt more like a bad dream. It wasn't until Randy yanked him through the doors of the office when things began to feel tangible.

The old lady behind the front desk gasped at the sight of them barging into the building. "That him?" she uttered the question so quietly that Randy couldn't hear it—but he understood that look of shock in her eyes, so he nodded in response.

He led Cody through the office to the interrogation room. He ripped open the door, throwing the fisherman inside the dark room.

Cody stumbled and slammed face-first into the wall, cursing under his breath.

Detective Dubois walked in after him, setting down a briefcase on the rectangular table in the middle of the room. He began taking out photographs and notebooks. He looked up from his papers, watching them.

Cody turned to Randy, fresh blood dripping from his left nostril. "You didn't have to do that," he said, feeling the tenderness in his nose.

"Shut your goddam mouth," Randy growled through his mustache.

"You're gonna be sorry—"

Out of nowhere, Randy's right fist came flying toward Cody, meeting his eye hard enough to send him crashing on the floor.

Detective Dubois rushed over that instant, standing between them to create space. "Look at me," he snapped at Randy, his eyes glaring. "If you keep this up, you're asking for a misconduct, do you understand?

Cody took a deep breath, looking up at them from the ground. "What the hell is wrong with you?!"

The Sheriff grabbed him by his forearm and walked him over to the chair across from the detective, forcing him down in the seat. He took the handcuffs off, placing them back on his belt.

"I need to call my wife. I'll be right outside the door," he grumbled under his breath, storming out.

Dubois just nodded and continued organizing the scattered disarray of notes and photographs.

Cody noticed a photograph that they had recently taken together. It was a picture of them sitting on the couch in their townhouse. Probably one of the last photos they had together. She had posted it on social media with a heartfelt caption. He remembered that night so clearly. The memory was still fresh. The emotions attached to it were still there. He could hear her light laughter as he stared at her perfect smile, feel her warm touch from their interlocked fingers, and even smell the faint hints of lavender from her shampoo.

That night was too recent to be a photograph in an interrogation room.

"I'm Detective Dubois," the detective started, noticing the fisherman staring at the picture. He cleared his throat. "Cody, would you like a lawyer before we go on?"

He looked up from the picture, locking his jaw.

"Look, I'm new here," he added. "I used to work in New Orleans, but I saw an opening here—and I thought the small-town life is what I wanted." He leaned forward, lowering his voice. "No one follows protocol here. Sheriff Jones makes up his own rules. The parish's office is a complete joke."

He looked at him, confused. "Why are you telling me this?"

"The Sheriff is gonna want you to talk. He's gonna want you to say everything you know—and he could care less if you have a lawyer or not. He thinks he can ignore the rules just because this case involves his childhood friend. But *if* you desire a lawyer, I can find you one. You do not have to talk or confess anything if you want a lawyer present."

Cody looked disgusted. "I don't need a lawyer. I ain't got nothin' to hide."

The detective paused, and then nodded. "Understood."

"You said Vivian was his childhood friend?" He couldn't recall ever hearing Vivian mention a male friend from her childhood.

Dubois nodded. "Do you know this case isn't even ours to solve? This case belongs to New Orleans's department since that's where she lives. But he told me we would be the ones to find her since she was his friend. Sounds childish, doesn't it?" He took a deep breath, shaking his head. "Anyway, let's begin. Tell me about the last day you saw Vivian Banks."

It was around this time when Randy entered the observation room and watched them through the one-way mirror.

"Where should I start?" Cody asked, scratching the back of his head.

"I want to know about the whole day. From the second you woke up."

He dropped his eyes to the table. "I left the house around six o'clock in the morning and went to work. She was still asleep. She's normally sleeping when I leave for work because she doesn't have to be at her job until nine. I try not to wake her. I normally text her when I leave—just telling her good morning and where I'll be and things like that."

The detective nodded.

"That day, my buddy told me he was closing the New Orleans location and focusing only on our smaller location up the river. Said he was ready to leave the city and something 'bout retiring from the tourists. He asked what I thought about moving and keeping my job with the fishing company. Offered me a promotion and such. Colter has been a good friend of mine for the past ten years, so I told him I would think about it. Getting out of the city sounded kind of nice. Only problem with that is... well, Vivian is in New Orleans. So, I asked her what she thought about it all later that night—"

"What time was this?"

"I don't really remember. I came home around six."

"Uh-huh. And how did she take the news of you being asked to move to Greenville?"

Randy noticed the change in Cody's expression. He looked beat. Like the memory of that night suddenly hurt to remember.

He hesitated. "Not very well. I told her about my promotion and that I wanted us to move to Greenville, and she—um. That's when the argument started."

"She didn't want to move?"

"That's correct. I took this personally and overreacted, and when she told me to leave—I did. I went to a local bar, and I don't remember anything after that. She doesn't like alcohol. You see, her parents died from a drinking and driving accident, so naturally, she was always against it. And before I met her, I had a few drinking problems myself."

"Drinking problems?"

"Yeah," he frowned. "And when I'm drunk, I'm not me. It's like I become my father when I taste liquor. My dad was a hard worker, a good husband and father—but he was human. He had his issues. When he came home smellin' like whiskey, we would hide in our rooms until morning. Like I said, he was a good father, but when he drank, he wasn't the same man."

Randy understood the trauma Cody talked of. He could still picture his own father stumbling in their trailer home, so intoxicated he couldn't even stand straight. He could still hear his old man screaming for him, blaming him for whatever bothered him that night.

One memory in particular stuck out to him when he heard Cody's confession. When Randy was ten years old, his father came home late, drunk as usual—but that night, a little drunker than normal.

He wasn't just drunk.

He was angry.

When Mr. Jones came home, he started calling for his son. Randy was in bed, sleeping soundly, when he woke to his father pounding on his bedroom door. He was so frightened; he thought the trailer might have been on fire or something. His father kicked open his door, running into the dark bedroom. He grabbed Randy by his pajama shirt, pulled him up from the bed, and stared at him with bloodshot eyes. Randy remembered how his father's face didn't look like his father's face. He looked possessed. All the boy could do was cry as he was trapped in his father's grip.

"Where're my keys?!" his father shook him hard. "Give me back my keys!" He let go of Randy. The boy fell off his bed. He scattered to his feet, confused and terrified.

"I don't have your keys!" he said back. "I promise!"

"Where are my keys?! I know you hid them from me! Tell me where you hid them, you little *brat!*"

"I didn't hide them!"

SLAP. The back of his father's hand met the side of his face with a hot burning sensation.

That was the first time he saw this version of his father. The version that made him hate the man. The version that made him want to be the father he never had. Not just the Drunk, but the Angry Drunk. From that day on, he would stay the night over at Margaret's trailer when his father wasn't home before eleven.

"I don't like who I am when I drink," Cody said, bringing Randy's attention back to the interrogation room. "But I got my feelings hurt when she told me she didn't want to go with me. I thought that she would be the one, you know? I was planning on asking her for her hand this year."

The detective nodded.

"Anyway, I promised Vivi I wouldn't drink, and I broke that promise. The next morning, I went back to our house, and she was gone. I tried calling her, but she didn't answer, so I figured she was still mad at me. So, I drove my boat up to Greenville."

Detective Dubois raised an eyebrow. "Did you try calling her again once you made it to Greenville?"

"Yes. Every day. But she ignored my calls and texts, so I figured she just needed the space to calm down, so I let her have space. I guess that was a mistake, wasn't it?"

CHAPTER TWENTY-NINE

"MARGARET," the woman chuckled sweetly, smiling down at her, her hand reached out. "Get up, silly. You're gonna get your Easter dress all dirty."

Margaret stared up at Mrs. Abel from the floor, the pain in her head snapping off like a light switch.

She was in another memory.

She sighed to herself. "What about Jane?" Her voice was small and high-pitched. She looked down at herself, at the dress Mrs. Abel warned her she would get dirty, and understood when and where she was in time.

It was a pink, fluffy, tutu-like dress with ruffles. She remembered this dress instantly, and the remembering caused a flicker of excitement to ripple through her.

It was her first *real* dress, the nicest thing she had owned at eight years old.

Her father had asked Mrs. Abel to sew her a dress like the ones the other little girls in church wore. He couldn't afford a brand new dress from the boutiques in town, but Mrs. Abel could sew a nicer dress than any store could sell. And she did it without charging him a dime.

It was Easter at the plantation. Mrs. Abel always threw a big party, inviting everyone in Belles Parish over after service for a breakfast feast and egg hunts.

Despite most of the townspeople pretending to detest the Abel family, almost everyone came.

She set out nearly a hundred tables and chairs in the front yard and hid eggs throughout the courtyard.

Margaret could hear everyone laughing and talking outside. She grabbed Mrs. Abel's hand and stood up. She looked down at her white tights and Mary Jane heels, smiling to herself. She was dressed like a baby doll—but back then, she felt like a princess.

"Mama," a little girl called from the kitchen table. It was Mary Grace. She was sitting at the table with Lucille and Vivian, all three of them dressed in similar fluffy material.

They were eating candy and swinging their short legs over the floorboards.

"Can you tell us the story of the Grandmothers?" Mary Grace asked before eating a chocolate egg.

Mrs. Abel smiled at her daughter, putting her hands on her hips the way she always did whenever any of the girls said something silly. "Didn't I already tell y'all that old story?"

Lucille pulled the lollypop from her mouth. "Oh, please, oh please!"

She glanced out the window and then back to the little girls. Her eyes, as deep and blue as the ocean, smiled at them. Margaret swore if she looked long enough in her eyes, she could see the waves.

"Alright, alright," she started with a light chuckle. "I'll tell you the story. But it has to be quick. I can't leave my guest for too long." Her red lips lifted into a soft smile, and those waves in her blue eyes sparkled.

Margaret climbed into the seat next to Mary Grace, feeling strange about how small she was in the chair. Thoughts of Jane tugged at her mind, but she knew she was stuck until the memory decided to let her go.

"A long, long time ago, four families lived in this house. Four men, four women—"

"Our great grandparents!" Lucille giggled in excitement, the sugar getting the best of her.

"Yes, dear."

"Why did the four families live together?" Margaret asked, realizing she didn't know the whole story. "I mean, how did the women come about magic and—"

"We'll save that story for another day, dear. Today, I'll tell the story of the Grandmothers," she told her. "A long, long time ago, four families lived in this house. Four men, four women, and four little girls—Beatrice Abel, Evelyn Morgan, Elizabeth Clifton, and Frances Monroe." Clifton was Margaret's grandmother. She had never met her, but she was always told she resembled her.

"These little girls grew up to be beautiful women, and they all had *amazin'* gifts. Beatrice had the ability to *read* minds. She was the first and only female police officer in Belles Parish at the time, solely because she could tell what the *bad guys* were thinking. She wasn't afraid of anyone. And Evelyn had the gift of *healing*. She could feel what others were feeling and make them feel better simply with a cup of *iced tea*. Elizabeth could see the *future*. People all over Louisiana came to her for her guidance. And lastly, Frances Monroe could *speak* to the dead. She—"

Mr. Carson knocked on the doorframe of the kitchen, stopping her midsentence. He was exactly how Margaret remembered him.

Mr. Carson was the nicest man in Belles Parish, as well as the tallest. He was easily six foot and seven inches and was skinny as a pole. He had a wide smile hidden underneath his curled mustache. His brown hair was slicked back, and Margaret could smell the hair gel from the table.

Mr. Carson wore his finest clothes not only on Sundays but every day. He was a natural businessman, and that year, he was running for mayor, so he always made sure he was looking presentable. He was elected that year and was mayor until the unfortunate day he met Death, five years later. He had a stroke and died in his sleep. It was sudden tragedy that broke Mrs. Abel's heart, stealing the light from ocean eyes.

He grinned at his wife. "Is Mrs. Abel borin' you girls again?" he teased, winking.

She squinted her eyes at him and shook her head as a warning.

He laughed, running a hand along his gelled hair. "Just kiddin', darlin'. I just wanted to tell the young ladies that the Easter egg hunt is 'bout to start." He had such a pleasant voice.

Margaret remembered a few memories of him reading to the girls on the porch during some evenings when they all slept over. He would read classic literature to them and tell it in a way that made them sit on the edge of their seats. He could make any story captivating.

"Thanks, Daddy," little Mary Grace smiled. "Mama's gonna finish this story, and we'll be right out!"

He nodded, giving her a side smile. "Alright, sounds good. We'll be waitin'." He walked out of the kitchen, and Mrs. Abel watched him.

She loved him with her entire heart. They were the kind of couple that people wanted to be. Never fighting—just deeply in love with each other like two high school sweethearts. She wanted to take his last name but wasn't allowed, really.

It was the Abel family's promise to never give up the name. This made the townswomen of Belles Parish talk and talk, but she kept her last name, regardless of what they said.

"The women all married handsome gentlemen, and the four couples lived happily in the plantation—"

"Why did they all live together?" Margaret asked. "I mean, I get that the Grandmothers' parents all lived together, but *why* did *they*?"

"That is a good question, darlin'. I guess the girls were used to living with each other, and they didn't see the need to leave. The property is so very big. It was nice to have the extra help."

"Then why don't our mothers live here with you?" Margaret asked. "I know my mother couldn't because she died when I was born, but why don't the other women live with you?"

This question baffled Mrs. Abel. She tried to find the right words. "Well, there's nothing wrong with living separately, darlin'. In fact, it's quite normal." She took a deep breath, obviously thinking of something else. She then smiled, hiding whatever was bothering her. "We should go outside now. They're all waiting for us. Come on, girls."

"But you didn't finish the story!" Mary Grace whined.

"You know how that story ends," she replied.

The girls, except Margaret, jumped from their chairs and ran outside.

Margaret pressed her eyebrows together, looking up at Mrs. Abel. When the girls ran out, she turned to the oven, stirring a big pot of green beans. She looked over her shoulder at Margaret, raising an eyebrow.

"You goin'?"

Margaret messed with the seam of her dress. She was starting to wonder when she'd wake up from this memory. In the real moment of this memory, she followed her friends outside for the Easter egg hunt. But right now, she did not want to participate in this memory any longer. She didn't understand the point. Nothing happened on Easter Sunday. She knew she probably should go along with her little friends, but she wanted to wake up. She stayed seated in the kitchen chair, wishing with all her heart she'd wake back up to Jane.

"No, I don't feel up to it," she answered after a long pause. Though she tried her best to sound serious, she couldn't take herself seriously at all with how small her voice was.

Mrs. Abel gasped slightly. "You sure, darlin'?"

She nodded.

A man and a woman stumbled into the kitchen, laughing and giggling. The man, smirking and grinning, leaned against the doorframe, crossing his arms over his broad chest. Margaret didn't recognize him. The woman with him sort of skipped toward Mrs. Abel, her blonde curls bouncing behind her back.

It was Lucille's mother, before the drugs and alcohol left their marks on her beauty.

She was a tall woman, even taller in the black pointed stilettos, her legs accentuated in her black pantyhose and jean mini skirt. She looked like her daughter. Almost *exactly* like her daughter, but there was something about her that made her look *nothing* like her daughter. Something dark and sad—Margaret could feel this heaviness dripping from the woman.

She was drunk, very drunk.

"Did someone have a few daiquiris?" Mrs. Abel asked, shaking her head as she faked a laugh.

She snorted as she laughed in response.

"Minnie, what are you doing?" she hissed, grabbing her friend's wrist. She tried to keep her voice low, hoping Margaret wouldn't hear. "It's Easter."

The blonde woman giggled, almost stumbling over. She pulled her hand away. She then asked in a very loud tone, "And am I not allowed to celebrate the resurrection—"

"Keep your voice down," she snapped.

The man behind her grabbed his stomach and laughed as if she had told them the funniest joke ever.

"Listen, I'm leavin' early. Is it okay if Lucille spends the night with Mary Grace?"

Lorraine pressed her lips together, a great weight of bitter disappointment and obligation washing over her. "Of course she can stay over." She looked at the man by the door, narrowing her eyes.

He wasn't as drunk as Minnie. She knew him from church. He was a father and a husband—and had absolutely no business leaving with Minnie. His family had traveled up to Arkansas to spend Easter with his parents-in-law, and he 'couldn't go because of work'.

She had seen plenty of these men with Minnie. They all had the same motive. They wanted fun with no attachments. And

Minnie, as heartbroken as she already was, would do anything to feel loved. Even if it only lasted a night or two.

"If you hurt my friend," she told him with a forced smile. "I will hurt you."

His stupid smile dropped slightly.

Minnie clapped her hands together, running for the front door. "C'mon, let's go!" she waved her hand at Mrs. Abel as the two drunks stumbled out of the kitchen. "Thanks again, Lorraine! I owe you one!"

She wasn't the least bit shocked by her intoxicated friend. This was normal behavior for Minnie.

Their chaotic laughter left the house silent when they slammed the door behind them.

Mrs. Abel stared at the door, praying for her friend's sake. She turned to Margaret, frowning a little. Before she could say anything, the front door opened again, and two other people rushed in.

Margaret had almost forgotten who these people were when she first saw them, but when she saw the woman's hollow eyes, she knew.

They were Vivian's parents. She hadn't realized how much Vivi looked like her parents until she saw them again. She had her mother's dark hair and her big, brown eyes that lit up when she smiled. And she had her father's pointed chin and long nose and high cheek bones.

"Lorraine?" Vivian's mother called. "Lorraine, where is Minnie goin'?" The question was coated in dread, and by the disappointment painted on her pale face, Lorraine was sure Vivian already knew the answer.

Mrs. Abel chose her words carefully. "She was tired, so Larry Franklin took her home."

Margaret held back a laugh. It was easy to read between those lines.

Vivian's mother looked over at Margaret and covered up her worry with a sweet smile. "Hey, kid. Why aren't you with the girls?"

Margaret could feel her heart shatter a little when the woman looked at her. "I... I'm just taking a break."

"Well, Vivi is waitin' on the porch for you. You know she needs your help," she told her, nodding. "Will you help her?"

Margaret's mouth was dry. She tried to answer but couldn't.

The words burned her, tortured her, and she wanted to cry because of its pain.

Slowly, she nodded, getting down from her chair.

Lorraine Abel stepped forward, kneeling down in front of Margaret. She smoothed her hair back from her face. "Thanks for looking out for Vivian. It's important that you girls stay together and help each other out. Don't ever forget that." She probably was telling her this to remind herself after the situation with Minnie, but it only hit the nail in the coffin.

Margaret nodded, her throat tightening.

"Claire, is it okay if Vivi stays the night? I think the girls need a slumber party—what do you think, Margaret?"

Vivian's mother agreed.

"That sounds fun," Margaret said, fighting the urge to cry.

"Good. Now, go find Vivian."

"And she remembers this dream she's having right now?" Jane asked, watching her mother mindlessly walk out of the kitchen.

Mary Grace followed her friend closely. "Yes."

"How come no one told me about this?"

Lucille sighed, "There are just some things your mother doesn't want to tell you."

"She used to have premonitions of the future, but ever since she came here, the past has been stalking her," Mary Grace added.

She sucked in a sharp breath. "Premonitions of the future?" She was in complete and utter shock by all this. Her mother used to see the future.

"Shhh!" Lucille snapped. "You might wake her!"

"How did she see the future, though? I mean—did she predict things that *actually* happened?"

"Yes, darlin'," Mary Grace answered.

"I can't believe this."

Margaret, her eyes still closed, opened the front door and stood there for a moment before stepping outside.

Jane looked at her mother's friends—her *aunts*. "I need to tell you guys something. I haven't be completely honest."

Lucille and Mary Grace turned around in sync, their focus solely on her now.

The cicadas hummed in the background, and she focused on the sounds as she thought of what to say. "Remember when I fainted? Well, I've been fainting a lot lately. And, I've been having nightmares every night. And I wake up feeling terrible. And scared. And confused. But the worst part is that I can't remember these dreams. It's like I forget them as soon as I wake up.

"I fell asleep on the ride to Greenville today, and apparently, I was—"she paused, looking around and biting her bottom lip.

This was harder to tell them than she thought it would. They didn't make it any easier, either. They stared at her like she was telling them that she murdered someone.

"I was talking in my sleep. It scared me a little," she finished, shuddering.

Mary Grace's eyes widened. "What were you sayin'?"

She hesitated.

"Jane, what were you sayin'?" She grabbed Jane's shoulders and looked into her eyes. "This could help us find Vivian. We need to know what you were sayin'."

"How could it help? I don't even remember the dream."

"How?" Lucille repeated, stomping her foot. "Because you're your mother's daughter. And whatever she has, you got *in you* too." She pointed to Margaret who sat on the porch's steps.

The heat outside warmed up ten degrees as she processed this. "You mean... like *power*?" Her hands shook as her nerves ran wild.

Mary Grace gave her a little shake. "You've got a gift, Jane. Just like your mother's. What did you say?"

"I said *dreams and visions will show you the way*."

The cicadas and crickets stopped humming.

Mary Grace let her go, turning to Lucille. "I told you! She *is* powerful!"

Lucille was speechless. She smiled in awe, putting a hand on her chest.

Mary Grace turned back to Jane. "Tonight, we're gonna help you remember your dreams. You don't have to fear them anymore, okay? I don't care what your mother thinks. You have the magic in you, and it's time you learn."

Jane was suddenly dizzy. "Magic?" she stuttered under her breath.

The corners of Mary Grace's lips turned upwards. She knew there was no point in hiding it anymore. "You're a witch, Jane Gardener."

CHAPTER THIRTY

THE AFTERNOON SUN painted the blue skies with gold streaks, littering specks of the gold on the Spanish moss-covered oaks. Cars and trucks were parked parallel on the driveway, all the way down to the street. The sweet smell of charcoal and cheeseburgers carried through the warm air. A large grill was set out to the right, with Belles Parish's beloved pastor grilling the patties.

The whole town was there in the front yard. Some people were eating at the tables, others were dancing to the radio that sat on the porch rail, but most of them were standing around, smoking cigarettes and gossiping like the townspeople did. They talked about how strange Lorraine Abel was, how nasty her sister Minnie was, and how odd and quiet her other sister was.

Being around all those people with the smell of the cookout lingering about filled Margaret with a nostalgic feeling she didn't know she had missed.

She looked over at her small friend sitting next to her. "So, you don't want to find eggs, either?" In the backyard, children screamed with joy.

Vivi shook her head, staring down in her lap. "No, I don't feel so good. My head hurts."

Margaret sighed, shrugging. "You probably need water."

"I just drank water! No, Mar. My head is hurting because of that woman over there." She shook her head again, keeping her eyes on her dress.

She looked around, searching for who she could have been talking about. She didn't remember this part of the memory.

"But if I don't look at her, she goes away."

"Who?" she asked, looking back at her friend. "I don't see anyone."

Vivian looked up, frowning. "She's standing behind the tree right—" she pointed her finger toward the tree closest to them "—there."

Margaret followed the direction she was pointing in until her eyes found who she was talking about.

It was like the woman appeared out of nowhere. She was middle-aged, average height, but concerningly thin. Her skin was dark, as dark as the nighttime sky. She was dressed for Easter, so she didn't seem to stand out too much. But still, she didn't quite fit in, either.

There was something wrong with her. Something terribly wrong.

"Who is she?"

The woman stared back at Margaret, and awkwardly, as if it was unnatural for her, took one step closer to the girls.

"Stop! Don't look at her. She'll come for us!" She grabbed her friend's arm, burying her face in Margaret's shoulder.

Margaret was shocked. She didn't remember this woman.

She didn't remember her because, in the real memory, she had gone with the other girls to hunt eggs. And Vivian was by herself.

The woman took another step, her right shoulder dropping forward. She took another one, rolling her shoulder back again. She looked like a baby horse learning to walk.

She looked weak. Tired. Hungry.

A sudden panic filled Margaret. She stood up, letting go of Vivian. "Stay here," she muttered, her eyes still on the woman in front of them.

She took three more awkward steps toward them, like some strange creature.

Margaret didn't know who she was, but she knew she was not human. She could see it in her empty eyes.

In the real memory, she was a child, playing carefree in the backyard while Vivian sat all alone with this ghost-like woman.

When she made it up to her, she immediately backed away.

Her eyes were completely black, like marbles set in her face. She could see her reflection clearly in them, her worried little face staring up at the woman.

She bent forward, reaching her bony hand toward her face. Margaret flinched but did not run away. She hovered his fingers inches away from her cheek. She licked her lips, opening her mouth to speak.

"When you grow up," she hissed in an evil whisper. "And when you and your friends break apart…" She didn't blink, and Margaret didn't either.

All Margaret could do was stare up at the stranger, speechless and frozen and mesmerized by her black eyes.

"And when your sweet, loving protector, *Lorraine*—" she said her name like it cut her tongue. "—dies off, I will come for you all. You, your friends, and your *daughter*." Her voice was rotten, hoarse, and soaked with death. Whatever she was, she was weak. Margaret knew she couldn't hurt her or any of them even if she wanted to. "And then all this," she waved her other hand around. "will be mine. The land, your souls, your *power*."

Her fingertips touched Margaret's cheek, burning into her flesh like scorching iron. She tried to back away, but the pain shot its way up to her temple, bursting in her head like an explosive. She screamed, and the woman smiled—or at least, she thought it was a smile.

The pain was tormenting her, which was the very reason she was grinning like some sort of monster.

"Stop!" Margaret cried out, begging her.

"I will come for you—" the pain sharpened with her voice. It was worse than any of her usual headaches. "—and your friends—" more pain "—and your *daughter*."

She shut her eyes and saw a vision.

It was like a bright TV screen in front of her face, forcing her to watch the quick picture.

There was a bonfire in the woods.

It was nighttime.

The flames roared toward the full moon, howling and hissing as it burned and crackled.

There was a girl a foot in front of the fire, levitating over the ground, her eyes closed.

The girl was Jane!

Was she dead?

A shadow behind the fire started to grow and expand like a black wall, towering over the fire and Jane.

The fire hissed. What was it burning?

Jane's face was expressionless and certainly not peaceful. She looked dead.

Margaret's eyes rolled in the back of her head, her lids stuck open as if she was staring at them.

She was screaming.

"Mom!" Jane yelled.

Margaret opened her eyes to the sky, howling her lungs out. She could hear her daughter's voice but didn't see her. She was completely taken over by the presence of fear.

"Mom!" Jane yelled again.

Margaret could feel someone grab her hand. It was the evil woman. She was coming for them—just as she had promised.

"Mom! Look at me!"

She stopped screaming, her senses coming back to her. She was shaking uncontrollably. Jane had never seen her mother so frightened.

Margaret looked over at her daughter, tears streaming down her face. She didn't utter a word, only embraced her with a hug, her fingers gripping the back of Jane's shirt.

Jane hugged her back, realizing she was also shaking.

Mary Grace and Lucille stood around them.

"Margaret, what did you see?!" Lucille barked the question, her eyes wide with panic.

Margaret hesitated, letting go of her daughter and turning to her friend. She hugged Lucille, bursting into sobs. "We're not safe anymore."

"Come inside. I'll make you something to calm your nerves, and you can tell us what you saw." Mary Grace was already walking toward the house. Lucille and Jane walked by Margaret's side.

Margaret took a deep breath, running her shaky hand through her hair. She didn't want to tell them what she saw. She didn't want to have to describe the vision she was burdened to see. Because she was afraid she would have to relive it all over again when she did.

"I've never been so scared in my life, Mary Grace," she said after she had taken a seat at the kitchen table.

She didn't feel safe anymore. She felt like someone was watching her. She could still feel the evil woman's black eyes locked on her. The house didn't even feel like a safe hiding place anymore.

"Someone is coming for us," she murmured, almost inaudible.

Lucille reached across the table and grabbed her friend's hand. "Who, Margaret? Tell us."

Jane was leaning against the sink, her arms crossed over her chest as she watched her terrified mother.

Mary Grace poured the boiling water from the kettle into the ceramic mug, watching the tea bag bleed out, turning the hot water a reddish brown. She picked up the mug carefully and walked over to the table.

"What memory did you have, Mar?" she asked, sliding the mug in front of her.

Deliberately, Margaret told them exactly what she saw. She told them about their mothers. About Vivian's parents. She told them how Mrs. Abel told her that they should always stay together. She teared up during this part. So did Lucille and Mary Grace. Jane stood by the counter, completely bewildered the entire time. She felt like she was dreaming. She couldn't believe this was really happening to her and her mother.

Her mother was a witch.

Jane was a witch.

When Margaret started to talk about the creepy woman hiding behind the tree, the house fell silent.

"Only Vivi saw her," Margaret trembled, the image of her black eyes in her head. "And she didn't even tell us. I don't understand why she'd keep this from us."

"Vivian always pretended everythin' was okay," Lucille said.

"That just doesn't make sense." Margaret shook her head. "And why would she only scare her?"

"You said this *thing* attacked you telepathically?" asked Jane.

Margaret lifted her eyes from the steamy tea and looked over at her daughter by the counter. "Yeah. What are you thinking?"

"She's the weakest out of the four of you," she replied. "Mentally. Cody told me she's always battling with depression. Maybe that's why this woman messed with her and not you guys. This woman you saw... she could be the kidnapper we're looking for."

They all chewed on the thought for a solid minute. Her mother nodded, taking in a shaky breath. "You might be right, Jane."

Lucille held back her urge to cry. "So, this is what that thing wanted. For us to drift apart, for our strengths to weaken. It makes perfect sense. She got Vivian alone when *we* couldn't protect her, and she took her. Son of a—"

"What is she, though? If she's not human, then..." Jane trailed off, feeling like the walls were watching her. Goosebumps rose on her arms and the back of her neck. Out of habit, she played with her hair, running her fingers through the short ends like a brush.

Margaret didn't want her daughter to hear any of this. It killed her to know she was putting Jane in danger by sharing all of this with her.

"I don't know," she breathed.

No one said anything else for a solid minute. The silence was just as terrifying as Margaret's screams—maybe even worse.

Jane went on, "But let's just say this thing can age, right?" The three women nodded, waiting for her to continue. "So that would mean we would be looking for an old woman now."

Margaret thought about it, then answered, "I don't think an old woman could kidnap Vivian that easily."

"We're not talking about a regular old woman, Mar," Mary Grace muttered. "If this thing has been stalking Vivi that long, she knows Vivian's weaknesses by now."

"We need to tell Mr. Jones about this," Jane nodded her head, feeling a sudden urge to call Bobbie Jo that instant.

"The house phone is broken," Mary Grace sighed. Jane felt a pinch of guilt for that.

Jane pulled out her phone from her back pocket, handing it to Mary Grace, and saying, "Here, use mine."

The woman gratefully took her offer, dialing Randy's cell. Fortunately, there was just enough service to call out.

"What else did Cody tell you?" Lucille asked Jane while Mary Grace was talking to Randy on the phone.

"Not much, really. Only that she had mental health issues. He's innocent, though. I don't know how I know, but I could just tell."

"Where is he now?" Margaret asked her, trying not to feel upset that her daughter went off on her own. She was frustrated that their conversation earlier was interrupted, but she knew it wasn't important at that moment.

Jane looked over at her. "He's at the sheriff's office."

Mary Grace ended her call with Randy, handing the phone back to Jane. "Randy said he hasn't seen any suspicious old women lurking around, but he's gonna tell his team to keep their eyes peeled. Oh, and Cody is being interrogated right now. Randy said he'll call back once he's done."

"Good," Lucille nodded her head, picking at her red, glossy nails.

"And, in the meantime," Margaret started, looking over at her daughter. "You're grounded."

Jane's eyes grew wide as she sucked back a gasp, "What? Why?"

"Well, I think what you did today deserves some sort of punishment—and I also don't want you running off anymore since you were in my vision."

"That's not fair!" Jane rolled her eyes. "You said it *could* have been me. It could have also—"

Margaret rubbed her temples. "There are people out to get us, Jane—I can not let you get hurt."

Jane thought about the postcard. "You mean the people you wrote about in the postcard?"

Margaret stared at her in disbelief and then glanced at Mary Grace. That postcard was supposed to be destroyed. "How—" She stopped herself, not having enough strength to worry about how Jane found that postcard. "Yes, I mean those people. And the woman in my vision. The point is, we're in danger." She sighed, taking a big gulp of her tea. She pictured the evil man from her memory, shivering. She looked up at her daughter, not seeing the young woman standing in front of her, but the little girl she remembered her to be.

"Who're the people, Mom?"

She drank the rest of the tea, setting the mug down cautiously. "Bad people. My head hurts—I'm going to lie down." She stood up and looked over at her friends. "I'll be down soon. I just need to rest for a minute."

CHAPTER THIRTY-ONE

WHEN THE SUN FELL and the sky darkened to a velvet black, a halfmoon rose above the plantation, shooting rays of silver below.

Jane gazed at the swaying Spanish moss, deeply absorbed in thought. So much had happened that day that it felt like days ago she drove to Greenville with Bobbie Jo.

She thought of Cody, the way his brown eyes pooled with tears when they told him that Vivian was missing.

She thought of her mother, the way she screamed as if fear itself had taken over her completely. She had never seen her mother so afraid, and it frightened her.

But out of everything that happened that day, her thoughts led back to what Mary Grace and Lucille told her.

She was a witch. It was unfathomable. Witchcraft had always been fiction in stories, yet it made sense. Everything made sense. Her forgotten dreams, her headaches, her fainting, her strange intuition— the way she *knew* Cody was innocent simply by looking into his eyes. It was as if her inner witch was always there. She just had to acknowledge her.

And her mother—she was a witch too. They all were.

It was unbelievable and absolutely shocking.

She had so many questions. But she knew she wouldn't get any answers just yet. Her mother surely wouldn't tell her what she wanted to hear, and she could only ask her aunts so much.

She shifted her weight in the rocking chair, patiently waiting for what would happen next. Mary Grace had promised her she would help Jane remember her dreams tonight, for whatever that meant.

Margaret was sound asleep in her bedroom, thanks to whatever was in the tea Mary Grace brewed for her.

"I know how strange all of this is to you," Lucille spoke from behind Jane, startling her.

Jane whipped her head around and sighed in relief to see it was only Lucille. Ever since her mother described the strange woman from her vision, she couldn't help but imagine the stranger lurking in the shadows, watching her.

Lucille sat down next to Jane and pulled out a cigarette, slipping it between her lips. She lit it and took a deep inhale, letting the smoke fill her lungs. "Your mother raised you to be a normal mortal, but unfortunately, we are anythin' *but* normal. Though we aren't related by blood, we're family, you know? My great-great grandmother had three best friends she called sisters, and so did my great-grandmother, and my grandmother, and my mother, and so do I."

"But I don't. The four-sisters-thing stopped with you guys. Why?"

Lucille sighed to herself. "I'm not sure. I think my mama's generation is what broke the long tradition of the sisters. My mama wasn't a good woman. She had problems—just like everyone else, but she let them get the best of her. So, she wasn't a good sister, let alone a good mother. And your grandmother died giving birth to your mama. Vivi's mama was a good person, but she died when Vivi was just a little girl. Mrs. Abel was the only true witch in that generation.

"And then the four of us were born. Mrs. Abel taught us to stay together, but... I guess we were just as bad as the generation before us. We drifted apart, closed up, and grew away from each other.

"Margaret found the man of her dreams right away, and then you came along. But Vivi and I weren't too lucky when it came to men, and Mary Grace was always too busy caring for her mother to settle down. I guess being a mother wasn't in my cards. I don't mind, though. I'd rather be the fun aunt than—" she stopped, her eyes dropping to the floor. "Anyway, I'm sorry you don't have your own sisters to help you out. But you got us, at least."

Jane reached over and touched her hand. "I'm grateful I have you, Lucille. You're the nicest person I've ever met."

Lucille looked at Jane with red, teary eyes. She sniffled. "Oh, do you really mean that?"

She smiled at her aunt. "Of course."

They talked about the day. Lucille asked about Greenville, and Jane asked her about her mother's *visions*.

"She's always had them," Lucille had told her. "Some things she saw would happen that very minute, but other things wouldn't happen for months."

She wanted to know why her mother threw away her powers. Why she bottled up her past and changed herself completely. But Lucille didn't seem to know. That, or she didn't want to tell Jane. She decided she would ask her mother why she left Belles Parish. Something must have happened. No one just runs away from their life for no reason, right? She wanted the true story, and she knew she'd have to hear it from her mother herself.

Mary Grace walked onto the porch, holding a candlestick with both hands. The light from the fire illuminated her face and eyes. She stared across the porch at Jane and Lucille. "Jane, come," she whispered. "There's no time to waste." She turned around and walked back into the house. Lucille jumped to her feet and rushed after her, flicking her cigarette over the railing.

Jane stood from the rocking chair and followed the women as quietly as she could. Mary Grace was walking down the end of the hallway, the fire's light turning the walls orange, filling the space with shadows.

"Come, come," she whispered, stopping at the end of the hall.

When Jane made it up to her, she held her breath. "My mom might hear—"

"She'll be asleep for the whole night if we're quiet and she doesn't fight the melatonin from the tea. Come on, follow me." She opened Vivian's door, stepping aside to let Jane enter.

"What are we doing in Vivian's room?"

Mary Grace pointed across the room, making Jane look in that direction. The bookcase that was pushed flush against the wall was now moved to stand in the middle of the room, revealing an open hole in the wall. It was a doorway with stairs leading up to the attic.

"This wasn't always Vivian's room, you know. This was originally built as the study, with access to the attic, more commonly known as our *covenstead*."

Jane stared at the stairs, suddenly nervous.

"Come on, child," Mary Grace smiled, walking across the room. "There's nothing to be scared of." She walked up the stairs with the candle, leaving Vivian's room pitch black. Lucille climbed the stairs next.

Jane chewed her bottom lip as she contemplated whether she should follow her aunts or not. The darkness of Vivian's room forced her to make her decision, and she quickly moved her way across the room to the enigmatic stairs. When she looked up, she could see the warm light of Mary Grace's candle moving farther into the upper floor. She held her breath and walked up the steps, bracing herself for whatever waited upstairs.

The attic was not like any attic Jane had seen. It was a massive room filled with odd collections and bewilderments from years ago. Open cardboard boxes of old photos crowded the doorway, along with other common attic things like holiday decorations and dusty paintings—but that was the only thing normal about the attic.

The room was a hexagon shape. Like one big honeycomb cell.

Right away, Jane's eyes fell on the circle of candles in the middle of the room. In front of the candles was a wooden lectern. Lucille stood behind it, studying an open book on the slanted top.

She looked up at Jane, a wide smile filled with pure excitement painting her face.

Jane looked around the room, letting out a gasp. Each wall, except for the one at the front of the house, was lined with tall, massive bookshelves. The many shelves contained a countless number of books and journals, jars filled with strange curiosities, candles of every shape and color, and other mysterious novelties. At the back of the room, there was an antique purple velvet couch, along with a glass coffee table and two purple chairs.

"This is a *very* sacred place," Mary Grace started as she watched Jane look around the attic in awe. "This attic was a sanctuary for generations of witches."

The word *witches* made the hairs on her arms stand. She looked down at the candles again. "So, what are we going to do?" She blinked, thinking to herself, *'Sacrifice someone?'*

"No, we don't sacrifice people, darlin'," Mary Grace answered.

Jane blinked.

"Don't be scared," Lucille told her, her smile softening. "All you need to do is trust us, okay?"

She nodded, awkwardly standing by the stairs. "You read minds, don't you?" she asked after a pause.

Mary Grace nodded. "That's not all I can do. We all have our strengths. Telepathy happens to be mine." She stepped into the circle of candles. "Well, let's begin," she announced.

Lucille took one quick glance at the book on the lectern and then walked over to Mary Grace's side in the circle.

"Come on. Don't be afraid." She handed the candlestick to Lucille, reaching out her hand to Jane.

Cautiously, Jane walked over to the candles and paused for a moment.

There was no turning back now.

When she stepped into the circle, she could feel a force pulling her in.

Lucille sat down on the floors, sitting crisscrossed. She patted on the floor with her free hand, smiling up at Jane.

Slowly, Jane sat down in front of the women and brought her knees to her chest.

Mary Grace moved to Jane, looking down at her. "I need you to lie down and relax," she said, kneeling next to her. Jane did as she was told but remained hesitant. "Close your eyes and take a few deep breaths."

The girl shut her eyes, breathing in the biggest breath her lungs could hold and pausing before releasing it.

Mary Grace started rubbing her hands together in a quick motion, letting the friction warm up her skin. She hovered her hands over Jane's closed eyes, taking a deep breath herself. She started to whisper something so quiet Jane could hardly hear what she was saying.

"Try to relax, dear. Focus on your breathing," Lucille commented.

Jane tried to focus on her breathing and not what Mary Grace was mumbling. But she couldn't help but wonder what she was saying. Whatever language she was speaking certainly wasn't English.

"Focus on your breathing," Lucille reminded Jane. "Relax."

Mary Grace closed her eyes, repeating the same strange words over and over again, her palms hovering over Jane.

A rumble of thunder sounded in the sky, turning the air in the attic icy. The candles' flames flicked one at a time but did not go out.

"It's working," Lucille said.

Mary Grace opened her eyes, putting down her hands. "She's asleep." She nodded her head.

Raindrops pattered on the roof as the wind outside began to moan. The rain then fell harder, crashing against the house.

"I didn't think it was supposed to rain," Lucille said, looking at the small circular window on the front wall.

"It wasn't."

Standing on each side of Jane, they held hands together, chanting the same words Mary Grace said seconds ago. They spoke it quickly, in a hushed tone, repeating and repeating until the chant sounded like a mush of melded voices.

"Enthüllen, was verborgen ist. Enthüllen, was unsichtbar ist."

A gust of wind blew through the attic, shaking the flames.

Lucille opened her eyes and sucked in a sharp breath. Mary Grace opened her eyes slightly.

As if a force was lifting Jane from the ground, she began levitating upwards. The women dropped hands but continued to chant.

Another round of thunder boomed in the distance, making Lucille jump.

"Don't stop! It's working!" Mary Grace called out, noticing Lucille's worry.

The room felt like it was spinning. Over and over, they chanted their words as Jane rose higher and higher in the candle circle.

Out of nowhere, a screaming crow burst through the round window behind them. Shards of glass spread across the wood floors, and the bird twitched in the broken pieces until it died.

The women didn't stop. Mary Grace could feel the power streaming from the girl, and so could everything else. Rain and wind blew through the broken window, invading the attic with a deadly chill.

Jane's eyes were still closed, and she continued to levitate higher.

An eerie layer of fog hovered carefully over the dark bayou. Thick clouds blocked out any sliver of moonlight, casting a sinister shadow on the cypress trees.

The frogs moaned, and the crickets softly laughed as the yellow-eyed alligators crept around the black waters like slithering snakes.

Out in the middle of the river, tiny air bubbles began to rise to the surface, a sign of life below the blanket of turbid water. Ripples formed circles around the popping bubbles before a figure slowly ascended, pale and drenched. Her black hair hung over her face, hiding all but her trembling lips. She was dressed in a white nightgown, discolored from the muddy bayou, matching the gray bark of the surrounding trees that stood like decaying skeletons dressed in Spanish moss.

The woman stopped rising when the water was just below her chest.

Her blue lips opened slightly, murmuring, "Dreams and visions will show you the way." The thin, shaky lips repeated this message again and again in a delicate whisper. "Dreams and visions will show you the way. Dreams and visions will show you the way. Dreams and visions will show you the way."

Her whispers echoed throughout the murky swamp until they began to morph into desperate cries.

"Dreams and visions will show you the way. Dreams and visions will show you the way. Dreams and visions will show you the way."

The women kept chanting. Faster and faster. They could hardly breathe.

Lightning struck a nearby tree, the room momentarily turned a wicked silver.

When the light from the sudden storm snapped off, Jane's eyes shot open. She arched her back, opening her mouth and inhaling as much air as she could. With her exhalation, her body fell to the floor, making a loud thud when she hit the ground.

She had been drowning.

Drowning in her own ocean of ignorance, and she could now finally breathe, seeing what her subliminal mind had hidden from her.

She could see the truth in her so-called nightmare.

And it wasn't a nightmare at all.

It was a message.

"Jane!" Mary Grace called out.

As if the storm had never started, the rain stopped, and the wind halted.

Jane raised her eyebrows and widened her eyes, the lightning's flash flickering in them as she stared at the ceiling. Her lips trembled as she found her voice.

"I remember my dream."

END OF BOOK ONE

Acknowledgments

I came up with the idea for When She Vanished two years before I actually began writing it. I was in the process of publishing my debut novel when, almost out of nowhere, a wave of sudden inspiration slapped me in the face. I didn't have a storyline in mind—all I knew was that my next story would involve a missing woman, the Deep South, and witchcraft. I was working on several novel ideas at the time, but I couldn't quite shake this one off. I knew I had to write it. But again, I didn't have a real story quite yet. After I published my first novel, I gave myself two months before sitting down to write again. I used this time to mentally construct the world of When She Vanished—and the minute I sat down and began writing, it was as if the story's characters took complete control. The prologue was the first thing I wrote. I didn't have the intention of writing the prologue first, it just happened. I had this dream-like scene burning in my mind, and once I finished writing it out, I realized I had written the opening of the book. And then, the story began to unravel, creating characters that will forever live in my heart.

There are so many people I want to thank for inspiring me to write this book and helping me polish up the words once they were on paper—but right now, I'm only going to shout out the important ones.

First and foremost, I would like to thank my family. Thanks for always putting up with my craziness and listening to my story ideas while I was writing WSV. You guys really helped steer the plot in the right direction, and I couldn't have done it without every one of you.

Here's a big thanks to my friends! You all were my first fans, and I appreciate you guys more than you can imagine.

I would like to thank the wonderful Brittney Kristina for helping me with this book. Your edits and your (sometimes brutal) honesty really helped shape this story into what it is today.

And lastly, thank *you*, Reader, for reading When She Vanished. I hope you liked it, and I can't wait for you to read what happens next.

Until Next Time,
Kaitlynn Flint